Fade

D.C Clemens

DEDICATION

To the best parents and sister in the world- and also to my own.

ACKNOWLEDGMENTS

I'd like to thank the wonderfully devoted team at Soul Food Independent Publishing for making this book possible.

A Brief History of Ex-humans

Ex-humans, the contracted form of "Extraordinary humans" and likewise used to imply "former" humans by Regulars, are defined as any person with the inherent capability to manipulate one's self or environment in any variety of ways. Some of the more common abilities are usually physiological, such as having great strength, high endurance, or sharper senses; however, there are abundant examples of other talents which involve the mind or natural elements. There are also highly variable degrees of proficiency for Exes sharing analogous powers. An easily digestible example would be where one Ex could lift a ton or more with little training whereas another Ex would still require months of vigorous exercise to lift half as much.

While the secretive nature of most Exes inhibits keeping precise data on them, recent calculations based on documented Exes has shown there to be a noteworthy gap among the number of males and females, with females claiming the majority of their populace at approximately sixty-five percent. The reason for the discrepancy is unknown and, as with all things associated with their existence, requires extensive study. It's also known that as much as five percent of the general population carry any one of the known Ex genes—the percentage will likely go up with the discovery of more Ex genes—but only a minority actually exhibit any of the superhuman capacities.

Ex-humans have undoubtedly existed during the Age of Antiquity, but accurate accounts of them are exceedingly scarce throughout this time period and are normally tangled within a heavy dose of folklore. It has been conjectured that a few prominent historical figures were possibly Exes, however, most researchers and historians are pressured by their governments and the general public to not explore the possibility that famous individuals like Cleopatra, Genghis Khan, or Leonardo da Vinci were anything but Regulars. Regardless, by the late Middle Ages, a growing number of societies began blaming these "unholy" beings for their misfortunes and many populations in Europe and Asia came to the conclusion that Exes were responsible for the Black Death and for the many failed harvests in the years leading up to what's now known as the Expulsion. In the span between the diffusion of the Bubonic Plague and the Age of Enlightenment, tens of thousands of individuals around the world were accused of being part of the "accursed" and thousands more were hunted down and executed in the name of both God and for the interest of ensuring Regulars remained the controlling authority.

Knowing Exes are a rare breed, projected to make up little more than one percent of the population at any one time, it's expected that a bulk of those killed were Regulars and became victims of the mass hysteria. Of course, some Exes fought back and gained supporters, but this only fueled the fire and served as "proof" of their violent nature. In the end, Exes had too few numbers and were too unorganized to battle back effectively. It was the intervention of the intellectuals during the Age of Enlightenment that finally permitted Exes and wrongly indicted Regulars to gain some level of reprieve from the cycles of paranoia. While large scale, blind purges never again transpired until the days of Hitler's crusade (though smaller scale expulsions remained fairly common) the effects of the era are still felt to this day.

At the advent of World War I, nations began to openly recruit Exes into their ranks, particularly when it became clear that the war wouldn't be a quick affair. Countries promised any Exes who volunteered to serve would attain equal rights with their citizens. This "Ex arms race" did not give either side a major advantage, as Exes who contributed in the war split fairly evenly between the Allies and Central Powers. At the end of the war, many people assumed the unprecedented bloodshed resulted from the use of Exes and saw them no better than the horrifyingly potent modern weapons that included machine guns, tanks, and poison gas. Despite the continuing negative sentiment from the public and nations only partly keeping their promises, if they kept them at all,

Exes were able to acquire their first noteworthy supporters since the intellectuals of the Enlightenment; war veterans. Many soldiers witnessed firsthand how there was little difference between killing someone with a gun or by using one of an Ex-human's sundry abilities. Despite the fact Exes were largely segregated from the main army, not trusting them enough for offensive engagements, a level of comradery did form when the military opted to use Exes in mainly defensive roles. In effect, many soldiers were often protected by Exes and many asserted that battles would have been bloodier without them. Nevertheless, in the duration between the world wars and the worldwide economic collapse, the standing of Exes remained largely unchanged from before the Great War.

Mirroring the first global conflict, countries started enlisting Ex-humans into their ranks when World War II began. To recruit as many as possible, Britain and the United States began promoting Exes as champions and protectors of democracy, seeing them as a necessary addition to contemporary militaries, especially given Japan and Russia were also encouraging Exes to join their side. Meanwhile, Adolf Hitler regarded Exes as impure as Jews or homosexuals. Many who were captured were horrendously experimented on in an attempt to find ways to control them or possibly find a weakness they could use to eradicate the entire race. Combined with news of these gruesome experiments and treating Exes as the defenders of their country, the end of the war brought the first sweeping international laws recognizing Exes as having the same rights and protections as Regular citizens, at least, in theory. A few of the more famous Exes did enjoy a more respectable standing with their respective country, but most were still, understandably, wary and chose to remain hidden instead of exposing themselves by registering and finding government vocations, which were primarily situated in the military.

The onset of the Cold War quickly rekindled mistrust between the races as both the U.S. and U.S.S.R struggled to control their growing arsenal of nuclear weapons and emerging number of Exes. In the late 1950s, a program, which would eventually become the peacekeeping Stewards, was created by the United Nations in an aim to combat the increasing trend of governments using Ex-humans to covertly influence another nation's politics or to eliminate targets. With the Stewards largely considered an important reason all-out nuclear war was averted on several, if mostly classified, occasions, public perception in the world's superpowers slowly began to ease in favor of further assimilation for the Exes.

The biggest consequence concerning Ex-humans when the dissolvent of the Soviet Union occurred was when dozens of highly trained Exes found themselves unclasped by the threat of nuclear annihilation. Some of these accomplished Exes used the Cold War as evidence of the Regular's inability to competently rule the planet and saw themselves as the solution. Numerous terrorist organizations started appearing throughout the globe within a few years, preaching it was time for Exes to subjugate Regulars. Since then, several assassinations of politicians and even multiple Stewards have been attributed to some of these organizations, along with a few major terrorist attacks.

Other Exes sought to build on the idea of cult worship. Since the time Exes first appeared, a handful have either actively advertised themselves as spiritual guides or have been freely venerated by Regulars. Pockets of these sects, while usually secretive and relatively rare, have steadily developed and gained influence throughout the world. Today, the best many Exes and Regulars can do is to tolerate one another and find their way in a still evolving world.

—An excerpt from a lecture by Professor Adam Gillman of Columbia University

Chapter One

February 10, 1999, is the day a nineteen year old named Felix Everett died. However, if he was feeling ironically upbeat, he observed it as his second birthday. More specifically, he was killed in what is sadly a not uncommon, run-of-the-mill, might just make the top of the news, drunk driving accident. He was not the drunk one, mind you, and wasn't much of a drinker to begin with. Felix was simply minding his own business, driving back to his residence hall in UC Berkeley under a waning moon, when his compact car was blindsided by a full-size pickup truck and its three drunken occupants, who were attempting the same goal. Despite the intensity of the collision, Felix held on tightly to life, even recalling the sounds of police sirens as he lied hemorrhaging on the asphalt. He was still at the outer edge of consciousness when the paramedics lifted him into the ambulance, though all was a hazy blur of red lights and innumerable iridescent streaks and spots.

Nevertheless, the injuries were far too severe for any hope of survival and it was a minor miracle he lived for as long as he did. Yet his memories and conscience did not end with his end.

His first clear remembrance since the accident were the words of one of the two male paramedics saying, "We've lost him. Time of death 1:38 a.m."

At first, Felix concluded there must have been another victim in the ambulance the paramedic was referring to, as he did not feel particularly lifeless looking up at the ceiling of the ambulance and hearing what was going on around him. *Could an ambulance carry more than one person?* he asked himself.

All the same, the more he thought about it, the more something did feel off. The first evidence indicating something was wrong came when he recognized he couldn't move any part of his body. He tried wiggling a toe, raising a finger, or turning his head, but his body would not follow his commands. He then wondered if he was completely paralyzed. The potential outcome absolutely terrified him and it was close to tempting him to give up on endeavoring to move an extremity, but endeavor he did. After a few minutes of vainly struggling to get something to move, he realized he was quickly becoming cold. Actually, cold wasn't the right word. He felt his body was rapidly losing heat, but he himself didn't feel much at all affected by it. It was mildly similar to holding a warm glass of water and sensing the temperature drop when the ice that was dumped in was taking its effect. The temperature change could be detected, but it had no negligible impact on the person holding the glass.

Felix next heard the second paramedic say, "Surprised he lived as long as he did. Hope he didn't feel any of that."

"The severe head trauma likely deadened the pain," said the first medic. "He barely even moaned."

They might have continued the conversation, but Felix suddenly began experiencing something very akin to severe claustrophobia, forcing his attention away from the outside world. He needed to move or he felt a something horrific would happen if he didn't. He tried thrashing with greater desperation, but to no avail, so he did the only other thing he thought he could do; scream. He expected to hear the outcry only in his head, given his apparent immovable condition, but much to his surprise, he heard himself yell out loud. He next anticipated hearing the paramedics respond to his desperate remonstration, but they remained silent. So he tried again. For a second time he heard his own exclamation as clearly as if he shouted in an empty high school gym. They spoke this time, but it was unrelated to him. Something about a new sports car one of them just bought.

Confusion and anger swept over him, which made him unconsciously move to get up. This unthinking action was, astonishingly, fulfilled. Before he could comprehend it, he was sitting up on the gurney and looking at the two paramedics, one blonde and heavyweight, the other slim and dark-skinned. They persisted in disregarding him. He was about to say something to get their consideration, when he noticed his right hand. It required a long moment to come to grips with what he was seeing, unable to understand how such a thing was possible, but there was no denying it; he could see straight through it. Instinctively, he checked his left hand and saw it existed in the same transparent form. He next observed beyond his translucent left hand that his legs were under a white sheet soaked with fresh blood. He slowly tried to grasp it, but to his horror, not only did he fail to grip any of it, his fingers were consumed underneath the sheet.

At this point, the ambulance came to a full stop and one of the paramedics opened the doors while the other grabbed the head end of the gurney. Although it was obvious before, it was only as they began to roll the gurney into the hospital did Felix truly start to comprehend his predicament. He couldn't be seen or heard and he had a sneaking suspicion he didn't want to see exactly what was below the not so white cover. In a decision that didn't quite feel like his, he hopped off the gurney and stood in the busy hallway, completely alone.

The vanished muscles in his legs started wobbling and his airless lungs began to hyperventilate. He slowly lowered himself to the ground until he was crouching low enough to see the small, dark blemishes on the otherwise bleached floor. What finally released him from his stupor was when a female nurse cut across him to get to a nearby room. There was an incredibly surreal sensation that surged over his entire being (whatever that was now) when the young woman crossed his body. Of course, this was a challenging sensation to comprehend given that no living being could feasibly experience what he just went through, but if he was forced to describe it, he would have said it was more or less like being pleasantly electrocuted. This also served as a slap to the face of sorts and he was able to briefly regain his bearings. He stood back up and actively avoided anyone who was heading in his direction. While the strange sensation was not exceptionally offending, it was much too strange to voluntarily experience a second time in his current emotional state.

Through the course of the last few minutes, the words were building inside of him and they finally came together when he knew not saying them any longer would eventually drive him insane.

"I'm dead."

Chapter Two

There was some relief in hearing those words, but there was still the matter of what the hell to do next. He then remembered his family. His immediate family consisted of his accountant father, a mother who taught high school math, an older sister, and a younger brother. An abrupt emotional pain made him tersely wish his family hated him so they wouldn't miss him. Every curse word he could evoke left his ghostly lips and combined them in mostly ridiculous ways.

Wanting to escape the bustle and noise, he wandered into a room down the hall with an out of the way stairway no one would use unless it was to escape a fire. After a moment or two of vacantly staring at nothing in particular, he felt like walking up the stairs rather than standing around doing nothing. When he tried placing his right foot on the first step, however, it simply phased through. Several more efforts provided the same result. Frustrated, he gave up.

"Okay, Felix. Calm down," he said out loud to himself. "You're dead, but not entirely. I mean, at least I'm not in a fiery pit right now, so there's that."

It helped him to hear his own voice, but he also was mindful that constantly talking to himself, even if no one could hear him, was still too close to crazy for his liking. He made a rule to do it sparingly, at least, for as long as he cared about remaining sane.

To make sure no one could hear him, he gathered some courage and walked down the hallway yelling, "Hello! If you can hear me, please say so!"

No one reacted to his cries. If he wanted to further investigate if there was anyone anywhere who might be able to perceive him, he would have to try upstairs or go outside. The outdoor option felt far too ambitious, so he went back to the stairs and decided to practice climbing them until he either conquered them or found it an impassable obstacle.

Why couldn't a ghost walk upstairs? he wondered.

He inhaled needlessly deep breaths and focused on the first step. Clearly, it was no longer a question of physical contact but…well, of something else. Dozens of failed approaches later, he had an epiphany. His mind was automatically stuck thinking his phantom body still had an impact on its surroundings when it obviously no longer did. On his next step, his mindset was *I'm not here.* Sure enough, his right foot held its ground on the stair.

"That's one small step for man, one giant leap for ghost kind," he said quietly, unamused by his own allusion.

Sticking with his new mentality, he was able to easily climb the first flight of stairs. It wasn't Waterloo, but it was a victory nonetheless. The second floor wasn't as hectic as the first, in truth, it was almost too quiet for the freshly made ghost. An elevator door opened nearby and out rolled an unconscious patient on a gurney being pushed by a male nurse. Though thankful it wasn't his own body, seeing this made Felix uncomfortable to go through with his yelling plan, so this time he decided he would go up to someone and concentrate on talking to them directly.

He found an older female doctor talking to an equally matured male doctor standing next to a room where the patient they were talking about was presumably in. Felix walked up to them and, while using a similar mindset from walking up the stairs, tried making them hear him. No luck. The doctors stood talking for a good thirty seconds, but no word of his seemed to reach either one in that time. In desperation, as they began to go their separate ways, he attempted to grab the male doctor's arm, but his hand did the traditional ghost act and he felt that electric-like and slightly enjoyable sensation travel up his own arm. It felt wrong to do this, and since it didn't elicit any reaction, he thought it best to continue avoiding contact; until he became desperate again, anyway.

Knowing he was in the hospital with sick and dying people started to advance his depression. It was uncomfortable to be at a place where death was a daily occurrence.

Wait, are there other ghosts around?

While an interesting possibility, he figured if there were any, he'd eventually run into one, for better or worse. All at once, his weightless body felt cumbersome. He sauntered slowly back downstairs and stepped outside the hospital door—waiting a few minutes for someone else to open it rather than walk through himself—found an isolated curb, and sat down. Emotionally, he was drained. The onslaught of tragic weirdness was too much to handle. He knew his ass was somehow sitting on the concrete, but he only assumed this was true, he couldn't confirm it with the actual touch. His very own body provided only the tiniest resistance to his own hands as they phased through his chest. He tried emptying his mind for as long as he could. Despite having a lot to think about, he did actually succeed in salvaging some composure, mostly by coming back to the idea that things could, theoretically, be worse. It was simply a matter of breaking his circumstance down.

First, he was still essentially himself, just minus the fleshly body. Next, there was the fact he wasn't in any physical pain. What also turned out to be a small consolation was recognizing he was in uncharted waters. Instead of being frightened by the unknown, he found himself a little excited by the prospect. There was also some hope in finding someone, dead or not, who could help him maneuver being part of the undead society.

I couldn't possibly be the only ghost ever, could I?

For now, he thought it best to find something constructive to do to keep busy, and that something had to be his family. While he wasn't too keen about seeing a distraught family, he felt it would be abandoning thing them if he wasn't there. There was also the idea that if anyone could sense him in some way, it would be a family member. He knew the four of them would undoubtedly gather at his parent's house and at his funeral. Both of those events would be held back in his hometown, a one hour drive north from where he currently was. Not wanting to keep on doing nothing next to an area where death was never far, Felix began walking towards his birthplace.

The air around him became less heavy as he walked farther away. The greater the expanse he was from the hospital the more extreme the difference was. He absorbed one last gaze at the medical building and came to one of two conclusions; either his imagination was quite powerful, or he was sure he could make out a melancholy, life-filled aura surrounding the building. As he continued onward, he noticed a similar aura around sparse crowds or in certain buildings, mainly apartments. After walking for almost an hour, there was little doubt in his mind that what he was sensing was similar to a sixth sense. He noted that the more people there were, the denser the air became. When dawn was approaching and the sleepy college town began to awaken with more individuals walking or biking in the streets, Felix found he was able to sense even these loners if he focused enough. The activity helped keep his mind off too many gloomy thoughts and he made steady progress to his destination.

As he anticipated, he didn't seem to be suffering from any kind of his exhaustion even after sprinting rigorously several times. There was also no sign of hunger or thirst creeping up on him, which he was grateful for until he came to the realization he would likely never be able to smell freshly baked bread, feel a cold Coke drench his parched tongue on a hot day, microwave some cold pizza in the middle the night, or experience the taste of sizzling bacon! For some reason, these relatively trivial losses upset him more than anything yet. Meanwhile, he kept his eyes open for anyone resembling a fellow ghost, even if it was just one of a squirrel; anything would have helped. The trek lasted the whole day and, besides being deceased, nothing eventful happened. A few ideas formulated on testing what he could do with his astral form, such as seeing if he could ride in a car, go through walls, go into a girl's locker room, or freak out animals, but he was not in the mood.

On further reflection, he also made up his mind not to go directly to his parent's house, but to wait for his family and friends in the cemetery where he would undoubtedly be buried near his beloved grandfather, his namesake. He couldn't be sure exactly why he wanted to be in the cemetery before anyone else, all he knew was that it felt like the best choice. Maybe he was prolonging the inevitable meeting with his living family, or perhaps he was feeling a ghost aptly belonged in a graveyard. Whatever the exact motive, he meandered towards the cemetery.

On finally reaching it, he immediately discovered the place to be oddly soothing, in spite of it being nearly moonless and echoing only dreary silence. Finding his grandfather's resting place in the night's embrace wasn't too difficult, seeing as the grave was situated near the tallest oak tree in the area. While hanging around an unlighted burial ground might be an eerie and time-slowing way of finding some sort of peace, Felix discovered time actually seemed to speed up. The sun rose to an overcast sky, but even without it as a reference to follow the passage of time, the next day and night terminated reasonably quickly. He practiced moving as a ghost during this lull period. He ultimately managed to jump and run on obstacles as if they were actually there to impede him and also accomplished climbing some of the large oak trees using the stair mindset.

On the afternoon of the second day, he saw two caretakers begin to manually prepare what had to be his grave and, on the succeeding morning, the funeral was held under a pristine sky. It was expectedly bizarre to see virtually everyone he ever knew mourning him. In a peculiar way, it was marginally gratifying to see that even in his fairly fleeting life he had dozens of people sadden at the loss. What naturally trumped everything was seeing his distressed family. Linda, his older sister, was acting resilient for their younger brother and mother. She was always a strong and independent girl. He remembered her behaving much in the same way when their cherished grandfather died six years ago. Viciously stamping out a great deal of expectation, he quickly learned that no relative or friend reacted to his touch or cries. Whatever was left of his soul felt as though it were tearing at the seams, ripping open to exclaim curses at his own entombment. He wished he could cry to bring about the relief only the end of weeping could bring, but even this respite was forbidden to him. He then wished he could somehow use his unique situation to help those closest to him, protect them like the heroes of the world.

The closed casket service lasted longer than he liked and was relieved to see it end. He was able to hitch a ride back home in the family SUV and stay with them in the coming days and weeks. He felt it was unethical to witness normally private moments and was only in the room if he thought his living self would enter. It was a conversation between his father and sister when he learned that no one else had died from the crash, the driver having been taken out of critical care the day after his burial was held. The news did not illicit any sentiment from the deceased teen.

After a couple of weeks haunting his grieving family and seeing them gradually move on with their lives, he spent more and more time exploring his neighborhood and tried exposing any more dormant abilities he might have. With training, the new apparition was able to refine his life sense perception to point out subtle and unique differences between individuals and successfully track them over a distance of dozens of yards, even if they were out of sight, behind walls, or in a crowd. Animals also could be tracked in this way, and whereas a majority gave no reaction to him, he believed a few showed possible signs of sensing him. One potential trace of awareness derived from an old stray cat that appeared to deliberately avoid crossing paths with him, though other attempts to force a similar response from the gray animal proved fruitless. More promising results came with crows. They didn't avoid him, but once in a while he was positive a murder of them would caw at his direction when he saw no reason for them to do otherwise. In any case, he was well aware he was grasping at straws.

Felix had a hard time believing there wasn't someone out there who could interact with him. Consequently, after a couple months inhabiting his mute town, he thought it was time to travel everywhere he could to find someone or something that would allow him not to inevitably lose his bloodless mind. The best place he figured he should begin his search was in a large city. So after saying an unreturned goodbye to each member of his family, Felix made for the closest metropolis; San Francisco. Instead of walking or running the entire way, he was able to shorten the trip substantially by hitching rides on various moving vehicles.

When he reached the city, he spent his desolate days trying to engage with everyone he could, including self-proclaimed psychics, holistic medicine men, ghost hunters, dentists, but no one he encountered responded to him. It was towards the end of his second day in the city did he first see, or, more accurately, sense his first Ex-human. Known only as Madam X to the public, she was among the few well liked Exes, due to openly working with the U.S. government and was an honorary member of the

Stewards—an organization made up of Exes working for the U.N. and whose express purpose was to create and preserve peace between Regulars and Exes, and, occasionally, among nations. Unlike other Exes, who wanted to remain hidden, become vigilantes, or turned to criminal enterprises, she was seen as an example to follow. Her power was top secret, but most guessed she was able to use telepathy. This gave Felix some hope. He had theorized that if anyone could see or hear him it would have to be one of the Ex-humans.

She was speaking in a park promoting goodwill between Regular and Exes. Felix glided past her security detail and stepped onto the wooden platform. She wore a navy blue mask over her eyes and forehead to hide her secret identity, otherwise wearing a simple blouse and skirt and kept her long, black hair in a ponytail. He guessed she had to have been wearing a bulletproof vest under the casual clothing. Going purely by her voice, she sounded about the upper range of middle age. Putting his lips right beside her ear, Felix yelled, "Mashed potatoes!" in the middle of one of her sentences, but she didn't skip a beat. Driving his entire body through her also provoked nothing except for a stronger life pulse. It was the worst psychological hit since realizing his own family couldn't interact with him. And yet, there was still a tiny bit of hope remaining in him. Billions of humans and millions of Exes were waiting out there waiting to be tested on.

If it wasn't for some of the perks, the misery would have been completely overwhelming. The biggest and most obvious advantage was going and seeing anything he wanted. He enjoyed standing in the infield during baseball season and seeing the action up close, not being at all bothered by the heat. Concerts and other sports venues were good hangouts as well. Seeing as his predicament was bleak, he did allow himself a few peeks of some high school or college girl's showers and the like, though he did not do this often, seeing as he lacked the ability to...express his gratitude.

The weeks and months clocked by with this same pattern repeating itself. In the year 2000, sometime in an August afternoon, he was haunting the Grand Canyon's North Rim when he heard an unusual crackling laugh. Following the curious cackling led him to the edge of the canyon wall. There he saw a shocking site. Leaning over a railing was a man dressed in a tattered uniform, which looked to be from the Union side of the Civil War, and, most striking of all, he could see right through him. Despite his maddening laugh, Felix crept closer and cried a greeting.

The fellow ghost only kept laughing until Felix stood directly behind him and shouted, "Sir! Can you hear me!?"

The ghosts stopped leaning over the railing and turned around. His face told he was about fifty or so and had a malnourished look to it. "Lincoln!" he said raucously. His voice sounded dry, broken, and echoless. "He's on the other side! Truman wants to see him right away! Did Eliot tell you about her new pot?"

The crazed ghost then ran through Felix as if he had just seen Lincoln and was urgently trying to catch up with him. Felix noticed that he felt nothing when the phantom passed through him. Attempting to grab the lost soul's attention was pointless and the weary, saner ghost had to give up his chase after several hours. Nevertheless, it was something different, even if it was a glimpse of his own future.

Chapter Three

April 8, 2014

"So, Charlene, what color nail polish will you wear for your big date?" Shelley asked her friend between their high school classes.

Charlene pulled out the needed algebra book from her locker, feeling a little annoyed her companion was still on this topic. Not that she was unconcerned about her looks, of course— any cursory glance would have informed anyone she cared about matching clothes, accessories, and shoes—she was just never one to talk about every detail, and Shelley had been going through the entire playbook.

"I don't know," Charlene answered nonchalantly, now regretting telling her excitable friend her boyfriend had a surprise for her. "I might borrow one of your red ones, actually."

Shelley noticed her friend's indifferent tone. "It's your two month anniversary. I can't imagine he won't expect a serious move from you. He'll probably take you to some romantic-"

"He doesn't expect anything," said Charlene defiantly. "Devin's not like that. I wouldn't be going out with him if he was."

"I don't know. I find it difficult to believe a guy that good looking won't get frustrated and move on."

"Are you trying to get me to sleep with him?"

"No. Well, I mean, if you like him so much and he's kinda really hot, then something's gotta give, right?"

Charlene only rolled her eyes as she turned to leave for her class. Shelley could really be a bit sex crazed, and the worst part was now wondering whether Devin was indeed expecting for her to take the final step. "Dammit, Shelley," she muttered under her breath.

Hours later, Devin came up to pick her up for their Tuesday evening date. From her second-story bedroom window, she could see him getting out of his black Jeep Wrangler, wearing nothing that indicated he was treating this particular day as special. She also imagined he would have let her know to wear something fancy if they were going someplace upscale. He rang the doorbell and one of her sisters answered.

She next heard her nine year old sister Ann yell out, "Charlotte! My future brother-in-law is here!"

That really irritated her. She despised it when someone called her by her real name. "Looks like Ann will mysteriously lose her favorite hat for a couple days," she mused to herself. Seeing no reason to change from what she outfitted herself with, she merely put on her most comfortable black leather boots to go with her jeans and emerald jacket and went downstairs. She saw her thirteen year old sister Emily, currently going through a goth-phase, talking to Devin, but didn't see Ann anywhere.

Emily must have noticed her older sister looking for her because she said, "I didn't see where she went."

"Well, you better find her eventually. Mom just texted me. She won't be back from her shift until two, so you'll have to feed her."

Emily's response was to collapse face first on their plush linen sofa and, in a voice stifled by the cushions, said, "I'll order pizza."

"Ann won't keep that a secret," warned Charlene.

"It'll be a veggie one," said the muffled voice.

"Yeah, right," Charlene said doubtfully. She turned to see Devin leaning by the door wearing a wily smile. "What?"

He shrugged and replied, "Nothing, you just look adorable."

Emily groaned.

"Shut up, Emily. We're going, and for the love for all that is holy make sure Ann doesn't get into the attic again."

She was sure Emily groaned again, but the door was already closing behind her and didn't hear it. As soon as she sat in the passenger seat, she began trying to read Devin's demeanor for any possible change. She cursed Shelley again for sticking this train of thought in her mind. Neither she nor Devin were pushing for sex. It would come naturally and not become obligatory simply because of a calendar date. But what if she was wrong? What if he did force the issue? What was his surprise for her?

"Where we going?" she asked Devin in a slightly nervous tone once they started for the road.

He didn't seem to notice the minor change in her tone, as he kept his usual aloofness. "Didn't I say it was a surprise?" A couple moments later he continued. "Guess there's no point keeping it any longer. Check the glove box."

She opened it and pulled out two tickets. When she read what they were for all her anxiety vanished and she began laughing. She was certain that he didn't know what the date indicated. It was merely a coincidence.

"Hey, what's so funny?" he wondered, looking a little perturbed.

"No, it's nothing, really. Home opener. Seattle Mariners. Should be lovely."

In hindsight, it all made sense. Devin played both football and baseball and loved to watch nearly any sport. Combined with the facts that neither of them paid much attention to their previous minor anniversaries, and that she liked to see games with him, she should have inferred his intention.

He still looked a little hurt she laughed at the tickets, so she leaned in and kissed his cheek, saying, "Trust me, I'm very happy right now."

She began thinking the night might end better than she first thought.

Chapter Four

Felix was glad to be back in the good ol' U.S of A. He would have arrived earlier, but he ended up hovering around an Ex for the last few weeks in Japan. This Ex was part of the Yakuza and had the ability to harden his skin and make it tough enough to deflect small arms fire. After stalking him for some days, Felix quickly discovered that he was actually an undercover cop, who was eventually able to gather enough evidence to arrest several high ranking members. Unhappily, the Yakuza discovered who had infiltrated them and had Yuuma, that was the cop's real name, assassinated by another Ex-human. Felix knew this assassin to be an infamous and brutal killer colloquially labeled in America as the Pursuer.

Felix had tracked him once before and was able to discover that the Pursuer was most likely of Spanish origin, given his loose resemblance to Antonio Banderas, and due to the nature of his profession, was constantly on the move. How he managed to be hired at all and avoid capture by even the Stewards was a mystery Felix would have to dedicate weeks to answering, however, he didn't much enjoy trailing criminals when he could do nothing to stop them. The assassin had superhuman senses and reflexes, which he combined with highly tuned martial arts to get close to any target and use any number of weapons to eliminate them. He specifically killed Yuuma by driving a long, thin blade into his mouth and, while he was wildly trying to pull it out, the Pursuer was able to trip him up and thrust a second long knife through Yuuma's eye and into his brain. This all happened in his Tokyo apartment while his wife watched and screamed. She was also executed shortly thereafter. It was after this sad episode that Felix decided to return to mainland America and take a break from watching what Exes were doing.

The plane landed in Seattle where he soon learned the Mariners were experiencing their opening day. It was a bit of good luck he thought. It had been three years since he last saw an American baseball game. He arrived in the beginning of the second inning and started going through the crowd to hear what we could of the latest baseball news. He could always trust to find groups of die-hard fans scattered throughout the stadium discussing hard-core baseball stats and news.

After a few minutes of wandering aimlessly through the stadium, something unusual struck his life sense. Fifteen years of traveling the world and sensing millions upon millions of living things made him familiar with virtually every kind of aura possible, but what he currently sensed was unlike anything he could categorize. This aura wasn't particularly strong and so could not belong to an Ex, but it was also far too unique to belong to the average human. From what he could tell, it was somewhere in the seats behind third base. Intrigued, he went down to search for which individual it belonged to. With his years of experience, it didn't take him long to pinpoint the person who owned the intriguing aura sitting on the eighth row and a couple seats inside the aisle, where he now stood.

His first reaction was to be briefly taken aback. The odd aura emanated from a stunning young woman, who looked to him to be either in high school or possibly a young college student. She sported shoulder-length, auburn hair that enveloped a gorgeous face, which held a pair of soft, amber eyes, an endearing button nose, and full, rose colored lips. Her body was lean and fit, giving him the impression she must have been active to keep up her figure. He had seen many, many women in his travels and she would unquestionably be one of the few whose image would be seared into his mind for some time, notwithstanding her exceptional aura. Sitting next to her was someone who could only be her boyfriend. A tall, good-looking guy with a dark mane of hair, moderately bulky muscles, and was carrying a tray of nachos they were sharing.

Seeing a happy couple was still one of the few things that

really depressed Felix. He became disturbingly emotionless to witnessing murders, domestic violence, bullying, and general injustices, but seeing something he truly yearned for greatly affected his temperament. He stared at the revolting couple for a few minutes in what could only be described as a semi-trance, or, if anyone could see him, as an eerie pervert. When he regained his faculties, he took a few steps towards the girl to feel what her abnormal aura felt like. It was the only sensation he could enjoy and this one promised to be interesting. Felix reached out to touch her left shoulder and on making contact, something so unexpected happened that he believed the blood he didn't have froze in his nonexistent blood vessels. She reacted.

She was slanting to her right so that she could comfortably wrap her right arm around her boyfriend's upper arm, but when Felix's fingers contacted her shoulder, she immediately straightened, much like someone would do if a small piece of ice were placed inside their shirt. Felix pulled away his hand in mild panic.

Noticing her reaction, Devin asked, "You okay?"

Grabbing her left shoulder she looked about herself, clearly very confused. "I-I'm fine. I just had this very weird feeling."

"Really? Like what?"

"You know, weird."

"No, I don't know," he said, half laughing.

"Just forget it."

The thing was, she couldn't forget it. The feeling was

undeniably the strangest she had ever felt in her remembered life. It was similar to a powerful sense of déjà vu combined with an instant, but brief, energy rush, and she saw nothing that could have caused it.

For Felix, the aura itself surpassed his expectations. Even after he had pulled away he still felt that electric-like pulse coursing his being. He also noticed her aura didn't let go easily. It was comparable to pulling a metal object away from a strong magnet. It required every measure of his being not to walk through her entire body or yell out something. If she could indeed feel him, or more excitingly, possibly hear him, then he couldn't be too rash and frighten her away. He had to choose his next actions carefully.

First, he waited several minutes before giving her a more subtle tap on her shoulder to see if she would react again, seeing as he had experienced false alarms before. This time she responded almost like a mosquito had bitten her, but seeing as her light jacket prevented bugs from stinging her, there was another troubled expression on her face. She rotated her shoulder, acting like their might be some type of nerve damage affecting her. Next, he wanted to check if she could hear him. He thought for a few minutes and came up with a simple plan. Felix had heard what her boyfriend's name was during his earlier gawking and decided to call it out. He walked a few rows behind them and prepared to holler Devin's name, but the crowd suddenly roared with excitement when someone hit a three run homer to allow the home team to take the lead. Frustratingly, Felix had to wait several more minutes for the inning to end so the crowd noise would die down. When the epoch finally ended, he was able to yell out Devin's name loud enough for her to overhear, if she could, but not loud enough to make it crystal clear. The exclamation had the desired effect.

Charlene turned around and examined the crowd behind her. "Did you hear that?" she asked her date.

"Hear what?"

"Your name. I thought I heard someone call you."

"No, I didn't hear anyone," answered Devin, looking behind him to check if there were any familiar faces.

"I guess I misheard."

She frowned slightly to herself. She was sure she didn't mishear it, and it struck her as odd that no one she looked at actually appeared to be calling anyone. Her hand unconsciously reached for her left shoulder again.

Felix, meanwhile, could scarcely contain himself. He rushed down to the couple after shouting the name and was able to clearly hear the girl's last sentence. He bounded from sheer joy around the couple's section, careful not to exclaim anything too loudly or risk her overhearing him. For the rest of the game, he preserved a constant watch over her, adamant to follow her to the ends of the universe or to any undiscovered dimensions she might cross. In that interval, he thought through different ways he could open up a line of conversation that would least freak her out. He had imagined this scenario countless and countless times, but there was a completely different methodology to his thinking now that it was so close to reality. He knew he would have to wait for just the right moment, wanting for them to start off with the best possible foot. But what to say? It didn't help that she was insanely beautiful and in his living days would be a couple leagues below her. At least she wouldn't see that.

Once the game was over, he followed the couple to a nearby Italian themed restaurant where they shared a large pizza for nearly an hour. It was here Felix first learned the young woman's name was Charlene. From what Felix could gather, Charlene was a bright young woman and Devin didn't appear to be simply a dumb jock or anything, not as smart as the girl, but still not your stereotypical buff moron. They were a sickeningly attractive couple. The more he scrutinized the girl of his hopes and dreams, the more he liked her. She didn't strike him as the type to act superior because of her looks, and if she did insult you, would accomplish it in a polite and charming way.

After their meal, Devin drove her to an upper middle-class neighborhood and stopped in front of a modern style, two-story home. For a while, Felix, who had sat himself in the back seat, was worried the two might enter the home and finish the night off with a bang. Over a decade of closely watching almost every kind of person turned Felix into a good people reader and he could tell Devin was regretting something going by his marginally nervy demeanor. Charlene was pretty much at ease until they reached the driveway. The air around them became somewhat awkward and he knew both of them were thinking about something they each had not evidently done before. The relationship exhibited both the signs of a first date and of an old married couple. The awkwardness ended as they kissed goodnight and Charlene exited the jeep alone, much to the relief of Felix.

The inside of the house was decorated nicely and comfortably, but wasn't anything too special. He had been in some very outlandish homes and was by this point numb to anything but the tremendously outlandish. The house was quiet and she moved in a way that wouldn't disturb a napping tiger. Much of the floors were wooden or tiled so she had to take off her boots to accomplish this feat. She appeared to be examining all the rooms. He had the notion she was hoping not to find something out of place. His aura check revealed there were two auras upstairs, neither of which possessed the unique aura Charlene carried. Satisfied with the condition of the first floor, she went downstairs into the basement, which was furnished as an entertainment center with a large flat screen TV fitted with a PlayStation 3, a dark leather couch, an old pool table, scattered board games, and some drums and guitars. Charlene didn't spend long here and went upstairs after only a hasty scan.

On reaching the second floor, the haunted girl ignored the room in front of the stairs and the room down the hall to the left. Felix could feel the left one was empty and the other was occupied by what was likely a younger sibling. She instead turned to her right and made a quick right, heading for the second aura, carefully opening the first door on the left side of the hallway and entered the mostly darkened room. She didn't bother turning on the light and began to drag her feet so she wouldn't step on anything that happened to be on the floor. In the other side of the room was a twin sized bed where Felix could see the outline of a child, which, going by the décor, was presumably a young girl. Charlene's destination was a hat rack in the farthest corner and she proceeded to snatch an old-fashioned brimmed hat with a rose-like flower clinging to the bowl.

After gaining her prize, she stealthily made her way back to the door and shut it behind her. She looked pleased at accomplishing this frivolous errand and entered what turned out to be her room, located beyond the bathroom and facing the street. Everything in the room appeared to be precisely put in its place and contained a few predictable feminine touches, like a couple stuffed animals and cute stickers of various cartoon characters, had the typical pictures of her family and friends, a few academic and athletic awards, and a small plasma television. Felix did enjoy the fact that the walls lacked posters of boy bands and that everything wasn't pink. The hat was placed in her backpack in a way that wouldn't fold or crush it. As soon as she answered a text, she started to undress. It was here Felix decided to leave her alone, not wanting to invade the privacy of the only person who might actually have a chance to befriend him. Another half hour later, the light in her room turned off.

He wandered the house, but found nothing specifying the

family wasn't anything but ordinary, however, due to the complete lack of any kind of father pictures, he theorized the mother divorced him at some point. When the matriarch of the all-girl home came in about an hour after Charlene went to bed, he confirmed that no one in the household could be expected to sense him any more than usual. The woman was as he projected the mother of Charlene to look like, middle-aged, but attractive, though she had longer, darker hair and was obviously very tired. The rest of the night he spent imprinting Charlene's aura into his mind to allow him to easily detect it amongst a crowd of a hundred thousand people from as far as five hundred feet away. The excitement meant time slowed down significantly, but Felix was by now an extremely patient entity and dawn ultimately came.

Charlene was the first to wake up. Once she washed up, she directed her legs into the kitchen and began fixing breakfast for herself and her two sisters, who awakened not long after. Felix was able to hear and sense the youngest dash out of her room and head for the kitchen to meet her chief sister.

"Where is it?" asked the little girl vehemently, still in her SpongeBob pajamas.

"You didn't hear?" replied Charlene, knowing what Ann was referring to. "It's in a farm living happily on a pig's head."

"Give it back!" exclaimed the youngest, though she didn't yell as loudly as she probably could, undoubtedly aware her mother was soundly asleep after a long shift.

Charlene still didn't appreciate the order and tone. "I

suggest you drop the subject if you don't want to eat burned eggs with untoasted wheat bread. Besides, if you're good today, I have a feeling the pig will bring it back."

The threat of unsatisfactory food quieted the child, but she still pouted her way upstairs. Shortly after this scene, all three girls were eating the eggs, toast, bacon, and biscuits Charlene had prepared. With the little one in a bad disposition, the middle child apparently going through a phase where she pretended to hate everything, Charlene still groggy, and all of them scarfing down their food, there wasn't much conversation to be had. It was at this time when Felix tapped on the other sister's shoulders to make sure they couldn't feel him. There were no reactions.

They all entered into a dark blue Camaro in the garage when they finished eating and the eldest dropped them off at their respective schools. Felix tried keeping his distance from Charlene to make sure a sudden movement from her wouldn't accidently contact him, so he sat in the backseat between Emily and Ann. Felix was tempted to talk to her when she came to be alone, but decided to continue remaining discreet. He didn't think she'd freak out and crash, but taking any kind of risk to her life was unthinkable. Nevertheless, he was becoming anxious and impatient for the first time in many years. All he could think of doing was blurting out, *I'm here!*

High schools hadn't changed in the last fifteen years since his death and Charlene's was fairly typical, though it did have an exquisite water fountain up front dedicated to someone he had never heard of. There was still time before class started, so she went into the cafeteria in the middle of the school to talk to a group of five friends in one of the tables. One of the girls in the group seemed especially interested in knowing how Charlene's date went. In any case, the bell signaling the beginning of school soon rang and the group split into smaller groups. Charlene walked to her homeroom with a guy Felix quickly identified as gay, though the boy didn't try to hide it or anything. The gay topic took a further and further back seat as more Ex-humans popped up and overshadowed it. Though being a homosexual Ex was an especially bad prospect in some regions.

Felix finally settled on a plan during her homeroom period. He would try talking to her in one of her classes. After studying her a bit, he was pretty sure she wouldn't simply run out screaming out of the classroom. The situation would instead force her to remain quiet while he was allowed to plead his case. As long as she didn't think herself crazy and immediately check herself into a mental institute, it felt like a decent plan. He didn't want to disrupt her entire school day, so he resolved to wait until one of her final class periods. Seeing her diligently listening to her teachers and completing her work with ease confirmed his hypothesis that she wasn't just looks, giving him even more confidence she would be able to handle the impending unique situation.

In the second to last period, a social studies class, Felix saw the opportunity he was looking for. The last ten minutes of the class was spent on a quiz. The room was quiet and he likely wouldn't be interrupted by any teacher instruction. He permitted Charlene a few minutes on the quiz, predicting she wouldn't need much time to finish it. The trust was rewarded when she finished in less than five minutes.

He moved to be adjacent the student sitting in front of her, gulped an instinctively tense breath and, perhaps a little too quickly, said, "Charlene, please stay calm. No one can hear me except for you, so please stay calm and just listen to what I have to say." He paused a second to gauge her reaction. She slowly straightened her back and her widening eyes attentively browsed the area she thought the voice was originating from, but she remained silent, so Felix continued. "I know this is insane and I don't want to scare you. My name is Felix Everett. I know this is a bad time to talk and I don't have time to say everything I want to say. I know this sounds disturbing as hell, but I need to talk to you, and since I'm sure you have no interest in declaring yourself crazy in front of people, I'll be waiting by your car after your last class to explain. Again, I know how this sounds, but please, just a few minutes of your time. Please." He, of course, wouldn't head directly for her car; he still planned to drift around her.

Charlene was understandably bewildered at what had transpired, so much so, she didn't hear the teacher tell everyone to pass up the quizzes and the girl behind her had to place the papers on her shoulder to get her attention. Once she began to actually think of what had occurred, she found she didn't know quite how to feel or what to do. She quickly dismissed the idea of telling anyone. No one in the room appeared to have heard the enigmatic voice and she was still unsure she had really heard it. She came up with several theories ranging from an Ex playing a trick on her to an intense daydream enacted by a hallucinogenic drug slipped in by one of the lunch ladies. Whatever it was, there was one unmistakable quality about the disembodied voice. He sounded painfully desperate.

Chapter Five

There was no forgetting the voice all through her last class period and, despite her best efforts, could not help but feel apprehensive when he said he would wait for her by her car. She did not like the idea of being alone with whomever the voice belonged to, so she formulated a plan she believed would work well enough. After the school day ended, she texted Isaac, a friend of hers, who also happened to be a car fiend, to meet her outside near the water fountain.

"Hey Charlene," said Isaac when he met her outside, a light drizzle dappling them both. "You asked for a favor?"

"Yes. Do you mind looking under the hood of my car? It could be my imagination, but it sounded a little funny when I started it this morning. I just want to make sure nothing's wrong."

"Yeah, I could take a quick look if you want. Would hate for that girl of yours to be feeling bad when you just got her."

They walked to her car and she popped the hood and he began taking a look. She acted like her phone was vibrating and answered it. She felt much more confident now that someone was with her.

"Hello? Are you there, Felix?" she asked, closing the car door so Isaac couldn't hear anymore.

Felix saw what she did and he couldn't help but love it. She was definitely something. In a way, it helped him to relax. "I'm here," he answered, phasing into the backseat. For a moment, neither one could come up with anything more to say, each absorbing the situation. Felix finally nervously added, "Thanks for coming."

"You are in *my* car. Who are you?"

Strangely, he initially wanted to respond with a joke – maybe he'd say something like "I'm your conscience" but he refrained and actually said, "Well, like I said, my name is Felix Everett, I like long walks on the beach, watching sports, and… I've been dead since 1999."

He waited for her reply, but before she could say anything, the stifled voice of Isaac told her to turn on the engine, which she did.

"You mean you're a ghost or something?" she asked a little dubiously, her eyes scanning the apparently occupied backseat through her rearview mirror.

"You can call it that."

"All right, let's say I pretend this joke is going over my

head and I just accept that you're a ghost. Why was I the only one to hear you back in the room?"

"I don't know. You're the only one who has been able to hear me after years of searching."

"Wait. How did you even know I could hear you?" wondered Charlene.

Felix wasn't expecting for her to ask that. "Oh, I, uh, tested it."

"When?"

"Keep in mind that I had to be careful in my position. For fifteen years I've been unable to interact with anyone until you, so I had to approach things carefully."

"When?" she repeated, with a more interrogating tone than before.

"The first time I met you. Yesterday's Mariners game. I called out Devin's name to see if you would hear it."

"*You* called him?" She tried to be understanding, especially if he was telling the truth about the fifteen years of no human interaction, but she still felt perturbed a ghost, or at least some nutcase, was apparently around her for nearly an entire day without her knowing it. She then remembered the strange sensation on her shoulder. "And you also touched me, didn't you?"

"This sounds bad, doesn't it? Yeah, that was also me. It was how I first knew you might have a chance at hearing me."

"By touching me you realized you could possibly talk to me?"

"Yeah, besides no one being able to hear me, no one can sense me in any way, even if I walk through their whole body. This goes for Ex-humans as well. Anyway, I touched you because you have this very remarkable aura. I've sensed countless auras over the years and none were like yours, so I couldn't help but feel it up close. It really shocked me when you actually reacted to it."

He would have kept talking, but Isaac slammed the hood down and went up to the window, which Charlene lowered.

"Everything seems to be in working order," said Isaac. "You probably just turned the key too hard or something."

Wearing an amiable smile that would charm Hades himself, she replied, "Probably. Thanks a ton, Isaac. I feel loads better. See you next time I need use of you."

Felix was thoroughly impressed by Charlene's ability to juggle the situations she was handling. Once Isaac was walking away, Felix said, "I thought you might make him stay longer."

It wasn't until Felix mentioned the obvious option did it cross her mind. A swift evaluation of her current frame of mind revealed she was bizarrely at ease with the situation. She had to assume it was because her common sense didn't yet fully grasp what was happening, conceivably thinking it was all a weird dream. Seeing no way she could simply leave now, she decided to continue the abnormal conversation after a deep inhale.

"I think you might be a sick creep, but not a dangerous one. Anyhow, you were saying something about auras?"

Her attitude and question told him she was already beyond

cautious anxiety and delving into the more entrancing realm of curiosity, significantly uplifting his mood. He said, "Every living thing has what I call an aura. Humans, animals, Exes, and they're all unique, like a fingerprint. When I touch someone I can feel their life energy and, admittedly, I take some minor pleasure out of it. It's the only sensation I can still feel, and yours is unlike any I've ever felt before."

That last part sounded like he was trying to give her a compliment, but not knowing how to respond to it, she ignored it and asked the first thing that came to mind. "You say you've been dead for fifteen years?"

"Yes."

"May I ask how you died?"

"Drunk driver. I didn't even make it to the hospital."

"I see. So you've just been wandering around?"

"I believe the politically correct term would be 'haunting,' and yeah, pretty much."

Charlene was quiet for some moments, trying to contemplate what being alone for fifteen years would be like. How could someone go unbroken after that? She had to admire him for staying relatively sane. Again, this was assuming he was telling the truth, or if he was telling the truth but still deviously crazy. She elected to ask what she was pondering outright to gauge his response. "What is it you want?"

"What we're doing now. Just some talking... I know it can't mean much now, but I swear not to be a burden to you. Even if you agree to only speak with me for once a year for five minutes at a time, I'll be grateful forever."

There was a level of heartbreak in his tone that she'd never heard anyone attain before. It was like if someone was timidly begging her for their life. She had to lighten the mood or she felt she would tear up, so she said, "Don't be silly, ten minutes a year should be fine."

If he still had the ability to cry, this little joke would have set off his waterworks, instead he psychologically choked up and didn't say anything.

"What do you plan on doing now?" probed Charlene after half a minute of silence.

"That's up to you, really."

"You already know where I live, right?"

"Yeah," he replied shyly.

She sighed and began backing up the car. If he had indeed been deprived of conversation for a decade and a half then she doubted he would merely leave her alone if she told him to buzz off, and, moreover, she didn't really want to.

"Where are you going?" asked Felix.

"I'm tired so I'm going home. You can come, I guess, but I do have some rules."

"Naturally. I assume I can't enter any bedrooms and bathrooms."

"Yeah, otherwise, we'll take this a day the time. I'll admit, if you aren't a crazy pervert or something, this could be interesting.

You must have picked up quite a bit of in your travels."

"A couple things."

"Well, go ahead, tell me something juicy. I have to get something out of this or I'm going to change my mind when I start thinking straight."

"All right, that's easy. You know the vigilante known as Hermes? The guy who can control gravity? From what I gathered, he was taught and trained by his parents at a young age. They wanted him to emulate the best of mankind or something. Anyway, here's the kicker, his name is Carl Myers."

"Myers? You mean from the Myers Corporation that owns, like, everything?"

"I'd put it at a fourth of everything."

"Do you know that who's responsible for his mother's death?"

"Before my time. I just know it was probably due to their support of Exes, but I haven't caught anyone openly bragging about it."

"Wow, that is juicy."

"Wait until I tell you about his girlfriends. Hey, can I ask you something?"

"Sure."

"Now, I swear I didn't see anything except for what I'm about to ask. I left as soon as you closed your door. I actually feel stupid for reminding you I followed you, but I'm in too deep now, so here it goes. Why'd you take your sister's hat?"

There was indeed a pang of aversion knowing she wasn't alone last night, but blew by it and said, "Oh, to teach her a lesson."

"What lesson?"

"She called me by my real name. I don't like my real name and she knows better."

"May I ask what it is?"

"Promise not to call me by it?"

"Of course. You can make me call you Queen of Canned Meats if you want. I'm just curious."

"Uh, Charlene is fine for now. My real name is Charlotte."

"Why don't you like it?"

"It sounds so old-fashioned. It's like nails on a chalkboard to me."

As she stopped at a traffic light about halfway home, she imagined going up to her mother, telling her she had found a ghost, and asking whether she could keep it. The thought made her crack a grin at first, until she realized Felix must have a family somewhere.

"Felix? Do, I mean, is your family out there?" After several seconds of silence, she thought she must have been too insensitive. "I'm sorry, I didn't-"

"No, don't apologize. Sorry, I was just thinking. I haven't seen my family in three years. Last I checked, my mother and father were still working, though at least one of them might have retired by now. My older sister is a prosecutor in San Diego, married with two kids, and my younger brother is a physical therapist and already divorced. Don't worry, I'm not going to ask you to talk to them."

She was going to ask why not, but checked herself. He probably would like to let his family know he wasn't completely gone, but perhaps didn't feel ready to trust her with a task wrought with emotional peril. What if they didn't believe her and only ended up hurting them? Even the best case scenario had them believing her, but then she would eventually have to return to her own life and essentially leaving his family hanging out to dry. They would have to treat the situation delicately and only if they fully trusted each other. She wanted to believe he really was a wandering soul and gave him the benefit of the doubt for now, but she had to remember this could still be a tasteless joke by an Ex-human.

Wanting to change the subject, and genuinely interested, she asked, "What can you do as a ghost?"

"As you've probably guessed, I can go through any solid object. I can't fly or float, though, no matter how much I've tried. I can fall from great heights without consequence. It's weird 'cause gravity doesn't affect me like it would you. I fall at this slow, constant rate. About as fast as a guy with an open parachute. Then there's the life sense I described earlier. It's always on, but when I really focus I can sense a butterfly fifty yards off and tell it apart from one of the same species."

"Impressive. Hey, are there are other ghosts like you?"

"Oh. Well, yes and no."

"How do you mean?"

"Remember they can't harm you or anyone else, well, I haven't witnessed a ghost harming anyone, anyway. There are a few I've crossed paths with, except none of them had all their marbles together. There aren't that many and I don't know why there aren't more and why we're ghosts to begin with. I also never met one coming from later than the hippie era and rarely where there are a lot of people. I think the density of auras bother them."

"I don't regret asking that at all," Charlene said sarcastically.

"Will you tell anyone about me?"

"I've been mulling that over. Proving I'm not crazy shouldn't be that difficult. You could tell me things I couldn't possibly know, like getting someone to write down an impossibly huge random number and you tell me what it is while I'm on the other side of the room, and other stuff like that. Would you mind if I told anyone about you?"

"Only if you don't completely trust them to keep it a secret. I don't want to go public or anything if I haven't told my own family. I assume you don't either. Even if you don't quite have the aura of an Ex, people will treat you like one."

"I won't tell anyone right away, I guess, not until I'm sure how this will work out. In fact, I don't want to be mean, but if I can be honest, I'm not quite comfortable having you in my house."

"I wasn't expecting you to be as welcoming as you've

been. I'll get out now and meet you anywhere and anytime you want."

She suddenly felt bad about expressing her distrust, but she needed a way to prove he was trustworthy. But how to keep track of a ghost? A little smile formed when a strategy began to materialize. She asked, "Do you mind staying in on one spot until tomorrow?"

"I'll spend three days hopping in that spot."

"I couldn't tell if you were hopping. I could have you constantly singing, but I'm pretty sure I'll regret that. No, I'm planning something else. When we arrive, just wait in the car a few minutes. To prove you will, I'm going to leave my phone and call it from the house phone and when I come back, you'll tell me how many times it rang."

"Sounds easy enough." Felix felt pleased he met someone who thought things through, almost as if he was the one who had chosen her.

She pulled the car up to her house a few minutes later and entered the garage. "Wait here," she ordered, leaving her phone in the passenger seat.

What seemed an instant later to Felix, her phone rang.

Charlene came back holding a digital watch not long after that. "How many rings?" she asked.

"Four."

"Good. Now then, I set up three alarms on this watch, which I'm leaving here," she explained, putting the watch on the dashboard.

"And you want me to tell you what times they go off," Felix surmised. "If I miss one, you'll assume the worst."

"Maybe not the worst, but it won't be good."

"Not a bad plan for someone with blood."

"Well, there are some perks to having blood in the brain."

"Then I've seen more ghosts than I thought."

Hesitantly, she left him in the car. She felt like asking him more questions, but thought it was better to step back a while and process what the hell she was getting herself into. When she walked back inside the house, she saw Emily in the kitchen making a sandwich. If making sandwiches was an art form, she'd have her own exhibit.

"Where are Mom and Ann?" Charlene asked.

"Mall," answered Emily, not looking up from her work.

Charlene was about to ask why she didn't go as well, but was reminded of her current phase by her dark clothing and makeup. She actually thought she looked cute as a goth and was pretty sure she was doing it to impress a boy.

"Say," started Charlene, "you by any chance haven't learned anything about spirits from the dark arts have you?"

After swallowing the piece of sandwich, her sister said, "Possibly. Why do you ask?"

"I'm being haunted by one."

"Like, by an old guy?"

"He sounded around my age, actually, but I suppose he

technically would be a bit older than me."

"Just threaten him with a sexual harassment lawsuit. That worked for one of my friend's mom. Got her boss to stop hitting on her"

"Truly, the dark arts are such a mystery to me."

Charlene went upstairs and found herself becoming more worried about Felix. It was just dawning on her that she really couldn't stop a ghost from going anywhere. She discovered she was more at ease talking with the inexplicable presence rather than not being able to personally keep tabs on him. It wouldn't have bothered her so much if she lived alone or if it was at least a female ghost. All she could do now, however, was wait and see, or more accurately, hear, if he passed her test... and definitely skip her evening shower.

Her apprehension grew enough so that she couldn't concentrate on her homework, pay the usual attention to her friends' texts and calls, or find the courage to go to sleep. In the long battle between her apprehension and her instinct to trust him, instinct and inevitability finally won out and she was able to sleep surprisingly effortlessly once she permitted her drowsy body to lay on her mattress a little after two in the morning.

Chapter Six

Though not as much of a snooze as she wanted to get, she was still amazed to see she had slept without waking up from anxiety. For a little while, she even believed the supernatural encounter might have been a potent dream. She surprised herself when she found herself wishing that wasn't the case. Seeing she still had some time, she mumbled, "Screw it," and decided to take a shower. Once she braved the quickest shower of her life, she went into the garage. "Felix?" she inquired as she opened the car door to retrieve the watch from the dashboard.

"I see what you did. Very funny. You only set up two alarms; the first at 1:23 and the other at 4:56."

"Did I say three alarms before? Silly me. By the way, I'm planning to ditch. No way can I focus with you around. I find it more productive to see if I can get used to you or discover your true identity."

Felix was tempted to say something comparable to "naughty girl" but figured she wouldn't be in the humor for sensual banter, so all he said was, "Fair enough."

"When my sisters come, sit outside or something. Even if they can't feel you, I'm not okay with your spirit or whatever contacting theirs, accidentally or not."

"Yes, ma'am," consented Felix, his manner purposely mimicking an obedient soldier.

Within the next hour, Charlene dropped off her sisters once their morning routine was done.

"So where are we going?" Felix asked when he reentered the car from his seat at the trunk.

"Nowhere in particular. Most public places frown on people talking to themselves, so I'll drive around for a while until I think of somewhere more appropriate."

"Won't your friends be upset you didn't invite them to your day off?"

"I'll just say I started feeling sick or something. I don't often do this, so I can get away with it a couple times."

For much of the early part of the conversation, Felix explained more in detail what he experienced after realizing he was dead and described a little of his living life. Charlene likewise confirmed her mother did divorce her father ten years back. It was an ugly split and she had not seen him at all the last four years due to his remarriage. He picked up a mildly downhearted tone during the explanation. Next, Felix, in an attempt to impress Charlene, explained how he taught himself to understand several languages—by usually haunting a linguistic school—and was able to speak fairly fluently in a few of them in his quest to make sure that if anyone could hear him, there wouldn't be a language barrier. To demonstrate, he spoke a little Japanese and told her about his recent trip to Japan, although, he left out the gory details when he talked about the Pursuer. The conversation continued to jump from general topic to general topic until Charlene stopped near a scarcely occupied park.

"I'm tired of driving. We shouldn't be bothered much here. Let's take a walk."

They didn't walk long before they passed an older woman reading a book about a nonfictional murder mystery while the even older looking man she was with was feeding some pigeons.

"That's always bothered me," said Felix when he believed they were far enough away from the old couple for Charlene to talk back.

"What has?" she whispered.

"Books."

"Books?"

"I mean that I can't read them at my leisure. If I want to read a book or article I have to find someone who's reading it and hope they read at my pace or finish it at all. I've gotten over the fact that I can't sleep, eat, or manipulate anything, but I can still learn. It's kind of a pain in the ass, if my ass could feel pain, anyhow."

"That has to be a perk. Not feeling pain, I mean."

"I suppose," he said unconvincingly.

She sat down on the next bench she saw and thought over Felix's predicament for a long moment. "I'll be blunt," she began. "I want to trust you. My instinct tells me I should, and even my mind is beginning to accept you as a nice guy. I don't want to get an ulcer every night worrying about you."

"What are you trying to say?"

"It bothered me last night that I didn't track you myself. I'm just saying I'm not going to do that alarm test again. I think you know when you can be around me and when not to be and, in the end, I can't stop you anyway. It'll drive me crazy trying to come up with different tests trying to prove you're somewhere."

She sounded a little depressed. As this was the first crack in the armor he saw in her, this melancholy greatly frightened Felix. He knew he couldn't really make her fully trust him with any encouraging words, so he did the only thing he thought would lighten any spirit. He told a joke. He cleared his omitted throat and said, "Two nuns are sitting on a park bench. A man in a trench coat runs up and flashes them. The first nun has a stroke. The second nun tried, but she couldn't reach." There was a succinct period of silence from her, but to his relief and delight, she laughed.

She tried holding it back so she wouldn't look crazy if anyone was watching, but she didn't really succeed. It didn't require much dissecting for her to figure out why he had tried making her laugh, and she was still giggling when she said, "You dumbass. But maybe I am being a bit too serious."

"It makes sense why you would be, but I know a million more whenever you start feeling serious again."

She sighed heavily. "Felix, I swear I will find every priest, wizard, and exorcist I can if you break my trust. Now, come on, I'm hungry."

She drove to a nearby burger place she liked, and since there was still some time before the lunch hour, there weren't many people in the restaurant. Even so, she still wouldn't talk out loud and instead texted on her phone to converse with Felix when necessary.

In the middle of shoving a mouth full of burger, Felix decided it was a perfect time for another joke. He was behind her so as not to see a disapproval glance from her in time for him to finish. "Okay, let's see. The Seven Dwarfs were all taking a bath and feeling Happy. Happy got out, so they all felt Grumpy."

The joke once again succeeded in its mission. She made sure to pick up her phone to make people assume she received a funny text. She also used her phone to show a note to Felix, which read '*Asshole.*'

"All right, I'm sorry. I couldn't help it."

A few minutes later, a few college-age guys and girls came in and sat close by.

Felix remarked, "The blonde one has nice hair, doesn't she? There's something about long hair in a woman that tells me she really cares about her looks." When he turned to look at Charlene, he was instantly reminded she had short hair. "Well, that's not to say shorthaired women don't care, of course. It's just my type, is all. Not that it even matters to me given my situation."

Charlene typed '*Shut up*' into her phone.

"Good idea."

In fact, they didn't converse until they returned to her car.

"Where to now, captain?" asked Felix, using his military tone.

"Mom should be out of the house by now. She likes to have lunch with some friends and run errands. We should have the house to ourselves until she comes back with my sisters."

Her prediction proved correct. They went to the basement where Charlene turned on the television and laid down on the dark leather couch. Apparently very comfortable, Charlene ended up dozing off.

Felix watched the sleeping beauty for a few minutes, liking the way some strands of her hair fell over her left eye, and then went upstairs to leave her in private. He was greatly encouraged to see that she already felt relaxed enough to sleep with him in the same room. This was progressing far better than he could have hoped.

Charlene squeaked a short cry when she opened her eyes and saw Ann's upside-down face hovering just a couple inches from her own.

After being pushed away, Ann asked, "Why didn't you take

me to play hooky to?"

"I didn't do anything."

"That's not what your clothes say."

"I just went out to eat then I fell asleep."

"Oh, dear sister, your web of lies only grows. Was Devin here? Did he make you pregnant yet?"

"That's it!" exclaimed Charlene playfully.

The older sister stood up, picked up the smaller one, slung her over her shoulder, and walked upstairs with Ann screaming for her to put her down. She was planning to set her down in the backyard, but didn't get that far, her mother stopping her before she could turn the knob.

"Put her down," said her peeved mother. "She's not the one who skipped school. You're not planning to do that again tomorrow, are you?"

"No, Mom," answered Charlene, putting her sister back on her feet. "I felt like a little break, that's all."

"Mommy, I don't have any homework today," said Ann. "Can I go to Connie's?"

"Sure, sweetheart. Charlene, go take her and pick her up before dinner. Oh, and don't literally pick her up again!"

Connie's house was only a couple blocks away, but Charlene knew her mother didn't trust society enough to let a young girl walk or bike that far on her own.

When the eldest sister saw that Ann made it safely to her friend's house and was turning to walk back home, she heard

Felix's disembodied voice say, "I like your family."

"I'm fond of them myself."

"If you ever decide to tell them about me, I think they'll take it quite well, even your mother."

"She's an ER doctor and is around death quite a bit. I'm not sure how well that would prepare her for the undead."

"You know, I've never been in the hospital since I died. It's one of the only places I've actively avoided. It's sad to feel weak auras fading away. Sorry, I'm being depressing."

"It's okay. Listen, I just got an idea. Remember you said you're annoyed you can't read properly? How about if I download some audiobooks on my laptop and you listen to them? Would that work for you?"

"If you won't even try inventing a book a ghost can handle, I suppose it'll have to do."

The first thing Charlene did when she entered her room was to fulfill her idea. "So which story do you want to hear first?" she asked Felix as she awoke her laptop.

"I know you don't like old-fashioned stuff, but I'll have to request *Don Quixote*. The only guy I found reading it gave up halfway through. I've been bothered by it ever since."

"I don't hate everything old-fashioned. I just don't like it associated with me."

In a terrible 1940s gangster accent, Felix said, "I bet you're one of those feminist dames. Listen here, missy, just obey us men and everything will work out fine, see? Now use your witchcraft on that magic box and get me *Don Quixote*."

"Use that voice again and I'll only stream C-SPAN for you."

"Damn, I wouldn't do that to terrorists."

In a few moments, Felix was listening to *Don Quixote* while Charlene caught up with texts and family life. He listened to the audiobook the entire evening until Charlene came back from the bathroom, wearing some fluffy pink pajamas, and turned off the computer.

"Wow, I didn't expect something so shockingly girly," commented Felix.

"Oh, it's all I have, otherwise, I'd be sleeping in my birthday suit."

He couldn't tell if she was kidding or not and she didn't appear to want to clarify any further.

Before he could respond with any quip, she flopped onto her bed and asked, "Can I ask you a pointless question?"

"As long as I can answer pointlessly."

"What do you look like?"

"That's easy. Imagine the best looking guy can think of on a scale of one to ten, like if Brad Pitt and George Clooney had a baby. Now imagine I'm like a six and a half on that scale, capped with shaggy, black hair, brown eyes, and, thanks to my mother, a brown tinge on my skin. Since I've been unable to see my reflection for some time, a few of the details may have changed. It's lucky you can't see me or you wouldn't be able to resist."

"I know it was a dumb question. I was only curious."

"Yeah, it was pretty dumb."

"Okay! It's time for you to go. Patrol the house like a good ghost guard dog."

The loyal guard dog bid her goodnight and went downstairs to round the premises. The night and following day went smoothly. Felix decided to not talk too much and let Charlene get back to her usual routine. He tried being realistic, which is an ironic way for a dead person to think, about how he had to be prepared for possibly going days or weeks without Charlene wanting to talk extensively to him. He could give her answers if she was having trouble in school, but she was smart and would likely resent any substantial help. If she was lonely he could be a constant talkative companion, but she had an assortment of friends and family to lean onto, not to mention her boyfriend. He also had to come to terms with one other thing. He had no doubt that he would fall in love with her. As a result, he knew that the next year could be more of a trial than the entirety of the last fifteen.

Chapter Seven

Even if they wanted to talk to one another for a considerable amount of time, she was rarely alone to do so for the next couple of days. After school on Friday, she went out with Devin and some mutual friends to the mall and movies. On Saturday, she hung out with her sisters for the afternoon, taking them where they wanted to go. Later that evening, she went with her friends again, ending up at a house party further into the night. The gathering was packed more with Devin's friends than her own, but a girl like her was rarely at a disadvantage socially. She wasn't shy about drinking a couple of beers and didn't seem fazed by the smoke of either cigarettes or weed she had to cross every once in a while. She mostly stayed near the pool talking to a couple guys who she knew best and was careful not to get pushed in the water by an overeager partygoer. For a little while, Felix followed Devin around to overhear some of his conversations.

"What's her name?" asked a skinny young man to Devin, who appeared to be a friend of a friend and also looked to be drunk or high, probably both.

Devin hesitated, but eventually answered, "Charlotte."

"Damn, she's fine if you don't mind me asking, I mean saying. Do you think I can have my turn with her when you're done?"

Devin looked ready to knock him on his ass, and forgetting himself, Felix encouraged him by yelling, "Do it!"

The skinny guy burst out laughing and said, "Be cool man! I'm just playing. You getting all serious and s-shit."

Devin ignored him the rest of the night, but Felix noticed he kept a steady eye on him and even came in between him and Charlene once. This happened without her awareness and, to Felix's knowledge, Devin never told her he kept an incapacitated moron from bothering her.

Great, thought Felix, *he's got looks, he's a nice guy, and he doesn't even brag.*

It greatly irritated him that her boyfriend might actually be worthy of her. He knew he should feel glad, but he wasn't. What deepened the sting was realizing he might actually have wanted to befriend Devin in is living days.

Sunday evening rolled in and the girl and her ghost were in her room as he listened to more of *Don Quixote*.

Closer to her bedtime, Charlene turned off the computer

and said, "You've been kinda quiet these last couple days."

"You were always with somebody."

"Yeah, but no one can hear you. I know you don't want to bother me, but like I said before, I'm more bothered when I can't keep track of you. Unless I tell you otherwise, I prefer you feel free to comment as you feel fit."

While grateful for her words, Felix felt the need to change the theme. "You know, Devin had to keep a drunken creep off you last night."

"Oh?"

"It wasn't a big deal. I just noticed he never mentioned it to you. He's a good guy. I think of all your friends, he'd handle the news about me the best."

"If I ever decide to tell anyone."

"Want to keep me all to yourself, do you?"

"The more I think about it, the more I doubt people can handle the situation. No one can hear you except for me. It's not like if I tell someone about you it will help anyone."

"And you're worried it will more likely hurt some relationships."

"Even if I can prove you're not just a figment of my imagination, some might find it disturbing that I'm not as disturbed about a phantom hanging around me. Hell, I'm a little disturbed that I'm not disturbed. They'll worry, and they won't be able to fully trust you since they'll only have my word for it."

"It's your choice."

"I know, but if I don't tell anyone soon, they'll feel bad that I didn't trust them sooner, then I'll feel guilty."

"You know, there's no rush. You can always wait a year or five to think things through."

"Keeping a secret for that long will still make people feel like I didn't trust them."

"I think it was in the early nineteenth century when mankind invented something called lying. You don't have to tell someone you knew me that long."

"Lying, huh? Sounds intriguing."

When Wednesday evening came, Charlene spontaneously decided to join Devin and some of his friends in a poker game he and his cohorts played almost weekly. After informing Charlene they played with real money and treated the game fairly seriously, she responded by saying, "I know. I'm not going just for fun. I feel like earning some extra cash."

"I never pinned you as a gambler," said Devin. "You know, a couple of the guys are really good and there won't be any mercy from them."

"No, they just *think* they're good. I'll show them a thing or two."

"You mean *I'll* show them a thing or two," corrected Felix, a little surprised and pleased Charlene decided to use her ghostly advantage.

The three hour poker game went as expected. She lost purposefully at times, but won most of the money by the end, leaving Devin's friends and Devin himself a little dumbfounded. She giggled like the schoolgirl she was after leaving the game with Devin.

"I'm serious, we should go to Vegas," suggested Devin as he drove her back home. "You'll bankrupt the entire casino!"

"Oh, I'm not greedy, and don't worry, you can tell your friends I'll give them another month before I take their money again."

Once Charlene was back in her room, Felix said, "That was fun."

"I thought so."

"You know, if you played strip poker I would've been against you."

"I'll keep that in mind."

"Why did you decide to partake in the art of deception?"

She shrugged. "I just wanted to have some fun. Plus, some extra cash should help me buy the perfect dress for senior prom."

"Ah, prom. Where teens pretend to be fancy."

"Did you go to yours?"

"Yes."

"Did you have a good time?"

"No. I went with a girl, but I actually went to watch the girl I really wanted to go with. I was hoping she'd realize what a douche her boyfriend was and I'd be there to sweep her off her feet."

"It didn't go as planned?"

"Shockingly, it didn't. I found out later on that she moved to Hollywood to become an actress. I think I saw her in a beer commercial some years back."

"Was she critically acclaimed?"

"Her performance was much like the beer; bland."

Chapter Eight

A very rare occurrence occurred that Friday evening; Charlene was home alone. Her mother was working, Emily went to a concert with friends, and Ann was at a sleepover. Charlene herself fell ill soon after the poker party, forcing her to be house ridden. Currently, she was sitting on the couch in the basement, or what her mother dubbed the "Quarantine Zone" whenever one of her daughters had anything contagious.

"Devin is not coming over, I presume?" investigated Felix.

"I didn't want to make him sick, which would have been easy given what we were planning to do. You were eager to see us make out, weren't you?"

"Dying to."

"Damn, how did I not see that coming?"

"You're sick remember? Don't worry, you'll be better by tomorrow."

"Specters can see the future?"

"No, but I've felt enough sick auras to know yours is already recovering."

"Auras can tell you that much?"

"I've had some time to study them."

"You once told me you could touch auras?"

"You know I can. You felt it."

"Yeah, I did," she said tentatively, shifting sheepishly on the couch.

He saw the alteration in her attitude and asked, "What's on your mind?"

"I was just wondering if maybe, possibly, I could feel that again?"

"Really?"

"I think it's the medication talking, but I'm curious."

"You sure you don't want to wait until you're not as medically impaired?"

"No, I'm fine. I just want to more closely examine what the sensation is like. Go ahead and touch my hand."

"If thou commands thee." In response to the knightly tone used by Felix, Charlene held out her right hand in front of her with her fingers pointed down in a queenly manner. "Here goes, uh, literally nothing."

He suspected he was more nervous than she was as he inched his faded hand closer to hers. Still, he kept expecting for her to pull back and change her mind, but she never did. When their fingertips were only a couple inches apart, both of them felt the odd magnetic-like pull that forced Felix to touch Charlene's aura quicker than he had planned. Even though he knew more or less what to expect based on his previous experiences, Felix was still staggered at the intensity of the life pulse tingling his being. Conversely, Charlene was able to hold her hand in place for a couple seconds before the incredibly strange tingling sensation forced her to jerk back her hand. She rubbed the hand with the other.

"You okay?" asked Felix.

"Sure."

"And?"

"Tough to describe. It was sort of cold, but it wasn't bad. Like if my hand was hot and dunked in cool water. There's more to it than that, but that's the part that's too odd to describe."

"Wanna go again?"

Chuckling a bit at the hint of a double entendre, she said, "Later. You were right before. I'll wait until I feel better."

After waking up from her medically induced nap the next evening, she found she felt mostly alleviated from her sickness. When everyone else went to sleep a couple hours later, she decided it was time to try detecting Felix again. They moved from her room, where Felix had been listening to *Moby Dick*, and went back to the basement, where she didn't have to worry about being overheard as much.

"Let's see if we can go a little further," she said. She found herself unusually eager to experience the sensation again. "Go ahead. Start with my shoulder, like that first time."

"You're not going to sit down?"

"I'm recovered. I can stand."

Felix wasn't as nervous as before, but he still couldn't help feeling a little restless. It didn't help that the action strongly sounded like something he couldn't actually participate in. In any case, he held out his arm and walked up to her slowly and deliberately. In a moment, Charlene felt the apparition's hand on her aura. She shivered slightly, but held firm. Seeing no sign of protest, he continued to enter her nonphysical force until he was encompassing about a third of her aura. She began giggling at this point and pulled away, unable to control her laughter for some moments.

She eventually calmed herself down and said, "Very freaky. It's like the weirdest tickle ever. Also, the more I felt you the more I felt... something else."

"Something else?"

"Yeah, I don't know. It was like I sensed something on top of me and, as you went further, I began sensing multiple of these somethings."

"Three of them?"

"Huh? How did you know?"

"I can feel that right now. It's the auras of your family upstairs. I think you perceived them like I could."

"Really? Okay, do it again. I want to concentrate better this time." The process was repeated. On this latest attempt, Felix enveloped about three quarters of her before she dragged herself away in another fit of laughter. "Damn it! I can't help it!"

"You're making me feel inadequate."

"Shut up. Don't get me started again. Mom's a light sleeper, and so is Emily. I don't want to attract attention."

"No one can sneak up on me. Just put on a funny movie or something."

"No, it's fine. I'll just say I remembered a stupid joke. Anyway, I did feel the auras better. I even think I felt the neighbors."

"Not bad, missy."

A couple more tries later and Felix was finally able to completely enter Charlene's aura, albeit briefly. For him, it felt like he was a puzzle piece fitting nicely in its rightful place. It didn't escape him how the two of them were virtually the same height. For her, it was much like putting on the perfect sized clothing, except it was inside of her skin, and instead of feeling warm, she felt an energetic coolness. In each attempt, she found she could sense the auras more sharply, however, she couldn't conquer her laughing attack, which only became louder, and they had to stop melding.

"Together we make up an Ex," she professed, catching her breath on the couch. "I wonder if there's anything more I can possibly do?"

"We might find out if you ever stop laughing." In any event, he loved hearing her laugh and it gave him almost as much pleasure as her aura's sensation.

"We'll try again later."

Three days zipped by and Charlene and all her family were at the mall picking out the dress for the prom. She tried several, without unanimous approval for any, that is, until she came out in a dark purple, strapless dress. For Felix, she emanated the right balance of sexiness and class. Unknowingly, her family agreed with the spirit and Charlene appeared to like it as well. Felix was so enthralled by her he forgot to say anything. He had given his own commentaries with the previous dresses, usually a disapproving "Boo!" but Charlene only heard his silence on this last one. By the time he realized he should have said something, she had went back into the dressing room. He did eventually yell out, "I liked it!" but that felt terribly insufficient given what he really wanted to say.

After Charlene put on her regular clothing, she and Emily went to the adjacent restroom while her mother and Ann bought the dress.

As Charlene adjusted her hair in the mirror, she asked her sibling, "Do you think I look better with long hair?"

"Are you finally planning on growing it out? I believe it suits you better. I don't think Ann is old enough to remember you the last time you had it long."

"It hasn't been that long," insisted Charlene.

Emily's shrug ended the topic.

Charlene was up for another round of melding when

Thursday night arrived. She was more prepared to handle the experience and, within a few tries, held the meld longer and didn't laugh, at least, not as much. She ultimately became comfortable enough to walk during the meld. They found the magnetic-like attraction exerted by her aura made it easy for Felix to stick with her, unless she made an unexpected and severe movement.

While melded, Felix suddenly felt Charlene's aura briefly disappear. Spooked, he rapidly pulled away from her.

"Hey, what's wrong?" asked a worried sounding Charlene.

"You didn't feel that?"

"Feel what?"

He thought for a moment. What did it mean? Suddenly, an old memory bubbled up from the recesses of his imperceptible cranium and popped to the forefront of his mind. He remembered the apparition of the Union soldier passing through him and how he had felt nothing. Was that it? Did her aura disappear by fading along with his? But how? And why at that moment?

"Felix? You're kinda freaking me out."

"Sorry, I was thinking. I think I felt your aura match my, um, spirit perfectly, so it vanished from my radar for a while."

"Sooo… what does that mean?"

"I'm not sure. This is new territory for me, too. Hmm, remember you wondered what else you might be able to do by melding? Maybe you can do more than sense auras. If your aura became one with a ghost, then perhaps your body can act like one."

"Like go through walls and stuff?"

"It's worth a shot, don't you think?"

"Sure. What do we have to do?"

"I guess we just meld again until we match up."

They held a complete meld for several minutes, but Felix didn't feel the vanishing sensation reoccur.

Charlene was getting impatient, as she could begin to feel the fizzing in her gut from the near commencement of a laughter session. She was about to call it quits until she heard Felix say, "Wait. When I first died, I had trouble climbing stairs and obstacles until I realized my mindset had to change. Yours must need to change too. Start thinking 'I'm not here. I'm a ghost. I don't affect anything.'"

Taking his advice, she did her best to think like a ghost, though she found it mildly sad that the advice was so depressing sounding.

After another minute of trying to mimic the vanishing sensation, Felix exclaimed, "There! Try and hold whatever mind frame you have."

Charlene thought she would laugh again, but was able to hold her concentration. "I think I got it," she said. "Is it working?"

"Yes. It's strange, your aura is gone, but I still feel its pull. Try walking around a little."

"Whoa, this is weird," she said when she began taking her first steps as a nonphysical entity. "It feels like I'm almost weightless."

"Try touching the lamp."

She slowly reached for the lamp she was standing next to. He felt her tremble slightly when her fingers were only a few inches away from the shade.

"You're holding it well," he said, trying to reassure her. "Nothing to worry about."

"Who's worried?"

"Nobody, apparently."

More emboldened, she quickly crossed the last couple of inches and she saw the tips of her fingers disappear behind the shade. She immediately hauled her hand back in astonishment. "Shit! It worked!" she shouted, quickly moving to cover her mouth to suppress anymore noise, but her spiritual hands went through one another, further freaking her out. "This is so fucking weird! Hey, if I'm ghost-like, can other people hear me?"

"No idea, though I can hear you talking normally. The ghosts I've met have this non-echo quality in their voices that I don't hear in yours."

Encouraged by her earlier success, she wasted little time in trying to touch the lamp again. On the second attempt, she was daring enough to see her entire fingers go through the shade. Inevitably, she began giggling, but a frightening comprehension stopped her. She asked her companion, "Hey, what would happen if my hand was in something and my physical body came back?"

"I'm assuming nothing good. We'll have to be very careful if we keep on experimenting with this."

"Yeah, but it's not that hard to keep the fade. It feels oddly natural."

They continued practicing their melding and fading for the next couple of weeks. Charlene was swiftly able to master feeling auras, phasing her whole body through doors and walls, climbing stairs, and only rarely burst into fits of irrepressible laughter. Unlike Felix, Charlene did not gain his transparent aspect while being faded and also retained the ability to be heard, though neither of them could answer as to why that was possible. They could only assume that her living body was not able to become as diffused as he was. The experiments also revealed that any object she held when faded, such as her phone, which stopped sending and receiving signals once she performed the spectral act, would immediately drop and return to the physical plane if she either let go of the item or held it too tightly. They also discovered the bigger the item she made fade, the more tired she felt when she returned to her fleshly self, which happened when she either changed her mindset or when Felix disengaged about a third of his spirit from her body. It wasn't too taxing, but their early practice sessions didn't have her carry anything bigger or heavier than a textbook to be safe.

Felix could see she was delighted at her newfound abilities. All at once, he started having some misgivings at letting this develop as far as it had.

Chapter Nine

Her excitement over these discoveries was temporarily numbed by the arrival of prom night.

Before she would get ready and thus have no time to openly talk to one another, Felix informed her, "In case it's not obvious, I'm not going with you."

"Why not?" she asked, surprised he was the one suggesting some time apart. Up until that point, she had been the only one to ever request separating from each other.

"Seeing a lot of happy young couples sort of depresses me. Besides, you shouldn't have to worry about me making snarky comments on your special night."

"I'm not taking it *that* seriously, you know."

"Trust me, we'll both be happier."

"If you say so."

She recognized that there had to be more reason for his not going and came close to arguing the point, but decided not to press him. Maybe he was simply feeling a little down? She had little time to contemplate on his mood any further as she and her mother prepared her wardrobe, hair, light makeup, and accessories. Shortly after finishing getting arranged, Devin, some of her friends, and their dates came in a rented limo to pick her up.

Felix sighed deeply when he saw her drive away.

The night unfurled perfectly for Charlene. Both Devin and her were the main attraction at the dance floor and were almost unanimously voted king and queen. Afterwards, everyone went to an unsupervised after-prom party in a rich student's mini-mansion of a house. She was swept up by the atmosphere of the night and when Devin sneaked her aside to a separate room and locked the door, she felt ready.

By the time she came home late that night, Felix could see she was different, and not by her aura, auras couldn't tell him everything, but by using his years of studying human behavior. It felt like seeing her for the first time after a decade away from each other. The change, and the probable reason for the change, created a not unexpectedly jealous reaction in him. In a way, he found the feeling to be a welcoming departure from his previously deadened dispositions. It was the closest he felt to being alive since his death. He saw her swivel her head around, looking like she expected to see or hear someone, but she didn't call out to anyone and shut herself in her room. He allowed her go up to her room unheeded, knowing she'd pick up on his gloom if he spoke.

As soon as she stepped out her door the following

afternoon, her mother and sisters wanted to slurp up every facet of her night, which she gave, all except for the most salacious detail. Felix was able to regain his normal tone during the night and commented as usual, with no signs of his earlier ache coming out for her to possibly scrutinize. There were few words spoken between them concerning her night's exploits, but it was a silent understanding that there was no reason to bring up the matter.

Chapter Ten

Charlene's senior class graduated within the next few weeks. As both an early birthday gift and a graduation reward, her mother and her L.A. living aunt paid for a beach condo in her aunt's city for her and her friends to use for two weeks.

While eating lunch at an outdoor café in the beginning of their second week stay in L.A., Felix noticed an acquainted aura coming to sit nearby.

"Hey, do you see that older woman sitting a couple tables ahead of you?" Felix told his host. When he saw that Charlene was looking in the proper direction, he said, "That's Madam X. Retired as of four years ago from her work with the government. She's aged pretty well."

Charlene discreetly glanced at the unassuming Ex-human woman a couple times, trying not to give the telepathist a reason to read her mind. She observed that one of the most famous and experienced of all known Exes was alone and enjoying an iced tea and a hearty soup, looking wearied, but composed.

A few minutes after discovering this Ex, she heard Felix say, "Holy fucking shit balls. Crap, don't try looking for him, but standing on the other side of the street is the Pursuer, playing a tourist it seems. An infamous assassin, in case you haven't heard. Fuck, he must be here for her."

After pretending to get a text, Charlene told her two friends, "Mom wants me to call her. Excuse me a sec." She rose up from her seat and walked out of their hearing range and farther away from Madam X. Pretending to be on the phone, but still talking low, she asked, "Should we warn her?"

"Getting involved will be extremely dangerous. That Pursuer guy is no joke. He'll probably watch her carefully for a while until he can gather all the info he needs. Anyone who gets into contact with his target will be marked. We, or I should say, you, can't simply walk up to her and say, 'Hey, across the street is a notorious assassin that probably wants to kill you. Take care!'"

"Who's suggesting that? I know I can't be stupid. It just seems wrong not to do anything when you have such important information."

"I didn't suggest doing nothing either. It's just a scary thought involving you in a very high stakes game."

"That's nice of you, but with you around me all we have to do is meld and nothing can hurt me."

"There's more than one way to hurt a person."

"Still, if we're careful-"

"I know, I know. Listen, I don't think there's a way to give her a message right now without inviting his unwanted attention. I'll follow her and find out where she's staying. Once I figure that out, I'll meet you back at the condo and we'll go from there."

"You sure that won't take too long?"

"No, but the Pursuer is patient, furthermore, she's not helpless, even at her age. For all we know, she already knows about him."

"Fine, we'll do it your way, but if something happens to her, then I'll feel guilty and be mad at you."

"Noted."

So instead of following Charlene and her friends, Felix followed the old hero while also trying to keep track of her dangerous stalker. Madam X was momentarily joined by two older looking women, and the three ate and talked for over an hour before going to some neighboring stores to browse. The other women were not Exes and seemed to have no idea who their friend really was. Felix theorized they were relatively new acquaintances and unconnected with her previous life. They chatted of mundane topics, though the veteran Ex seemed to enjoy the humdrum subject matters. The women called her Fran and although Felix never discovered what her real name was, he highly doubted that "Fran" was anything but a cover name given to her after she retired. He wondered how strange it must have been to always be called something other than your original name for much of your life.

The Pursuer never came much closer than he did in the café and he actually dropped out of Felix's radar for some time until Madam X arrived at a house later that evening, evidently belonging to the oldest looking of her friends. It was an old-fashioned, blue painted, two-story wooden home in a neighborhood about a quarter mile from the beach. With the address memorized, he made his way back to Charlene's condo. By hitching rides with unsuspecting drivers and his talent for untiring running, he made it back much faster than any regular person could, reaching his destination well before any vacationing teenager's bedtime. Felix found Charlene with one other cohort, feeling the others were at the beach.

Once he hurried up the three flights of stairs, he broadcasted his presence by shouting, "Honey, I'm home!"

Hearing him, Charlene excused herself to use the bathroom, and knowing she wasn't actually going to use the little girl's room, he followed her. To keep from being overheard, she put on some loud music on her phone after closing the bathroom door. He told her the address, which she then looked on her phone's internet.

"Not too far. You said that's a friend's house?"

"Yeah, all three of them were there. I searched for a phone number or email address, but nothing was posted on anything. The Pursuer was close by, but still appeared to be in a lookout state."

"Sounds like we have to go personally." Her supernatural acquaintance remained silent. "You don't like the idea, do you?"

"Can't you just anonymously call the police? They'll be able to get the Stewards once you tell them about the Pursuer."

"Getting the Stewards may take too long and that's *if* they take me seriously. I think it's best to warn her personally so she can do what she feels is appropriate. I also doubt she'll like the police barging in, probably thinking she's an Ex-human herself, and likely attract the media."

"She might not like dying either."

"What's the problem? Even the Pursuer can't hurt me if we meld."

"Going through a door is one thing. Making sure you can survive attacks by an elite assassin is quite another. And even if he can't physically hurt you, what happens if he finds out who you are?"

"That's why heroes have masks right? Plus, it's not like I'm going in my 'Charlotte Fields is my name' T-shirt."

"Fine, if this is how you want to do this," he assented. "When do we go?"

"Like, ASAP."

"I assume you have an excuse ready?"

"Of course. I'll say I have to see my aunt, who my mother told me was feeling ill."

They were in her Camaro a few minutes later, stopping by a cheap clothing store where she bought a makeshift disguise, which consisted of a black hoodie and a thin, blue summer scarf. She parked the car in the parking lot of a closed Chinese restaurant about a mile from their destination.

"Should we meld now?" she asked.

"No dinner first?" Felix teased as he began to meld with her. "The restaurant is right there. No foreplay? Nothing?"

As he was melding with her, she put on her newly bought hoodie and put her sunglasses and scarf in the pockets, seeing no need to wear them yet with no Exes in the area.

"So how do we approach her?" she asked her partner. "You know her. What do you think?"

"You have to get her alone to explain everything without her reading your mind. She's a smart woman who worked in the underground world of espionage. Just talk to her in code."

"Code? Wouldn't it be easier if I let her read my mind? That way she would know I'm not lying."

"Maybe, but what if someone reads her mind someday? Look, I might be acting paranoid, but I settled on warning her personally, you can at least give me this."

"Alright, I'll fade when we meet her. So what coded message should I come up with?"

"Since her friend will probably answer the door, it's best if you hand her a written message and tell her to give it to Fran."

"What do I write down?" she asked, retrieving a pen and yellow pad from the glove box.

"Some sentences with a bunch of x's should be fine."

"That's not exactly code."

"Well, it's not supposed to be uncrackable."

"Right," she said indifferently. She began writing down the message. It read: *Dear Fran, I bring important and private information that a madam of your stature needs to hear. It concerns an ex-friend of ours. Please permit me to explain more.*

"That should do," said Felix admiringly.

They exited the vehicle and began walking. Felix felt no sign of the Pursuer and the enemy remained absent all the way to the front door, allowing Charlene to merely wear her hood up and not having to wear the other items of her masquerade. She rang the doorbell a few times and, at the behest of Felix, faded thereafter, not wanting to take the chance that Madam X would try and read the mind of whoever rang the doorbell. The porch light was turned on after a couple minutes. An irritated looking woman opened the inner door, but left the screen door sealed.

"Yes? Who is it?" asked the woman suspiciously.

"I apologize for disturbing you, ma'am, but I have an urgent message for Fran," answered Charlene as she held up the folded piece of paper. "Can you give this to her?"

Mentioning her friend's name softened the wary woman's features, but preserved her guarded tone when she replied with, "Okay." The woman opened the screen door to retrieve the note. Charlene fleetingly restored herself to hand the note over. "May I ask who this is from?"

"She won't know who I am, just say-"

"Oh, say Melanie sent you!" interrupted Felix.

"Melanie. Melanie sent me. I'll wait for her response."

The old woman nodded and went to find her friend, closing the door.

Knowing what she was wondering, Felix enlightened Charlene, explaining, "Melanie was an alias she used once. She was in Italy at the time, during the Humans First Conference."

Mentioning the conference brought back memories for Charlene of seeing, for the first time in her early life, tangible evidence of violence between Regulars and Exes. A bombing set up by Exes killed over three dozen people, mostly European politicians, and helped blaze a fresh trail of resentment between Exes and Regulars. The party responsible was a couple of radical Exes, who were each caught by the Stewards a year later.

They felt the Ex's presence on the second floor where it was shortly met by her friend's aura. Before long, both auras came down, but the Regular split off at the first floor and went towards another room, heading for the other occupant. The door reopened and revealed the retired agent wearing a black nightgown wrapped in a red bathrobe. She cast a quick up-and-down glance at Charlene.

In evident frustration, and perhaps a little startled, Fran asked, "Who are you?"

"You're in danger, ma'am," said Charlene candidly. "I know who you are and so does an assassin who's been tracking you, as far as I know, since this afternoon when you were having lunch at the café."

"How do you know this? You still haven't answered my first question."

"Ask her if she still checks her room for bugs," Felix recommended.

"Do you check your room for bugs?" Charlene asked the retiree. "We can speak more comfortably and more privately in your room." She looked over Fran's shoulder to see her friends gawking at them. Madam X turned to see them as well.

"Your name first," insisted Fran.

"Charlene," she answered, feeling lying to the seasoned woman wouldn't work.

"You might as well have brought that shirt of yours," said a somewhat exasperated Felix.

"Wait here," said Madam X as she opened the screen door to let her visitor in.

Fran next met her friends, spoke to them, and turned back around, gesturing Charlene to follow her upstairs. They entered her room, staged very much like an elderly woman's room, and shut the door. There was a fan on a stand she turned on to its highest setting and then proceeded to turn on a small TV to an infomercial about an acne product, setting the volume just above conversation level.

"They are sweet ladies, but my God are they nosy," said Fran. "As for other possible snoopers..." The Ex opened a bottom drawer, and under some heavy clothing, pulled out a thin, book-sized electronic device with a blue light turning on when she pressed a button. "This disrupts most wireless signals for a few yards. Now then, explain yourself, young lady. How do you know who I am and why I'm in danger?"

"In all honesty, I was told who you really are by a friend of mine. He pointed you out at the café, but he also pointed out the Pursuer."

"The Pursuer, you say?"

"Yes, and though I don't sense him now, he was close by a while ago."

"You can sense him?"

"Yes. Once my friend tells me of someone, I can keep track of their, uh, aura. My friend has this ability as well. It's how he recognized you and the assassin."

"So you're an Ex-human then?"

"Sort of, but I'm useless without my friend."

"I wouldn't say useless," said Felix. "You're definitely a tiny bit smarter."

Charlene couldn't help but twitch a slight smile at the compliment.

Madam X sighed and closed her eyes as she absorbed the information, eventually saying, "So you don't work with any government or organization then. You're what? Just a concerned citizen?"

"Pretty much. I couldn't just stand by and do nothing when I learned the Pursuer was stalking you. I wanted to warn you earlier, but-"

"But then one of the most dangerous men in the world would have likely learned about you," finished the experienced woman. "Cautious girl." Madam X shrewdly smiled at this last statement. "Well, if the Pursuer is targeting me that brings up a whole host of questions and problems."

"Your friends," cited Charlene.

"Yes, they'll be targets as long as I'm near them. Like any good assassin, and he's one of the best, he will eliminate potential witnesses and possible intrusions."

"Do you think he might use them against you?"

"Like hostages? No, not his M.O. He kills quickly and efficiently, with the least risk and exposure to himself. They'll be safe if I leave. What's your situation?"

"My situation?"

"If I leave right now, can you join me?"

"Oh, um, I can get away for a day or so without too much trouble."

"I hate to ask this of you, but if you really can sense him, then we'll have the upper hand. I'll use every advantage I can until I can contact some people and get out of this mess. Are you sure you're okay with this?"

"I wouldn't have come if I thought I could get hurt. Wanna see something I can do?" Charlene walked up to the fan and passed her arm straight into it.

"Show off," said Felix.

"That's quite an ability," declared the veteran.

"I've never tested it with fire or bullets, but I assume they'll pass harmlessly through me, too."

"I see, that explains why I can't read your mind. Your brain has phased out of my range. You're a higher-level Ex than I am if my ability is unable to affect you. Your potential is impressive." Madam X appeared as if she was going to say something more, but stopped. As an alternative, she acquired a cigarette case from her bathrobe pocket and lit a cigarette, not bothering to ask if her guest minded.

After a brief silence, Charlene asked, "Now what?"

"I would like to get a safe house agents sometimes use, but I don't want to possibly lead him to one. How far can you sense him?"

"Five hundred feet or so."

"Hmm, not far enough to guarantee he's still not able to follow me. We'll go to a motel and I'll make arrangements there. Once I'm sure I'm protected, I'll run you off. How's that?"

"Sounds good."

"We'll go in a cab. Did you come in your car?"

"Yes, but it's parked a mile off near a restaurant."

"You are a vigilant one. I'll give you some money to take a cab back to it or if they tow it for some reason. I have to turn off the jammer to call the cab, and I'll assume you're smart enough to figure out what not to do."

Charlene nodded. After turning off the jammer, Madam X began disrobing to change.

"Can I use your bathroom?" asked a quick thinking Charlene.

"Just outside the door."

"How dare you deprive me of an old lady stripping show," said Felix disingenuously when Charlene reached the bathroom.

When she believed enough time had gone by, she went back into the room and saw the Ex had already dressed in a gray blouse and a long, black business skirt.

"Our ride will be here shortly," said Madam X.

There wasn't much talking to be done with the jammer turned off, so, in the meantime, they went downstairs where they found the two other women in the kitchen. Fran explained to them that a family emergency had to whisk her away and she had no idea when she could return. Meaningful conversation didn't start between the older and younger women until they were in their motel room. Charlene didn't go into the lobby to keep off any possible cameras, per Felix's request.

"Who did you text in the cab earlier?" Charlene asked.

"A friend at the agency who can get the ball rolling. I didn't mention you. You're involved enough as it is, and I assume you don't want government officials to know about you. Apparently, they don't even have the decency to wait until I die to stop protecting my identity, but I guess I shouldn't blame them prematurely. Maybe someone dug it up somewhere else or I slipped up at some point, though I find that unlikely."

"Why would someone want to kill you?" wondered

Charlene aloud.

"Ha!" said Felix. "So naïve."

Madam X wasn't as tactless. "Oh, any number of reasons. I imagine I've pissed off a lot of people, in fact, I don't have to imagine it. A lot of things that didn't go reported, of course, but a great deal goes unreported during war."

"War?"

"Not open war, mind you, even if it's come close to that from time to time, but what else would you call it when groups of people fight and die for a cause they believe in?"

"Like in Italy?" asked Charlene.

"Your friend told you about that?"

"Just that you were there."

"Your friend sounds like he's been around," said Madam X, lighting another cigarette. "He's an Ex-human, right?"

"Only when he's with me. We're really very useless alone."

"Where is he now?" She evidently huffed too much smoke and began coughing.

When the retired agent recouped her air, Charlene replied, "He's nearby, which is why I can use my power."

"Have either of you thought about registering and joining the government or the Stewards?"

"Not really. Would you recommend it?"

"I'll be honest, it's a pain in the ass so big it's not funny. Much of it feels like it does now. Your life and the lives closest to you are constantly in danger, but, if you're like me, you can't help but get involved in a situation you know you have the power to change, whether for good or ill. The fact that you're helping me out of your own accord is not a good sign, dear, and in my experience, vigilantes rarely last long."

"It couldn't have been all bad."

"Of course not. It's never dull and the number of strong, dashing men is never in short supply, plus a woman or two sprinkled in."

"Oh God," said a queasy Felix.

"It's tempting, but I'm happy where I am now," said Charlene.

"If you really are happy, then I have to strongly recommend you stop using your power or whoever's power you're using. Once you start using it-" Another coughing attack struck her. "Excuse me. What was I saying? Oh, yes. I was saying using your power will eventually get you in too deep and you will *never* be able to get out. The world is still not ready to simply let Exes live normal lives. Joining one side or another is unavoidable if you keep helping little old ladies like me."

"I'll keep that in mind."

"Tell your friend this as well."

"He warned me about doing this."

"Then he's looking out for you. I know it's difficult for young people to listen to caution, but I swear half this world's problems would be solved if they did."

A few minutes later, Charlene noticed the old hero was coughing more and more and it only became viler sounding. "Are you okay?" Charlene asked her.

"I've tried smoking less, but-"

Madam X was cut off by a severe coughing attack that wouldn't stop. She bent over with her hand on her chest.

Charlene sat next to her at the foot of the bed and exclaimed to both Felix and Madam X, "What's wrong?!"

A white substance leaked out from the corners of Madam X's mouth. Moments later, she stopped coughing altogether and collapsed to the ground. They then felt her aura quickly begin to diminish.

"Felix, she's dying! Do I try CPR?" she asked, preparing to start the act.

"Just chest compressions, but if she has what I think she has don't do mouth-to-mouth."

"What? Why not?" she asked, beginning the chest compressions.

"I think she's been poisoned."

"Poison? You mean we were too late? He got to her!?"

"Probably, but I don't know when. I never felt him get close."

Charlene eyed the still burning cigarette on the floor. "The cigarettes?"

"Maybe."

Seconds after her heart stopped beating, her aura

completely vanished.

"Well, shit," said Felix after a moment's silence.

"Fuck," reiterated Charlene, nearly inaudibly.

"We have to go."

"Just leave her?"

"Unless you want the U.S government thinking you had a part in a famous Ex-human's death. Remember, she didn't mention you and they can't be that far off by now. We did what we could. He must've planted the poison cigarettes or whatever before we saw her at the cafe."

Charlene seemed to be a little dazed and lost in thought as she stared at the motionless body. He let her try and compose herself for a minute, but when he felt a group of auras heading toward them at the edge of his radar, he shouted, "Charlotte, it's time to go!"

Perking up, she left the room by going through the back wall to make sure she didn't leave a trace. She ran in the opposite direction from the group of auras until they were well out of range. She walked in silence for some time, not really paying attention to where she was going.

There was little Felix felt he could do but stay melded with her and make sure she didn't wander too aimlessly.

After a while, she hailed a cab near a bar to take her back to the restaurant, where she discovered her car untouched.

"Are you going back to your condo?" Felix asked.

"No, it feels weird to go back there. I'll go to my aunt's."

"Are you all right?"

"Not really. I know we did what we could, and they'll know the Pursuer did it, and I couldn't help any further, but I can't help feeling shitty."

"Sorry for calling you by your real name," Felix said quietly, trying to ease her mind as best he could.

"Oh, don't worry. I was out of it, and we did have to go. I just need some time."

"I know it sounds counterintuitive, but be glad it affects you. I've been numb to a lot of bad shit and I feel crappy for it."

When she entered the car, Felix thought about separating from the meld, but something told him to wait. Charlene called her aunt to let her know she was coming over and used the pretext that she had a fight with Devin and was punishing him by leaving him for a night. Her aunt greeted her warmly when she opened the front door to her modest single-story home. Felix thought Charlene resembled her aunt more than her mother, probably due to the more similar hair color and being a little more in shape, despite being a few years older than her sister.

"I hope I'm not bothering you too much, Carol," said Charlene.

"Nonsense," answered her aunt. "Mark's sleeping, but you know how he slumbers. A sonic boom wouldn't be good enough as an alarm. I hope you're okay."

"Oh, it's nothing. Only a dumb fight. I need time to cool off, that's all."

Carol looked at her niece a little doubtfully, but kept her opinion to herself and said, "You can use Gabby's room."

"Thanks. I'll probably be gone by the time you come back from work."

"Whenever you like."

They kissed each other's cheeks goodnight and Carol went to her room while Charlene headed for the kitchen to grab a bottle of water from the fridge. She next entered the bathroom, where Felix knew he had to disengage from her. He heard the shower running a few minutes later, lasting about twice as long as the usual amount. She came out wrapped in a towel and entered her temporary bedroom, locking the door. He thought she might lock him out all night, but after she dressed in some of her cousin's flowery pajamas, she unlocked the door and opened it ajar. When Felix entered, he saw her resting on the bed with her back turned to him.

In a murmur, she asked, "Can you stay with me? At least, until I fall asleep? Just talk about anything."

He obliged. He gabbed about random stories he believed she would find soothing, such as the time he saw a boy with cancer crying from joy when he went to school and saw some of his friends had shaved their heads to make him feel welcomed, or the time a soldier came home to surprise his girlfriend and successfully proposed to her. In the quiet of the night, he eventually heard the rhythmic breathing that conveyed someone was sleeping. He was glad to bring her some measure of comfort, but knew she wouldn't have needed consoling to begin with if he never opened his mouth, or wasn't around at all.

Chapter Eleven

Charlene was sullen for the next few days, but hanging out with her friends and Devin helped her not become too down. Apparently, the government kept Madam X's assassination under wraps, and the public wasn't even informed of her death until a week later when they reported she died of natural causes. Once she returned home, a lot of time was spent preparing Charlene's future after high school. Through several conversations between her and her mother, Felix gathered she was going to rent a student apartment near college and still wasn't set on a career path, despite earlier indications she wanted to go into the medical field. Her mother looked disappointed at her daughter's sudden hesitation to follow in her footsteps.

"I shouldn't have said I had second thoughts," Charlene said to Felix while on her computer. "She had such a hurt look on her face."

He knew the cause of her shifting outlook was witnessing

the old agent's death, and he was worried she'd start seeing him as a way to start fulfilling a desire he saw growing within her since that day. "It's a noble profession and it pays well, I hear," he said after a moment assembling his thoughts.

"You want me to be a doctor, too?"

"Anything, as long as it's not what you're currently thinking."

"Oh, and what am I currently thinking?"

"I don't know. Just forget it."

"You think I want to join the Stewards or the government, don't you?"

"I think you see a whole new world of possibilities. I don't blame you for thinking about it. I just hope, for both our sakes, you stay your usual, thoughtful self. I'll even come right out and admit it, I don't like that you're even considering joining a cause you don't have to be a part of, but I won't abandon you either. Just think everything through carefully."

"Whatever you might believe, I don't want to simply throw myself in harm's way. Her death did change my perspective a bit, and with you around, my prospects have changed as well."

"Why not go to Vegas, enter a poker tournament, and live off that?" he asked half seriously.

"Not exactly a satisfying life."

"No, but you could amass a fortune and give yourself more time to think, then you can throw it all away."

"Your suggestion is noted. You know, I'm thinking of

telling Devin about you. If we're really going to be a serious couple, I have to know how he'll handle you. Even if we break up at some point, I think I can trust him to keep you a secret."

"I don't think you have to worry about that. Even with the weird-ass powers some Exes have, I don't think he'd sound too sane if he began spreading the news that his ex-girlfriend talks to ghosts."

"Good point. It's also easy to deny you."

"Well, at least I'll have someone else on my side when it comes to your thoughts of grandeur."

A couple days later, Charlene did indeed decide it was the right time to tell Devin about Felix. They were in his jeep driving to her home after a Saturday night movie.

"Devin, I love you and I need to tell you something before our lives become a little more stressed."

"I told you already, you don't have to worry about college changing our relationship," her significant other reassured. "It's only a place."

"No, it's not that. It's slightly more serious and… bizarre. You have to promise me that no matter what, you'll keep what I'm going to tell you a secret."

"Secret, huh?" Never one to submit to a serious situation easily, and trying to lightheartedly guess her secret, he asked, "Do you have an STD?"

"No, Devin," she answered, more than a little annoyed. "I need you to promise me or I can't tell you."

"All right, I promise. Cross my heart and hope to die."

"Ha!" said Felix, who was in the backseat. "How appropriate, or inappropriate, depending on how you look at it."

Charlene overlooked the apparition's remark and continued to place her concentration on her date. She sighed and said, "Even with your promise, I'll understand if you find this a little overwhelming."

"Damn, I get it," said Devin a little impatiently. "Enough with the suspense."

"I, for one, hope it will last," said Felix.

"Okay, okay," relented Charlene. "The last few weeks I've discovered I have a couple of Ex-like abilities."

"Yeah? No shit? Like what?" Devin asked, his raised eyebrow displaying his intrigued state.

"For one, I can sense people."

"Sense people?"

"Yeah, sort of like a radar, but better, because I can sense someone and track them through walls and buildings."

"Like x-ray vision?"

"No, I can sense people, not see them."

"Oh, okay… cool."

"There's something else. I can go through objects and walls."

"Really? Can you show me now?"

"Sure."

Felix heard his cue and melded with her. Then, with Devin

watching while he stopped the jeep at a red light, she made her hand pass through the glove box and pulled it out.

"That's fucking amazing! I don't know what you were so worried about. I think this is badass. You know I've never had a problem with Exes."

"Well, that's the thing. On my own, I'm just a regular girl."

"On your own? What does that mean?"

"That's the possibly upsetting part. Someone else is giving me these abilities."

"Who?"

"His name is Felix."

"Felix?" There was a gap of dialogue, which lasted as long as the stop Devin had made at a stop sign. The rerolling of the tires restarted his power of speech. "So, he's really the Ex-human and he, what, just gives you your power from the goodness of his heart?"

"He's not really an Ex-human either. Only together are we effective."

"If you just used his powers, then does that mean he's close by or is this a time limit thing?"

"He's close."

"Tell him I'm punching him in the face right now," teased Felix, though he was actually punching him.

"How close?" asked Devin.

"He's in the jeep."

Devin looked around uncertainly and asked, "He's

invisible?"

"He's invisible, but he's not physical. You can't feel or hear him, only I can."

"Not physical? He's like a ghost or something?"

"Yes."

"Serious?"

"Yes."

Devin was contemplating in silence for a moment, checking the rearview mirror several times, until he asked, "So he follows you around?"

"Sometimes."

"Since when?"

"Since you took me to the Mariners home opener. He discovered me there. I would've told you earlier, but I was getting used to it myself. You're the first I've told anyone about this."

By this time, the vehicle had pulled up to her driveway.

"Now I can see why you were worried. This is... freaky. You're the only one who can see and hear him?"

"I can't see him, only sense and hear him."

"Right... and he's in my car. A dead guy."

"Do you believe me?"

"Hmm, I *did* just see your hand go through my car, and you could have left it at that instead of telling me a crazy sounding explanation, so yeah, I guess I believe you."

"You're not upset?"

"Upset? I don't know what I'm feeling exactly, but I'm

definitely not upset. It's just odd knowing someone's been watching us all this time."

"He's only here now because I asked him to be, he's not around when I don't want him to be."

"How do you know if you can't see him?"

"I can sense when he's nearby."

"That's a nice lie," said Felix.

Devin began laughing.

"What's so funny?" Charlene asked him.

"The poker game where you cleaned us out, that was your friend, right?"

"Maybe," she replied coyly, beginning to laugh with him.

Felix joined in with mocking laughter, which instantly broke up Charlene's merriment.

She explained in more detail Felix's circumstance, but left out particulars like Madam X and reinforced the idea she could sense his presence.

"You promise to keep this between us, right?" Charlene queried Devin as she prepared to enter her house.

"Of course. You can trust me. You're not going to make him follow me, are you?"

"Only if I think you're cheating on me."

"Emily and Ann are watching you through the window by the door," informed Felix, who had separated from her by this point.

"I have to go," she told Devin.

"We'll talk about robbing a bank later, then," Devin said just before he kissed her. It would've been longer and more passionate if he didn't remember he was being watched.

As he drove off, Felix said, "I think he took that as well as a sane person could. Do you think he'll call the men in white coats to take you to a nice padded room?"

"I'll have to consider breaking up with him if he does."

Entering the house, Charlene saw Ann running up the stairs while Emily stayed by the window.

"You didn't make out much," Emily pointed out. "Relationship trouble?"

"None of your concern."

"It looked like a serious talk."

"I'll tell you when you're older."

"Was there trouble in the sack? Was he premature?"

"Just get Ann into bed and worry about the guys chasing after you."

Chapter Twelve

The rest of the summer passed by quickly as everyone prepared for the new stage in their lives. Many of Charlene's friends would move too far for anything but social media contact. They talked about how the distance wouldn't affect anything, but she knew most, if not all, would find new groups of close friends and they would slowly drift apart. She was grateful a couple of close friends would follow her and Devin to the same college. In Devin's case, they had already known even before they started officially dating that they would go to Washington State.

Devin seemed to be adjusting to his girlfriend's revelation. He appeared to trust Charlene's judgment enough not to try and interfere with the peculiar relationship. It helped that Charlene didn't often talk with Felix in front of him, knowing it would still be an odd sight for an outsider. Devin did enjoy seeing Charlene go through doors and objects, which amused and placated him. For now, the trio had an understanding, but Felix couldn't help imagining the future, particularly the image of Charlene and Devin at the altar in front of a priest saying, "Do you, Devin, take Charlene and her ghost pal as your lawfully wedded wife and phantom?" In any case, Felix didn't see either lover taking that leap any time soon, and was content with the current state of affairs.

Charlene's twentieth birthday on the fifteenth of July was basically a going away party, and all the girls, including the usually unfazeable Emily, shed tears at the impending separation, despite their older sibling's insistence that she was close enough to visit fairly often and come at a moment's notice. Her birthday was a somewhat uncomfortable day for Felix. He knew Charlene couldn't expect anything from him besides a "Happy Birthday," but that's exactly what ate at him. It was a full day of being reminded how he couldn't give her anything more than what he already provided. There was some solace knowing no one else could give her the talents he donated and that she did seem to find enjoyment from it, but he wasn't too thrilled her sense of adventure was starting to surface as a result.

She was soon set up in her new abode, a room in one of the off campus student apartments, and she was in her first day of class before she knew it. It was when she was walking to her second class, psychology, that Felix perceived something interesting. He melded with Charlene so she could sense it as well. He was tentative at first, but decided keeping anything from her would make her wrathful if she learned of his secrecy.

Without needing for Felix to verbally point it out, she could sense an aura that could only belong to an Ex. The aura was currently static and she was walking towards it... then she was in the same building... then in the same auditorium. Sitting alone at the corner seat, three rows down from the entrance, was a young female Ex. Charlene didn't hesitate to go down and sit next to her to better evaluate who this person was. A quick glance showed she had an Asian heritage, which Felix assumed was Korean, as evidenced by the Korean word tattooed on her left arm. She was also rather skinny and likely didn't stand taller than five foot three, making her a full three inches shorter than the girl now sitting next to her. Though spoiled by Charlene, Felix could still see that she was very pretty and, in a bygone era, he would have been greatly interested.

Knowing Charlene wanted to strike up a conversation with her, Felix recommended, "Ask her why she tattooed 'Harmony' on her arm."

Charlene obliged.

"You know Korean?" asked the shy sounding girl, a trifling hint of her accent escaping her.

"A little," answered Charlene. "I have a friend who knows some and teaches me what he can."

"Oh. I just think it's a nice concept, to answer your question, I mean."

"I've always wanted to get a tattoo, but I can't for the life of me decide what to get or where to put it. When did you get yours?"

"Just before coming here, to America. I lived in South Korea all my life up until a year and a half ago when my father was transferred, or reassigned, whatever you call it."

"He's in the military?"

"Yes. My father is an American airman officer and my mother is Korean. She was a translator."

"Where's he stationed?"

"San Francisco."

"That's pretty far. Why are you way up here?"

"A friend of my father's is letting me stay free with her. She's an economics professor here, too."

"I'm Charlene by the way."

"Hannah."

"Ask what her Korean name is," said Felix.

"Oh, it's Kim Eun-Sun, but I prefer Hannah," responded Hannah once Charlene inquired for Felix. "No offense, but Americans have a hard time pronouncing Korean names. They also think 'Kim' is my first name and I don't want to correct everyone I meet."

Before they could go any further, the grizzled looking professor demanded silence as he started class.

On her iPad Charlene typed, '*Do you think she knows she's an Ex?*'

"I think the fact she tattooed 'Harmony' means she does.

I'm guessing she'd keep it a close secret since her father is in the military. Governments may like to use Exes, but most don't particularly trust them or anyone associated with them. It probably won't go swimmingly for her father if they find out about her."

The two girls had become friends within the next few class meetings, though if Charlene wanted to be friends with you there wasn't any choice in the matter. Hannah was a little introverted, enjoyed American rock music, and had a surprisingly voracious appetite, particularly when it came to pizza with anchovies. She was currently studying to be an electrical engineer.

As thanksgiving break was nearing, Charlene learned Hannah wouldn't join her family for the break. She explained that her parents would be working for much of the time anyway, and the break wasn't long enough to justify the hassle of the long drive to San Francisco. In addition, they never observed the holiday in Korea. Not wanting her newest friend to spend the break alone, she insisted she spend it with her family.

Chapter Thirteen

When they were a couple of blocks away from Charlene's home, both she and Felix (they often melded when she drove to be prepared for any possible accidents, making each feel safer) felt a lot of auras gathered near a house in the neighborhood. Three of those auras belonged to her family. She drove past her house and soon saw police cars and dozens of neighbors assembled on the yard and street. She parked a stone's throw away and jogged up to the crowd, specifically, to her mother and sisters.

"Mom, what's going on?" Charlene asked the back of her mother's head.

"Oh, Charlene!" cried her mother as she spun around and embraced her daughter. "Thank God you're here! Take your sisters back home and stay with them."

"What happened?"

"One of Ann's poor little classmates is missing," answered her mother. "Remember the Turner girl? Jodie? She was playing outside with her little brother and then she disappears when he went inside for a few minutes. I didn't want to leave your sisters home alone, but now that you're here, you can stay with them while I help in the search."

"I want to help in the search, too." Charlene vaguely recognized Jodie's aura. She felt it when Ann went to her birthday party during the summer, though the two little girls weren't great friends, more like associates than anything else.

"I know you do, but I'm not leaving your sisters alone when a possible kidnapper is out there," retorted her mother.

Charlene instantly regretted not telling her mother about her power before leaving to college. "Mom, I have to tell you something, like now, but not here."

"Can't it wait?"

"No, it's important. Trust me."

"All right, let's stop by home then."

"By the way, this is Hannah. She's the friend I told you about. She's going to stay with us during the break."

"Welcome to our neck of the woods, Hannah. Sorry it's during such a bad time."

"Me too," said Hannah as everyone entered the Camaro.

When they arrived at the Field's residence, Charlene and her mom went upstairs to her mother's room, whereas her sisters kept Hannah entertained in the living room.

"What is it?" asked her mother a little peevishly.

"Mom, if you don't want Emily and Ann alone, then I think

its best you stay with them while I go search with Hannah."

"Why is that?"

"I should have told you this sooner... Mom, I'm an Ex-human."

"What?" she stated with a modicum of disbelief.

"I'm an Ex-human. I've known for a few months now, but I've been too nervous to say anything to you before, but with Jodie missing, I know I can use my ability to help. I have a power to sense people and I know I can sense her if she's nearby."

Charlene could see her mother was a little overwhelmed at this news as her birth giver sluggishly sat on the bed. Charlene sat next to her and draped her arm on her mother's shoulders.

Contemplating to herself, her mother said, "An Ex-human? Sense people?"

"Mom?" said Charlene uncertainly. She had probed her mother before about Exes and received encouraging replies, but no one really ever knew how someone would react to the news.

Her mother responded by embracing her and saying, "I love you so much. I can't believe one of my girls is an Ex-human! I'm terrified and proud at the same time. Thank God I left your father, he would've hated this news. I don't know if you remember-"

"Mom," said Charlene as concisely as one could a one syllable word, reminding her time was of the essence.

"Right, right, I'm blabbering. Okay. If you can really help with your, um, power, then I suppose you'll be more useful in the search. Your sisters don't know about this, do they?"

"No. I know they won't be able to keep it a secret for long. Well, maybe Emily, but she'll probably tell Ann and I know she won't help but brag it to anyone she sees."

"Okay, I won't say anything. I keep forgetting you're not just the oldest daughter, but a grown woman now. Go help in the search. Find that poor girl and I'll stay here."

They hugged again.

"I'll be fine. I actually have another ability that will keep me safe. I'll show you later."

With that said, she went downstairs where she hugged her sisters and asked Hannah if she would help in the search. When she said she would, they left in her car.

"I thought your mom told you to stay with your sisters?" said Hannah.

"I convinced her we would be more effective."

"Really? I don't know this town, you know, and wouldn't your mother be more knowledgeable?"

"Under normal circumstances."

"What does that mean?"

"I'm going to tell you something I just told my mother and only one other person. We haven't been friends long, but I know I can trust you."

"Oh, thank you?" was her friend's unconfident reply.

"I can help find her because I can feel her presence if she's within my range. It's one of my powers."

"Huh? Powers? You're an Ex?" Charlene nodded. After

deliberating with herself for some moments, Hannah, in a wobbly tone, said, "Oh man… Charlene… so am I."

Charlene quickly reflected whether to say she already knew, but decided there would be time later for that and wanted to focus on finding Jodie, so she simply said, "That's why we're the best hope for that girl right now." To exhibit their enriched bond, Charlene placed her hand on Hannah's and gave her a comforting smile, which Hannah did her best to return.

Felix, even with the missing child in the background, was dangerously close to ruining the moment with a degenerate observation, but somehow held in the impulse.

"We're just going to drive around then?" asked Hannah.

"That's the best plan I got. I can sense people from about five hundred feet away in any direction, so we can cover a lot of ground this way."

"I hope she's close by."

"I think I heard most kids are kidnapped by people they know, which means they likely live around here."

"We don't know for sure if she was taken, though. What if she's just in the woods and not in the neighborhood?"

"There will be dozens of people already looking there, besides, the largest patch of forest is more than half a mile off. I doubt she made it that far on her own without anyone noticing. I'd rather assume the worst and not waste any time roaming too aimlessly."

Keeping with her plan, Charlene drove in an ever-expanding circle during the next couple of hours. She was forced to drive slowly due to both being in slow speed limit areas and because the auras became blurred and unfocused if she moved too quickly. Felix was better at detecting auras in motion, but he admitted that he didn't have Jodie's aura committed to memory and needed time to make sure a particular aura wasn't hers. Meanwhile, Hannah explained her power involved the ability to create and manipulate electricity, but didn't have perfect control over it as she rarely had the opportunity to practice privately. No one knew she was an Ex-human until she told Charlene, even her parents and younger brother didn't have a clue.

"I suppose this means we are sort of like sisters now," asserted Charlene.

"Or at least cousins," inputted Hannah matter-of-factly.

This was as light as the conversation became. When the search began to go into increasing darkness, they became tenser. Finally, as soon as the sun hid all its light, Charlene felt a child's aura that had to be Jodie's. They were in an average middle-class neighborhood about eight miles from their starting point. When she drew closer to the aura, she realized there was something irregular about it.

Felix sensed the disturbance as well and said, "She's drugged pretty heavily, I think."

Charlene stopped the car near the one-story house where the aura was coming from and, handing her phone to Hannah, said, "Look up the anonymous tip line for the police station, call it, and say you know where the missing girl is and give them that house's address."

"What are you going to do?" asked Hannah as Charlene opened the door.

"I'm going inside. Don't worry, no one's in the house. Take my car back to the last gas station. I'll join you back there."

She didn't give Hannah a chance to ask any more questions. Charlene closed the door and ran up to the house before Hannah could blink twice. A few seconds later, Charlene saw her Camaro drive off and, a few seconds after that, was inside the criminal's home. Felix didn't see the need to go inside the house, but feeling no apparent danger in it, he didn't express the sentiment. Since Jodie's aura was emanating below ground, Charlene looked for a door that led to the basement. Before she found it, a picture on the living room wall caught her eye or, more specifically, a person in the picture. The image was of a group of elementary age children gathered in front of their teacher in his classroom.

A dismayed Charlene whispered to herself, "He was in the crowd with... Oh my God. That's a teacher at Ann's school."

She forced herself to recover from the realization to continue to her goal. Upon phasing through the basement door, she discovered the light was already on and it revealed a disturbing room. The entire basement basically resembled what a typical ten year old girl's room would be. A large dollhouse was the first item she saw in front of the door and her eyes hastily perused over posters of horses, various Disney characters, and an ice dancer. There were two twin sized beds on either side of the room. One incorporated some stuffed animals and dolls while the other held Jodie, who was outfitted in a pink dress and red shoes that was obviously not the attire she originally had on. Charlene kneeled beside the bed and examined the little girl, who merely appeared to be peacefully sleeping.

"What can I do?" she asked Felix.

"Uh, there's nothing you can do. Only a medical professional can help her."

"But her aura is so weak."

It was in that moment did Felix realize why she came down herself. He had forgotten she wasn't yet familiar with how drastically a particular aura's strength could scale, especially that of a child's. "It's a little weak, but it's stable. She's actually fine. She should be healthy once the drug wears off. Trust me, her aura can get quite a bit weaker than this before real danger sets in."

She exhaled a sigh of relief. She lightly touched the girl's warm face, moving some strands of golden hair behind her ear. "You sure?"

"If I could bet my life, I would."

"I guess I'll just leave the doors open for the police."

Indecisively, she stood up and unlocked both the basement door and the front door, using her sleeves so as not to leave prints. She saw police cars make the turn to the street a few minutes later and left to the backyard, phasing through fences and bushes to easily escape detection by anyone, except for a couple of dogs who barked at her.

"You freaked me out when you told me she was heavily drugged," Charlene told Felix as they walked on the sidewalk.

"I probably should've followed that up with 'But she's fine.' My bad."

"It's okay. I'm happy we found her. Now I hope that perverted fuck didn't have time..." She couldn't finish the sentence.

Trying to lift her spirits, Felix said, "It looks like his plan was to kidnap the girl and help in the search for a while, keeping any possible suspicion off himself. Because of you that girl won't suffer anymore."

"Because of *us*."

"Yes, that was implied."

Inside the next hour, Jodie was recovering at the hospital and the story of her discovery was on the nightly news. It was during the newscast when Charlene learned that the teacher had shot himself in his car after finding out they discovered his prisoner. It was a little surreal knowing she was indirectly the cause of someone's death, even if the person deserved it. Her mother was overcome with emotion during the broadcast, knowing her daughter was integral in the young girl's safe retrieval. Later that night, when Emily and Ann were asleep, Hannah, Charlene, and her mother were in the basement where Charlene further explained and displayed her fading ability. Hannah also allowed her friend to tell Ms. Fields that she was an Ex-human as well, for the sake of easier communication and to alleviate the suspicious glances.

"Don't worry Hannah, I'll keep your secret, for all our sakes," said Ms. Fields. "I'm happy you have each other to go through this." Then, turning to her daughter, "You think your sisters could be like you as well?"

"No, they're not. I can tell the difference between a Regular and an Ex. I'm sorry Hannah, I've known since we've met that you're an Ex-human."

"That's okay, I guess," said Hannah, her tone generating a mixture of relief her secret was out and dazed at how fast other secrets were being distributed. "It's part of your power. I trust you and your mother."

"Oh, you girls make such cute friends!" exclaimed Ms. Fields.

"Mom," grumbled a slightly embarrassed Charlene.

"What? You do. I feel better that you won't be alone when you go back to school. It isn't easy for Exes out there. Support is very important."

Disingenuously, Felix said, "Hey, why not put her further mind at ease and tell her a phantom makes sure you're never alone."

"Does Devin know?" continued Ms. Fields.

"Yes," answered her daughter. "He's the only other person who knows, outside this room, anyway."

"That's good too. Now, I don't mind you helping people, but please be careful, honey."

"Trust me, I know."

"God, I wanted this to be a special Thanksgiving, but this is maybe *too* special. I'm going to take a sleeping pill. See you girls tomorrow."

"I wish I could be sure my parents will react like your mom," submitted Hannah when Ms. Fields had left.

"Whenever you decide to tell them, we'll be with you," said Charlene.

"We? You think your mother would come?" wondered Hannah.

Charlene recognized she was actually including the unrevealed Felix. Electing to get it out of the way, she began telling her friend about her unique situation. Her friend listened patiently and didn't ask any questions during her explanation, even when learning the ghost was in the room at that very moment. "Well?" asked Charlene when she had finished, eager to get her take.

"Umm... Hi, Felix?" Hannah greeted, not sure exactly where to look.

In response, Felix asked Charlene to repeat some Korean words. She did her best to accomplish the request. Hannah proceeded to chuckle.

"What did I say?" Charlene asked.

"Only that you desperately wanted to strip down and make

out with me," Hannah clarified.

"What a coincidence, that was going to be my Christmas present for you, Felix," said Charlene mockingly.

"He's funny," said Hannah.

"If I thought he was joking, I would agree," deadpanned her friend.

"What's he like?"

"What's he like?" echoed Charlene. This was the first time she had to think about describing his personality. It never really occurred to her that someone would treat Felix like a genuine person rather than a supernatural force.

This wasn't lost on Felix either and he was curious to know her answer, so he didn't comment.

"Oh, well, he's a nice guy, especially considering he was alone for such a long time and could have gone crazy. He likes sports and hearing audiobooks. I mean, really, besides the dead thing, he's kind of normal. He thinks he's funnier than he actually is, but as far as ghosts that could otherwise have haunted me, he isn't so bad."

"That's the kindest thing anyone has ever said about me," said Felix, faking a sobbing voice.

"You're lucky," said Hannah. "Even dead people become your friends."

"What do I keep telling you? You have to stop comparing yourself to other people and be more confident."

"Tell her I'd do her in a heartbeat if I was alive," added

Felix.

"Felix agrees, and he says you're beautiful, though he was crasser about it."

"Now go ahead and kiss her," instructed Felix.

"You're pushing it," warned Charlene.

"Then you take off each other shirts-" he continued, unabated by her warning.

"What's he saying now?" wondered Hannah.

"Like I said, he's your regular, simpleminded guy."

The rest of Thanksgiving break went smoothly. Charlene's family visited the Turner's home when Jodie returned from the hospital, acting no worse for wear. It was confirmed the drugging was the only physical harm the kidnapper placed on the child, causing everyone to feel infinitely better. Despite the good feelings brought about by Jodie's safe return, Felix had to come to terms with the fact that Charlene would invariably keep involving herself in situations he didn't want her to be a part of. So instead of vainly trying to dissuade her, he resigned himself to try and become as sensible an advisor has possible, unless it was exceptionally dangerous, of course.

It was a few weeks later that Devin, Felix, and Charlene were in her apartment one snowy January afternoon when Devin brought up a question Charlene and Felix had been pondering since they first found she could fade objects.

"Could you make people fade with you?"

"I don't know. I never tried making anyone fade before.

Hypothetically, I suppose I could, but I don't know what would happen exactly."

"Do you want to try with me?" asked Devin, enveloping his arm around her waist.

"It could be dangerous."

"Nothing bad has happened to the objects you made fade."

"Come on, you know that's different."

"Either it works or nothing happens. It's best to know now, isn't it?"

"Your boyfriend sounds like he wants to be your guinea pig or something," assessed Felix.

"Devin, I'm not taking any chances with you. I won't forgive myself if something went wrong. I'm curious too, but there's a lot more to lose than gain."

"Okay, okay, sorry I brought it up," said Devin, disengaging his arm. "If you change your mind, or if you find out you can make a person fade, then I'm ready to help you practice."

"What do you think that was all about?" Charlene asked Felix when Devin left for class several minutes later.

"I've actually seen this before. After Exes reveal themselves to their family or friends, then the Regular folks, that don't report them, attempt to become special in some way themselves. Devin might be a bit jealous of your power. It's only natural. I personally think there are more people jealous of Exes than outright fear them and that's where a lot of the hatred comes from. Regulars are no longer the special species on this planet. Not that Devin hates you, of course. He's in the low end of the envy spectrum. He probably just wants to go through walls or something. I call it 'Envious of Exes Syndrome.'"

"Envy, huh?"

"Yeah. To be honest, I'm surprised you didn't make the connection yourself. Men tend to want to stay the dominant one in the relationship and your power diminishes that in his view. I think he was showing you how brave he was by offering himself to be an experiment."

"That's stupid."

"If it's stupid, then you can be sure a man has thought about it."

Chapter Fourteen

A week and a half before spring break was set to begin, Charlene entered her Wednesday afternoon biology class and found Hannah wasn't there yet, which was unusual considering she was always there first and happened to know her friend was in campus. Her confusion increased when class began and she still had not arrived. She texted her. A few minutes later and she received a response asking her if she could come meet her by the Owen library. Knowing it had to be important, she complied with the request.

"What happened?" she asked when she saw Hannah standing alone by the building.

"It's my brother, Paul. He hurt someone at school and he ran away. They think he might be an Ex-human!"

"Well, shit," said Felix, both for Hannah's situation and knowing what was coming.

"Are you going to your parents then?" asked Charlene.

"Yes."

"We'll go with you," said Charlene.

"Are you sure?"

Charlene embraced her friend and said resolutely, "It's not even a question. I can go now. Are you ready?"

With neither girl having any imperative obligations, they were each in their respective cars within a few minutes and began what would be a marathon of a drive, the Camaro following the red Volkswagen.

An hour into the journey, Charlene called Hannah using the hands-free mode of her phone and asked, "Have you learned anything more?"

"The police found his phone dumped in a truck, so no one still has any idea where he might be. God, he must be terrified, wherever he is. The guy he hurt is in the hospital. He was hurt pretty bad. He's unconscious, but stable now."

"How are your parents?"

"They're looking for him. I don't know what they're feeling. They've just been giving me updates. I can't imagine what my dad is thinking."

"I'm sure it's only about finding your brother safe." A dubious silence crossed the line. To break it up, Charlene next asked, "Do you have any idea where to start looking?"

"No, and America is so much bigger than Korea."

"Don't worry, he couldn't have gone too far. We'll find him." A few seconds after hanging up, she said, "You've been quieter than I like."

"What can I say?"

"Just be honest."

"Okay, he's probably fucked. We both know him running away was exactly the wrong thing to do. He still has a chance if he comes to his senses and turns himself in, otherwise, he won't be protected by the Stewardship Act and will be treated worse than the average criminal. Best case scenario, we find him first and convince him to turn himself in. He'll serve his time and be forced to register. Worst case scenario... everything else."

"You think the Act would be more lenient on a scared fifteen year old."

"The Act was created *solely* for scared fifteen year olds. Luckily, the guy he hurt is alive or he'd have no chance at a decent life."

"It's not fair that people treat Exes like uncontrollable weapons. Forcing them to register when they're discovered and either work for the government or never get a good job at all."

"Please don't start focusing on all the injustice in the world," he pleaded. "Let's just focus on Hannah's brother and hope he doesn't become a sad statistic. Do that for me, please."

"I'm sorry. You're right. I'll focus on Paul."

"By the way, to focus away from Paul, why didn't you invite Devin?"

"How you feel about involving myself in these types of situations is how I feel about involving Devin."

"He'll probably be a little peeved you didn't invite him to

help. He'll think that you think he's, um, weak. There's a better word I want to use, but I can't think of it right now."

"Well, he'll have to understand that I can fade away and he can't, and that I love him too much to put his life through unknown dangers."

"Useless! That's the word I wanted to use! Yeah, no matter what you say, he'll think he was useless, so I would already start thinking of a better argument than," imitating a high-pitched girl's voice, "I love you baby, kissy, kissy."

"You can be a real bastard sometimes."

"I'm only trying to warn you about a possible argument that *will* happen. Believe me, I've seen enough relationships fail from lesser issues. Tread lightly on a man's ego, it's a fragile thing. I should know, I used to be one."

"Really? Then I lost a bet."

"Look who's being a bastard now."

Not long after this conversation, Charlene answered a call from Devin, which Felix overheard, as she didn't tell him not to.

"Hey babe, where are you?" asked Devin. "I thought we were meeting at your place to study for my mid-term?"

"I guarantee we weren't going to accomplish much studying," said Charlene, trying to keep his disposition upbeat. "Hannah has a family emergency I'm helping her out with. We're going to her home now."

"Don't her parents live in San Francisco? What's the emergency?"

With Hannah's permission, with the promise he would become another trustworthy friend for her, Charlene had already informed Devin about her new friend's situation, so she felt no qualms telling him details of the current state of affairs.

"Here it comes," Felix prophesied once Charlene was done explaining.

"Why didn't you take me with you?" asked Devin.

"And there it is."

Adept at disregarding the dead man's comments, she answered, "I want you with me, but I don't know what could happen if someone catches you helping a runaway Ex. Or, even if he doesn't mean to be, he could be dangerous if he can't control whatever power he might have. I'm already worried for Hannah's sake."

"But you should leave it up to me whether I want to involve myself. What was the point telling me about your power and hers if you won't let me help when shit happens?"

"He has a point there," said Felix, knowing he was walking a very delicate line.

Conscious of the ghost's input, she proceeded to say, "When there's time to think and plan out our actions, then we can become involved with these kinds of circumstances."

"And a day's drive isn't long enough?" disputed Devin.

"Devin, please understand. How would you feel if our roles were reversed?"

After a short pause, Devin gave an audible sigh and said,

"Whatever. There's no point arguing about it now. Just be careful and give Hannah my best. I love you."

"I-" Before she could finish, the line cut off.

Felix could tell saying what he wanted to say would be detrimental to their relationship for this trip and beyond, so he endeavored to comfort her by saying, "He'll get over it. I haven't met anyone who could stay mad at you for long, dead or alive."

"But like you said, he does have a point. I shouldn't have expected him to simply sit idly by after I told him of our power. Anyway, there's time later to deal with my little problems. Let's drop this."

"So what else are we gonna talk about for the rest of the drive?"

Not much talking transpired until the trio parked at a rest stop, where they agreed to rest a short time before entering California. Only thin streaks of daylight remained to illuminate the lower half of the sky, but despite the tedious journey, neither woman felt too fatigued yet.

"What are you going to do once we get there?" asked Hannah as the two sat on a picnic table, eating the snacks they bought from the vending machine.

"I'll leave you to be with your family and then Felix and I will start looking. I guess we'll start from his school and move out from there."

"How long will you-"

"As long as it takes," said Charlene.

While reentering her car, Felix said, "You know, even with our power it's going to be a bitch to find him. We don't know his particular aura and there will probably be a few Ex-human auras in the city that will sidetrack us."

"Oh, really? I guess I'll tell Hannah I just realized how hard this might be and I'm going back."

The sarcastic response was more or less obligatory and Charlene was correct in thinking Felix would not take offence.

He simply replied, "I honestly thought someone would have found him by now. He must have found the ultimate hide-and-go-seek spot. His face must be all over the news, and I doubt someone could be helping him."

"Any theories to where he might be? You've been to San Francisco."

"It's been a long time. Your idea of expanding from the school is the best option. I have followed a runaway before. A young kid, about twelve or so, discovered he had the ability to create powerful sound waves and accidently burst the eardrums of some of his family. He was found pretty quickly though."

"What happened to him?"

"I'll just say I hope Hannah's brother isn't in Iran right now."

When they finally reached San Francisco early the next morning, the Camaro followed the Volkswagen to Hannah's home and separated from there, making Charlene rely on her phone's GPS to find the middle school. For the next couple of hours, she drove much like she did when trying to find Jodie, but this time she had driven nearly a dozen hours longer.

"You need to take a break," advocated Felix.

"In a bit," replied a surprisingly alert sounding Charlene.

When Felix's definition of "a bit" passed, he repeated his last declaration.

"I'm fine, Felix, really. I can go another couple hours, no problem."

"Another hour and I'm breaking off the meld. You haven't had a decent meal in over half a day. I may have forgotten how to feel hungry, but I'm pretty sure a living person still needs food every once in a while."

"Okay, in an hour. Christ, you know it's unfair you get to use your deadness to guilt me into agreeing with you."

"It's also unfair I'm-"

"I know!"

Chapter Fifteen

At the end of the hour, Charlene was stretching her legs in the backseat while she ate her McDonald's cheeseburger and fries with her car parked in the lot.

"You need to pace yourself," lectured Felix. "We could be here for a good while. You can't help anyone if you don't have the energy."

"Something I've noticed. When we're melded, I seem to have more energy. I'll admit I'm a little tired, but as long as we don't separate, I think I can keep going for the rest of the day before I have to sleep."

"Even so, I stand by my earlier advice, well, I'm technically sitting, but you know what I mean."

Shortly after restarting their sweep, they felt the aura of an Ex, but it turned out to be a homeless woman.

"I wonder what her power is?" contemplated Charlene.

"You can't tell? She can give herpes to anyone who crosses

her path," Felix wisecracked.

"You're disgusting."

"Hey, I'm not the one giving herpes to everybody."

The duo were driving near downtown San Francisco no more than an hour later when each of them abruptly felt three fast moving Ex-human auras approaching them. In the following moment, they could see two motorcycles carrying the distinct auras zip past them on the opposite side of the street. The first yellow bike held two people and all of their faces were concealed under their helmets.

"Follow them," said Felix, conveying a tone that suggested he wanted her to do anything but heed his recommendation.

"Do you think one of them was Paul?" Charlene asked, trying to find the next opportunity to make a U-turn.

"I really hope not. I recognize two of the auras. The one you might have heard of is Sol. He's a big British guy who can absorb sunlight and then use it to burn or even, um, melt people. And while he might sound charming, it's the other I'm much more worried about. Her name is… Hold on, give me a second… Anashe! She's a powerful telepath who usually resides in South Africa. Mostly around Johannesburg. She secretly controls a good chunk of the diamond industry there. Sol acts as her bodyguard and occasional lover."

"What are they doing here?"

"I don't know. I haunted Anashe for over a couple weeks and she never needed to leave the region. Whatever brought her to the States can't be good, but I wouldn't be surprised if she found out about Hannah's brother and decided to pick herself up a new recruit while she was here. She's a big supporter of anti-human groups and likes to add to her mini-army when she can."

By this point, Charlene was able to make her turn and keep the targets at the edge of her radar. "Shit. So what now? Sounds like calling the police will probably get somebody killed and we don't even know if that's really Paul with them."

"Don't do anything yet. Just keep your distance for now and let's see where they go. Remember, assuming that is Paul, she couldn't and wouldn't have crossed half the world only for him. She's definitely here for another reason."

"Which means she'll probably leave him somewhere so she could take care of her business."

"Unless they go straight to her private jet, in which case, we're screwed."

Charlene carefully trailed the trio for the next ten minutes. The amount of traffic became denser as they headed closer to downtown, which they hoped meant the car remained inconspicuous. The mild pursuit came to an end when the two motorcycles entered a private parking garage near the Hilton across the street.

"Well, that's great," said Felix sardonically. "I thought if she left him anywhere it would be in a crummy motel, but it looks like she likes to keep her luxury."

"It's better than her leaving."

Charlene was forced to drive a couple blocks farther down to find a place she could park. She found one at the lot of a mall, but it was just out of range of their spiritual radar. They walked towards the hotel until they could sense the trio again, who were inside the building by then. They found a park bench at the perimeter of their range to sit and deliberate the situation over. The day was crisp and bright, so she didn't look out of place wearing her sunglasses and having her hoodie up.

"First things first," said Felix. "Let me go and confirm who's with them."

"Yeah, go ahead."

Felix slowly separated from the meld. "You okay?" he asked when he divided from her completely.

There was an immediate decline in her energy reserve, making her answer, "Just be quick, if you can."

Felix glanced at his hostess before leaving, but her sunglasses prevented any real conclusions of her physical state. He simply had to be glad her aura remained strong as he started rushing as fast as he could to the target auras. For the first time in a very long time, he prayed, and he ardently prayed for the third aura not to belong to Paul. Before he reached the apartment, he felt Anashe leave her fourth-story room and head back to the parking garage using the underground passage the hotel offered. Not taking any time to closely observe the layout of the building, he was momentarily standing outside the appropriate door. After another short prayer, he phased through the entrance. As expected, the room was updated and modern looking. Felix paid little attention to the décor, however, and stared at the two people currently in the living area, where Sol was eating some pizza he had evidently just heated, while the thin stranger was looking out the window with his back turned to Felix.

"You sure you don't want anything, kid?" Sol asked his roommate in his gruff English accent.

The aforementioned kid turned around and answered a bit sullenly, "No thanks. Maybe a little later."

Of course it's him, thought Felix.

The fifteen year old boy's shirt and jeans looked like he had gone through mud at some point, and Paul himself looked worn-out, but didn't otherwise appear to be in distress.

"Too nervous to eat, eh?" continued Sol. "I understand. It's quite a transition you're making, but you'll see, life with her will bring you more opportunities than life out there."

"Yeah," replied Paul, keeping his gloomy tone. "I just wish I could tell my family something, especially my mother and sister."

"Someday you'll go back to them a new man and you'll be able to give them anything they want. Anashe treats her friends real good."

Felix didn't stay to hear anymore. He paid more attention to the layout on his return run, in case it became necessary to enter the apartment building, but he didn't anticipate returning. Back at the bench, he found Charlene lying on her back with her left arm supporting her head.

"You awake?"

In response, Charlene raised her phone to her ear and answered, "Barely. What did you find out?"

After melding with her, he said, "It's him. He's with Sol while Anashe went off somewhere. He looks unhurt. And going by his attitude, it didn't seem like he was forced to go with them. I know you don't want to hear this, but, Charlene, he's out of our reach for now."

"What? We haven't even tried making a plan yet."

"Even if we somehow managed to retrieve him, it won't solve the problem. Anashe won't simply let him be. I know she began seeing him as her property as soon as he joined her, and she's not the type to let people get away with taking her stuff. I haven't seen many more people as prideful as she is. She'll have no trouble finding him or his family if we save him now and she'll do who knows what to them. I've seen her rewrite a man's memory so he would kill his own brother, and I didn't even know of a real reason for her to do it, except for her own amusement."

"So you want me to tell Hannah we found him, but there's nothing we could do?"

"There's nothing we could do *for now*. You can at least assure her that he'll be relatively safe."

"First you say she's unstable, but now she's safe to be around?"

"I don't know what she has in mind for him, but he's young, so I doubt she even knows herself what she wants out of him. He'll likely be raised to be a loyal devotee, laying down his life at her whim, telepathy or no. This gives us some time to plan for his future liberation."

Charlene was silent for a few moments as she contemplated over what Felix recommended. She handled what he said seriously. She was sure he wasn't simply trying to scare her away. Different scenarios went through her mind, but none guaranteed Paul or his family's safety, well, excluding one, but it was not something she believed she was capable of, not even for her friend's, or the world's, instant benefit.

"We can't leave him with her," she said timidly.

"I see Hannah as a friend, too, and I'll be more damned if I allow her brother to become that woman's puppet. Anashe needs to be out of the picture, and we'll need some help to accomplish the feat."

"How do you mean?" asked Charlene, perking up.

"If the Stewards knew more about her, then they could intervene and release South Africa's balls from her grip."

Charlene sat up. "Sounds like quite a project. You have an idea, don't you?"

"A starting point."

"And?" she asked irritably, knowing he was purposely dragging it out.

"I know of someone who has the resources, the skill, and most importantly, the connections to aid in our cause."

The information was enough for her to venture an educated

guess. "Carl Myers?"

"And Bingo was his name-o," confirmed Felix, reasonably annoyed at the path they had to take.

"So he'll be able to get the Stewards involved?"

"They might not officially work together, but he has supported the group from time to time, so they tolerate his vigilante justice."

"There's no way to inform the Stewards directly?"

"They work through governments and there's a much higher chance a lot more people will become interested in you if you get their attention directly. Carl will at least act as a buffer and as a reliable voice to our problem."

"If you're sure there isn't another way-"

"If you haven't thought of another way, there isn't."

"I feel bad for Hannah and her family though."

"Unfortunately, her parents will have to remain completely oblivious about his whereabouts, unless we tell them everything, which includes you."

Charlene gave a defeatist sigh.

"Come on, cheer up. No one would ever know anything without you. He has a chance now, and we can get rid of a demented Ex while we're at it."

"I'll feel better after some sleep. I guess we should go."

Reluctantly, and not without continuing to find a more speedy solution, she walked back to her car. The first thing she did when she entered it was to call Hannah and telling her they needed to talk in private. Hannah suggested they meet at the parking lot of a seafood restaurant near her home. Charlene spotted the red Volkswagen already waiting for her twenty minutes later. She parked her car next to Hannah's and met her friend in her car. As with anything told to her, Hannah listened attentively as Charlene explained the situation, but before she could fully explain the initial plan to try and get Paul back, Hannah began crying. Charlene hugged her and consoled her confidante as best she could. It was a minute before she fully composed herself.

"I'm sorry. I can't help but think of my mother. She's been worried to death and I can't say anything. What were you saying?"

"That Felix and I think we can get the Stewards involved to bring him back. We haven't worked out the details yet, but it's the only plan that doesn't endanger all of your family."

"How will you get them involved?"

"Do you remember who I told you Carl Myers is?"

"Hermes?"

"Yes. I'm not positive, but I'm pretty sure I'm going to have to use a little blackmail to grab his attention, and then I'll tell him about Anashe."

"God, when I see Paul I'm going to strangle him for causing so much trouble," said Hannah, attempting to recover some self-possession.

"And I'll need you to kick his ass for me," said Felix, more seriously than not.

"Are you going back home?" asked Hannah.

"I haven't planned that far ahead. I expect I'll rent a room somewhere and talk over with Felix what our next step is."

"Okay. Thank you for everything you're doing. I don't know where else I could look to for help. And don't hesitate to include me in whatever plan you come up with. After all, he is my brother." Hannah opened her palm and an arch of electricity discharged between her fingers, briefly illuminating the inside of the car in a flash of light. "I've been practicing more. It would be nice to test it out on that bitch."

Charlene didn't choose to remark on Hannah's last statement, seeing it more as her friend letting off steam than preparing to go on a war path. "I'll keep you up to date. Go home. Your parents need you more than I do."

After another embrace, they parted.

Chapter Sixteen

Going with her design to rent a room, Charlene searched for an affordable place on her phone. She found a motel not too far away and headed straight for it. As soon as they separated from the meld after renting and entering the single bed room, she felt a rush of exhaustion wash over her and collapsed on the dingy bed, not caring that the place was damp and had a mildewed smell to it. Felix only shook his head and watched over the premises until she awoke to the waning daylight several hours later. Her hunger being overbearing, she ordered a pizza.

"You there?" she asked.

"In spirit."

"That's getting really old."

"One would think."

Knowing it was futile to convince him otherwise, she moved to a slightly more important subject, saying, "I'm assuming you used your time wisely? How am I going to contact Myers?"

"It's clear we can't call or email him. Without us to supervise him, we can't be sure he'll take you seriously. There's also less chance he can track you and find out who you are."

"You don't trust anyone, do you?"

"You should understand why. Once a camera catches your face or a tweet, text, or email is traced back to you, then the whole world will know about another Ex and your life will become more complicated than it's already becoming. So, no, I don't trust anybody in the world of Myers and Exes."

"Then I should just go up to him covered up and with my face hidden?"

"Yeah."

"I'm pretty sure he'll think I'm robbing him."

"I'm sure your womanly charms will win him over. Check if you can see his itinerary on your magic device."

She complied. After a couple of moments searching, she said, "He's going to be at a cancer benefit in Chicago over the weekend."

"Anything after that?"

"Hold on... Nothing they put online."

"That hopefully means he'll be back home in Boston after that and stay there a bit."

"Boston? I have to drive all the way there?"

"I think I just found a reason to bring Devin with you."

She giggled. Pretending she was talking to Devin, she said, "Sorry babe for not bringing you with me. How 'bout driving me cross-country to make it up to you?"

Her pizza arrived a few minutes later.

After taking her first eager bite, she asked, "As far as you know, who else knows of Carl's hobby?"

"Let's see, there's his father, Victor Myers, a couple old family friends, one of whom acts as the head housekeeper. The other is a doctor and vice-president of the company or something. I didn't really follow them around. The only other person I know who knows of his side career is a former girlfriend of his. She's actually a daughter of one of the big shots on the board of his company."

"He trusted her with that information?"

"She's *very* good looking. In any case, I got the impression he was forced to tell her, but I don't know the exact circumstances."

"Okay, so when we reach his house, then what? Knock politely and hope he doesn't fly away?"

"There's a security guard at the gate entrance, but he should be easy to avoid, the trick is getting passed all the cameras without the alarms being set off. Some woods surround the place, but it gets cleared up in all directions for a hundred yards around, so they can see things coming from a good distance. We could first talk to the head housekeeper, a Ms. Gretchen something, and get her to help us, but she lives in the estate and doesn't leave very often. However we get in, the point is to get him alone without him escaping us. If he sees you, assumes you're a threat, and is able to evade us, then it could be some time before he comes out of hiding."

"This would be easier if you didn't have me *looking* like a threat, or if you could make me invisible."

"I'm sorry, let me go back to the ghost fairy and tell her she forgot to give me another power I can share."

"Jeez, you don't have to be a dick about it."

"I don't think I was being a dick."

"Maybe not for the undead, but for the living, that was dickish."

"Alright, I'm sorry, but I'm serious about the disguise part."

"I know. I'll make due, I guess."

The two remained in deep thought for several minutes as they each tried formulating a decent plan to achieve their goal without disrupting the Myers household too much. After all, they wanted to be on his good side. Charlene was the first to speak.

"What if we don't care if the alarms went off?"

"What are you getting at?"

"I'm saying we run up to the house and try to talk to Carl or Gretchen before they can get the police over. It must take them some time to get there and all I need to get them to listen to me is say, 'Hermes.'"

"We'll call that plan, 'Sure, why the fuck not?'"

They continued thinking up designs, but they were either too elaborate sounding or involved expenses she couldn't afford.

Once she satisfied her hunger, she acquired the courage to take a shower in the musty bathroom. Coming out of the bathroom, while drying her hair with a towel, she experienced another "This is a strange situation" moment, which still hit her every once in a while. She was hundreds of miles from home, standing in a crummy room, staring at an old, boxy TV, currently on ESPN for the sake of someone she couldn't see.

Observing she had paused at the bathroom doorway and seeing an introspective expression on her face, Felix asked her what she was thinking about.

"I was wondering what would happen to me if I was alone for fifteen years," she answered, sitting on the bed as she did.

"Don't bother. It's not exactly a pleasant prospect."

"You've never really talked about it."

"There's not much to say. I've had good days and a few more bad ones."

"What kept you going?"

"I really didn't have a choice. It's not like I can kill myself. I even went in a church once and pr..." He stopped himself, realizing he was treading back to something he had no desire to return to.

"Felix?" asked Charlene after a few seconds of his silence.

"What?" he replied, his usual levity intact.

She frowned and said, "You can be serious with me you know. It's not good to keep things bottled up."

"You're right, my blood pressure could start existing."

"If you can't talk to me, then who else?"

"Celebrities, marine biologists, cats-"

"Whatever! Forget it."

She grabbed a cold slice of pizza and began nibbling it so she had something to do.

Some moments of reflecting later, Felix decided he needed to explain himself. "Look, as soon as I found you, I felt those fifteen years were behind me. It wouldn't have even mattered if you agreed to speak with me or not. Simply knowing there was someone out there who could hear me was enough to ease my mind, and I didn't see the need to bother you with dreary details once we became friends. I still don't."

"Then you've obviously forgotten what friends are for. I'm only saying it'd be fine if you wanted to vent."

"Thank you, and I appreciate the support, I really do, but I'm not going to."

Charlene shrugged and finished her pizza.

He wasn't completely sure why it hit him now of all times, but an undeniable gust of emotion he once thought he would never feel again surged through him more powerfully than any aura had the ability of producing.

Yup, I'm in love with her.

Chapter Seventeen

They were driving back to Pullman within the hour and the first thing Charlene did when she arrived the next evening was to give Devin the details she didn't feel comfortable texting. He was much more curious than upset at that point. If there was any resentment left, it completely thawed away when she told him she wanted him to go with him on the next phase of the trip.

"He sure is excited about being your glorified chauffeur," remarked Felix when he saw Devin's reaction.

"What did he say?" Devin asked Charlene.

"You mean Felix? How did you know he said something?"

"You smirked a little just now. I'm guessing he commented."

"Oh, he did. He only mentioned how he hoped you enjoy long drives."

Devin appeared to want to say something more, but quickly

regained his nonchalant demeanor and instead asked when they would leave for Boston. It turned out Charlene had a test the next morning, so they decided to go right after, seeing as they estimated they would then line up with Carl Myers returning home, if he did go back to Boston, at any rate.

"I'll be sure to make it up to you," Charlene promised Devin as they began the outing in his Wrangler.

"Its fine," said Devin. "I mean, you can still make it up to me, but this is important, right? I wouldn't trade this for anything." He leaned in to kiss Charlene.

Felix began singing, "Infinite bottles of beer on the wall, infinite bottles of beer, if one bottle is taken down and passed around, then there are still infinite bottles of beer on the wall..." bringing to light how long this road trip was going to feel for him as the third wheel.

Charlene did not express or display any sympathy.

By changing places every few hours, and only stopping to fill up their gas tank and stomachs, they made steady progress over the vast terrain of Middle America. The jeep did suffer a flat near Chicago, but Devin was prepared with an extra tire and promptly fixed it, buying another spare soon after. They were finally close to their destination at the end of two days. Seeing as there were still a few hours of daylight left, they rented a motel room to wait for the cover of darkness, plus, they thought it more likely they would find Carl at home during the night. Of course, they knew he might not be there, but they were prepared to wait for as long as they could afford it.

When the stars began making their appearance, Devin drove Charlene and Felix as close as he could to the estate, located at the outskirts of the Greater Boston area situated on several dozen acres of land and isolated from major roadways. To be safe from any possible cameras ringing the border of the property, he had to drop her off half a mile from their goal.

"Here's fine," she told Devin, wrapping the blue scarf around her nose and mouth. "I'll call if anything happens, but don't call me, I'll have my phone off. Drive around for thirty minutes or so. Any longer and wait back at the room until I call you to pick me up here."

"Yeah, I will," said Devin. "You know, it's amazing what a few pieces of clothing can do. You look good all in black."

"Emily would be proud." She stared down at her black hoodie and the newly bought black beanie she held in her hands. She was finding herself increasingly nervous ever since they reached the east coast. A person's future and her friend's peace of mind depended on her convincing a Myers, or one of their acquaintances, about the threat posed by Anashe. However, this only made her more resolved not to turn back. Her will was further fortified when Felix melded with her. "I'll see you in a bit." She exited the jeep once she had donned her beanie and pulled up her hood, disappearing into the nearby woods surrounding the estate property.

Using the fading ability made it easy to traverse the dense

foliage and pass through an old iron fence, apparently kept there to help further deter potential trespassers before relying on more modern security measures. The woods cleared shortly after crossing the fence, revealing the outline of the imposing home about a football field away. Only a few lights were on and the cloud cover blocked much of the natural light, but it was enough to obtain a general rendition. The center of the house contained much of the original stone structure with the two more updated wings extending from each side, though Charlene noted they blended in well. The high roof gave the illusion that the two story building was twice as tall. Being well in range, they each could feel six auras scattered about the house.

"Can you feel him?" Charlene asked the apparition.

"No, but his father is in there, along with Gretchen. He must be waiting for junior."

"What makes you say that?"

"He ordinarily prefers to live and work in the city while he lets the son use the house."

"Do you think we should talk to him or Gretchen?"

"The older Myers normally takes care of the business side of things, not the 'go to South Africa and rid the world of a maniacal telepath' side."

"No, but it might be best to have him on our side so he can convince his son, unless you think Carl trusts the maid more than his father."

"I'm not saying it's a bad idea. It's probably the same

either way. The night is still young, though. Continue scouting the area and let's wait to see if a few people leave."

"It's always waiting with you."

"We have to pick our moment carefully. I would rather wait for Carl to show up, or at least wait for more people to leave."

Charlene circled the perimeter of the woods encircling the estate during the stakeout, careful to remain behind as many trees as possible. Victor's aura remained situated in a second story room for much of the time, leaving only once for what was probably a bathroom break. Sure enough, three of the auras belonging to the strangers left in the next hour, leaving Victor, Gretchen, and, presumably, another servant watching the house, not counting the solitary security guard by the gate entrance. In the interim, the sky became hidden behind a growing number of dark clouds. A steady rain began to fall by the end of the first hour.

"It's so strange not getting wet," said Charlene. "I don't even really feel the cold."

"I once let myself sink to the bottom of the Atlantic. I think I was about a hundred miles off the shore of North Carolina. I spent the next two days trying to find my way out, maybe it was three days, I forget."

"What were you trying to do at the bottom of the ocean?"

"Testing what I could do. I did that three years after my death. Ever since then, I've been content with walking over water than under it."

"Are you saying I can learn to walk on water too?"

"Maybe, but I imagine it'll take quite a bit of practice. Water is nothing like the ground, obviously. It takes much greater focus to even cross a calm swimming pool much less a fickle lake or ocean."

"That could be useful to learn. Why only bring this up now?"

"Like you said, it's always waiting with me. Hmm, though I guess this could also mean you'd be forced to wear a bikini for me."

"Whatever. I think I'm ready to go in."

"Who you going for?"

"Victor."

She was staring at the backyard of the grand home, as it appeared to be the shortest distance between the open plain and the house. She hoped the dark sky hid her approach, but she knew there must have been night vision cameras capable of easily picking her up once she exited the shelter of the woods. She unfaded to draw in a lungful of humid air and put on her sunglasses. Refading, she took her first step into the unavoidable. She spanned the grounds quickly. Before she had much time to process it, she had phased through her first wall to enter an unlit room. With her eyes already well adjusted to the dark, she could quickly surmise she was standing in a kitchen.

Before she could finish wondering if her approach had been discovered, an automated female voice announced, "Intruder detected. Lockdown option selected. Entryway doors and windows have been locked. Police have been contacted. ETA, five minutes."

"Fancy," said Felix.

Gretchen and the other aura were on the first floor, both of them moving away from her. Under Felix's guidance, Charlene rushed through the house looking for the stairs, successfully finding them in no time at all. Victor's aura had seemingly moved into an adjacent room and remained there.

"Intruder has infiltrated the building," informed the house's voice.

Charlene phased into Victor's presumed chamber, but her first glance showed he wasn't in the dark bedroom, nonetheless, she could feel he was nearby. The chamber itself was a large bedroom fitted with an impressively sized bed, and was modestly furnished with a vanity in the far right corner, a work desk, some chairs surrounding a coffee table, and a couple of shelves. Victor's aura was radiating behind a shelf to her left, which held various humanitarian awards and academic memorabilia.

"That's adorable," said Felix. "He thinks he can hide from us."

Charlene stepped up to the shelf and walked through it. Almost instantly, she was staring into the elder Myers' stern-looking windows to the soul. The black eyes were sunk into a face of worn white granite, which was crowned by a healthy shrub of silvery hair. He was wearing an expectedly expensive gray suit, sitting by a console overseeing some monitors at the wall opposite to where she was standing. She happened to notice that one of the screens showed a feed of the very bedroom she had come from.

Without the slightest show of fear or surprise, Victor raised his right arm and pointed a pistol at Charlene. Seeing a gun targeted at her sent an involuntary shiver of fright in her, making her hesitate and allowing for Victor to begin the correspondence with a deeply daunting voice.

"An interesting ability. One more move and I'll be forced to test if you can go through bullets."

Knowing his bark did indeed have no bite, her courage returned and, in in the calmest tone she could muster, said, "I'm here to ask for Hermes' help. I've come to you in the hopes you can help me convince him without him getting the chance to… fly off. I would like to request for you to call off the police so we can talk, um, more leisurely."

It seemed remarkable to her how little his expression changed and yet still see a fast working mind processing all she was saying.

"Proof," he said half a moment after she finished.

"Proof?"

"I assume you have something to back your claim, unless you think you can get somewhere in the blackmailing business without it."

"Maybe Gretchen would have been easier," said Felix.

"I can assure you, Mr. Myers, I don't have proof," responded Charlene. "And I'm no mind reader, if that's what you're thinking. I'm simply aware of who he is, and I know with his resources he can help me remove a problem that concerns not only me, but a great deal of other innocent and not so innocent people. I know you and his mother taught him to be a good man, to help the world however he could. I won't stop pestering him, you, Gretchen, and everyone else who knows about him until I get his support."

There was a longer pause at the end of her plea. It was broken by the house announcing, "Intruder in premises. Police ETA, two minutes."

"It sounds like you have two minutes of my attention to say what you have to say," said Victor coolly. "So out with it. What is it you risk exposure and capture for?"

Charlene went on to explain as best and as fast as she could about Anashe's connection to the diamond industry, the powerful telepathy she used to obtain it, and how she had come to America and taken a young, wayward Ex with her, leaving out her specific link to the boy. Victor listened with great alertness and expelled a small sigh once Charlene had finished.

He lowered his gun and turned to the console. Leaning into a microphone, he ordered, "Ms. Travis, please call off the police. Tell them a security malfunction was to blame."

"Sir?" responded an elderly woman's voice through the intercom, clearly baffled.

"Do it, Ms. Travis."

"Yes, sir," said the woman resignedly.

"I appreciate it, sir, I really do," said Charlene.

Turning back to look at his uninvited guest, he said, "If we can confirm what you say is true, then this is a worthy case to investigate, but I'll have Carl hear your account and leave it up to him to see how he wishes to proceed with this, and if he does, whether he lets you aid him."

"I don't plan on giving him a choice."

The faintest hint of a smile formed on his thin lips. "I suppose not." He stood up for the first time, putting the gun in a holster inside his suit, and regained his rigid countenance. "Until he returns in a few hours, I advise you wait in the bedroom and allow me to explain to Ms. Travis I'm not under the influence of either alcohol or telepathic manipulation."

He pushed a button on the console to permit the shelf wall behind Charlene to slide open softly. She stepped aside to let him pass. He turned on the bedroom light, which were already dimmed to half their full brightness. Before he left the room, he turned to face Charlene and said, "I'm indulging you because it's apparent you're desperate, given the fairly brash actions you've taken, such as breaking and entering and revealing your aptitude of going through walls. You mustn't let a desperate situation force you to use desperate tactics."

"I do what I have too, sir."

"My son used to say something similar."

After Victor closed the door, Felix said, "That was something."

In as low a whisper as possible, Charlene asked, "Should

we trust him?"

"Probably. More than anything, I think he wants Carl to deal with you. I think he doesn't see you as an immediate threat and is biding his time until his Ex-human son arrives. By the way, are you okay?"

"Yeah, I'm perfectly cheesy."

"Cheesy?"

"I don't know. Okay, maybe the gun thing freaked me out just a teeny, tiny bit."

"Me too, but you did well."

They were only alone for a couple minutes before Victor and Gretchen came into the room.

Gretchen, who appeared to be old enough to be Victor's mother, looked Charlene up and down and stated in a surprisingly robust voice, "So you're the Ex? As usual, Mr. Myers overlooks the finer point of things. He didn't get your name, or rather, the name we should call you."

"Oh, you can call me, uh… Fade."

"Makes sense," approved Felix.

"What more are you willing to tell us, Miss Fade?"

"You don't have to grill the girl, Ms. Travis," interceded Victor. "I received enough information to satisfy me. Carl will handle anything he wishes to know."

"You're too easily swayed, Mr. Myers."

"Carl will decide if I was or not. I'll keep an eye on her in the meanwhile."

"*We'll* keep an eye on her."

"If you insist. As for you, Miss Fade, is there anything we can get you?"

"No, thank you."

"Very well. If you two don't mind, I still have some work I would like to clear."

Victor went over to the desk and opened a surprisingly old looking laptop, instantly typing away at something.

To Charlene, Gretchen motioned to the three chairs by the window facing the front lawn and said, "Please, have a seat, dear." Charlene chose to sit on the chair that would allow her to face away from the camera that was apparently above the entry. After sitting opposite of her, Gretchen then asked, "How did you find out about Carl?"

"I'm sorry, but the answer is a little personal."

"Well, this is personal for me, too. Mr. Myers said you mentioned you knew how *I* knew about Carl."

"I understand your concern, but I promise no one else alive is privy to this information." She couldn't help smiling under her scarf at her reference to Felix. "It was happenstance, really."

"Could you at least take off those obnoxious sunglasses?" requested Gretchen. "It's much more comfortable talking to someone when you can see their eyes."

She hesitated to do so, but Felix gave his permission, so she removed them.

"See? Isn't that better? You have lovely eyes, young miss.

How old are you? Can you at least tell me that?"

"Twenty."

"God, I hate seeing young people, especially beautiful young women. Don't tell me you're beautiful as well?"

"Just say yes," said Felix. "Put her out of her misery."

"I may have heard myself being described as so, once or twice," Charlene answered.

"I thought so."

"Ms. Travis, you can stop your teasing," urged Victor.

"It's not teasing, it's preparing. You know you're son does anything for a pretty face."

"I have no intention of showing him my face," assured Charlene.

"Maybe not. Of course, it's not only showing him your face I'm worried about."

In a more serious tone, Victor said, "Gretchen, another word trying to offend our visitor and I will send you away."

"Yes, Mr. Myers. I hope you forgive my candor, Miss Fade."

"It's not a problem," said an unoffended Charlene. "It's understandable you'd be protective of this family."

"I suppose that was well said." She stood up. "I'll leave you be for a little while, at least until I think of something else to probe you with." She went up to Victor, whispered something in his ear, and left.

Chapter Eighteen

The next couple of hours had Victor barely exchange a word with Charlene. He seemed perfectly at ease with the silence overtaking the room, having the tap, tap, tap of the rain lightly hitting the window pane and the tap, tap, tap of Victor's fingers ceaselessly typing away being their only company. For a girl who was almost always conversing with somebody, the situation was slightly awkward. She wanted to ask him some questions about Carl, but felt she had no right to pry when she was being so secretive herself. Even Felix found himself unable to say anything constructive during much of the interval, afraid to make her illicit a reaction that would make her seem like she was weird or simply crazy. Gretchen came in several times, but was more agreeable than before and brought Charlene some iced tea and water. She drank a little of both when she was sure no one could see her do so. She also stretched her legs a few times by going over to the window and staring purposelessly at the rain. The only event worth noting in the first hour of the wait was the unidentified aura withdrawing from the premises. Near midnight, Victor received a text that made him stand up and close the laptop.

"Carl isn't far off," he said, moving to the door. "I'll have him met you here."

Evidently unconcerned about keeping a personal vigil, he left her and the ghost to their own devices. In another minute, Charlene felt a Regular and an Ex reach her radar. She went to the window and saw the outline of a black SUV drive up to the front and saw Carl Myers exit the back seat. He went inside and she could feel him meeting with Victor and Gretchen at the entrance while the car drove off. She eventually sensed Carl going upstairs. She put on her sunglasses again and stood near the door when he opened it, ready to greet him.

She of course knew how he looked like from internet articles, television, and magazines, but seeing him in person reminded her of how good looking the thirty-one year old was, not really her type, but still attractive. Under the blue sports jacket, she could tell he was lean and well-toned. He must have been only an inch or two taller than Devin, but his slender physique made him appear much loftier. His neatly trimmed, light brown hair capped a boyish face, making him look considerably younger than he was. It was apparent Carl had received more of his physical traits from his mother than his hard looking father.

Leaving the door open, Carl skimmed Charlene's frame with his energetic black eyes and said in a soft, deep tone, "Follow me. My room doesn't have a camera. It'll be more private." They trekked past a few rooms until they entered one much like the one they left, except it looked more lived in and personal, having more pictures of family and friends and some Red Sox and New England Patriot collectables scattered about. Carl led her to two hefty, red leather chairs on either side of a small round table, where they each procured a seat. "My father says you know quite a bit about me, including several people who know about my extracurricular activities." Charlene was about to intercede, but knowing it was coming, Carl held up his hand and continued. "I'll let slide how you came upon this information if you don't wish to reveal it just yet, but I do need to know if someone else can possibly find out the way you did."

"I can pretty much guarantee no one will learn of your secret the way I did. If they did, I would really like to meet them myself."

"Well, however you found out, the fact is, you do know, and so I find it sensible to at least evaluate where we stand. Apparently, you have some interesting information to impart about a certain telepath you want assistance in dealing with."

"Your help and that of the Stewards, if we can get it."

"Not a simple request. A vigilante billionaire and the Stewards are usually busy trying to clear one task or another. It would take a substantial threat to immediately divert our attention. You have no evidence I can use to start this investigation, I presume?"

"Except knowing which Hilton room she's staying at, if she's still there, but like I told your father, I also know the Ex known as Sol is closely connected with her."

"Not unexpected if this Anashe mainly works from South Africa like you say she does. He's known to travel throughout Africa, especially Johannesburg, however, he's proven elusive to regularly track. I've always suspected he's been receiving help from some unknown source to evade the authorities so effectively."

"I know it's Anashe who helps him, and she uses her influence to support anti-human groups."

"You also accused her of controlling a large part of the diamond industry."

"She uses her mind to control the right people. I imagine she has several aliases and gets the money indirectly. She's practically invisible. I know it won't be easy to even confirm she exists."

"Telepaths have always been troublesome, even the decent ones. A telepath with possibly as many resources as I have is a frightening thought."

"So, will you help?"

"I don't believe you're lying, but I find it a little puzzling how you could have obtained this much information without giving me something physical to start with. You didn't find out what she could have been doing in America?"

"No, sir," said Charlene downheartedly.

His air instantly became less severe when he said, "Ah, I'm going to request you don't refer to me that way. This is an informal meeting and I only let Gretchen and old farts in board meetings call me 'sir.' It's 'Carl' or at least 'Mr. Myers' until the old man kicks the bucket."

"Very well, Mr. Myers. What's the next step?"

He gave an almost imperceptible sigh. "Work. I can't ignore a possible menace this formidable. First, I'll check the Hilton and see if she's still there. Then I'll contact a few acquaintances to see if they've run into anything that sounds like it could be Anashe or maybe even already know of her."

"I want to help."

"Going by what I've heard, no."

"I know you think I'd be a liability, but I have a personal investment in this, plus, with my fading ability, I'm not affected by her telepathy, or any power, for that matter."

"If you were in trouble, would you want a team filled with seasoned professionals saving you, or the team with an inexperienced member?"

"Maybe 'help' was too strong a word, but I want to stay in the loop."

"A more reasonable request. I suggest we take this one step at a time and see where this ends up going."

"I could live with that. How long before you can update me about your inquiries?"

"Depends when they get back to me. Meanwhile, I suppose

I should try looking more carefully at my business ventures in South Africa for any anomalies, though, if I know my father, he's already started digging on that front. What do you plan on doing now, Miss Fade? Will you be staying over?"

"No. I already have a place in town. I'll be staying there and come tomorrow night to check on any updates you can give me."

"Are you sure it's not easier for you to stay over? I can pledge your privacy and have no interest in turning you in, for the moment, at least."

"It's not that I don't trust you, and I appreciate the trust you've already shown in me, but I have prior engagements."

"Then, before you go, let us try to build on that trust you've mentioned. The way you found out about me, is that the way you learned of Anashe?"

She paused a second before saying, "Sort of."

"I'm going to push this a bit, but you don't have to respond. It sounds to me like you acquired your information from another source, specifically, another person."

She remained silent.

"You understand why I inquire? Do you still insist my secret will remain undisclosed?"

"If you promise to involve me in everything concerning Anashe, then I'll tell you everything."

Carl laughed lightly. "I have a feeling you want to tell me out of your own accord. If we work together a little longer, I predict we won't have to make any deals for some personal information. If you can't think of anything else to pursue, I trust our meeting has concluded."

Not thinking of anything noteworthy to say, she let him walk her out to the front door, and after refusing an umbrella, Carl saw her dissolve into the rain.

Chapter Nineteen

"That went as well as we could have hoped," evaluated Felix when they reached the woods.

"I can't wait to tell Hannah we have an Ex-human billionaire on our side."

Devin showed up in his jeep a short wait later. When they reached the room, Felix asked Charlene if he should spy on Carl.

"That sounds very distrustful of me. Sure, go ahead. Make sure they aren't talking bad about me."

Once they separated, she instantly felt the effects of the near constant fading and promptly went to sleep.

By the time Felix reached the Myers estate, he found the elder Myers was still working in his own room and Gretchen was in bed. Carl was in his room staring at a computer screen full of financial gibberish Felix couldn't make heads or tails of. He retired to bed within the next hour while his father left in his own car shortly thereafter. Carl never left his vast home throughout the next day and Felix did hear and see him contact several people in reference to South Africa, which Felix informed Charlene of when he returned to her the next evening.

Though she was sure he could give her little information, she decided to give a quick check anyway, given that she had told him she would do so. She was standing at Carl's front door by ten o'clock that Monday night, attired in yesterday's getup. Gretchen opened the door and led her to a cozy dining room. Carl was in the middle of eating some steak and fried shrimp with a glass of red wine.

"I hope I'm not intruding," said Charlene.

"You seemed to have little trouble intruding last night," retorted Carl with a sly smile. "Care to join me? The steak is perfectly cooked if you like it medium-rare."

"Tempting, but I don't plan on staying long, besides, I prefer it bloody as hell."

"What if I say I have an hour's worth of information on Anashe?"

"Behind my disguise is a frown, Mr. Myers."

"I know I'm sounding much like a guy trying to convince his date to stay over, but it's not every day I meet someone new who knows my alter ego, and a fellow Ex no less! Do you know many Exes, Miss Fade?"

"Not many, no."

"Don't get me wrong, I have nothing against finding solace in Regulars, but it's always reassuring to know there are some who can relate."

"You're right. I often want someone to talk to about my multi-billion dollar corporation."

"A fair point. I guess my dream of finding a billionaire Ex to relate to, dies tonight."

"I'll be sure to mourn. Do you actually have anything on Anashe?"

"Not yet. I peeked at the Hilton's database and discovered the room you said she was in was unoccupied the last few days. I suspect she told someone to either erase the information or never had them put it in the first place. In fact, the more I think about it, the more I believe any paper or digital trail declaring her current existence will not be discovered using conventional means. Of course, I won't give up if that's the case. I'll simply be forced to apply more hands on techniques."

"I'll give you two more nights before I return."

"If you wish." He stood up and walked up to her. "Until then, please accept this contribution in the hopes it makes your wait more comfortable." He laid down a thousand dollars at the edge of the table. "As you astutely pointed out, we're not all billionaires."

"I would say thank you, but I suspect you could leave me a million dollars without you ever feeling the weight leave your pockets."

"You'd be correct. Who knows, maybe when you return, I'll be feeling less stingy."

As they were waiting for Devin, Felix said, "I think he might be smitten by you."

"He doesn't even know how I look like."

"That's part of your allure. Trust me, that guy likes his challenges. Play your cards right and you could be Mrs. Myers."

"Maybe being his mistress will be easier."

"For what it's worth, I think you'd make an excellent mistress."

Felix spent much of the next two days haunting Carl. As expected, he was usually busy with his corporation, despite his father handling much of the load. At other times he was preoccupied with another mission involving his Hermes' persona, concerning a senator's possible ties with an anti-Ex organization. A few hours before Felix had to return to Charlene, Carl received several emails with attachments relating to Sol. At one point, as Carl was speed-reading through the multitude of files, Felix saw Anashe in a grainy still from a security camera. She was standing next to Sol meeting with what appeared to be several militants, though Felix couldn't tell from what specific group. Carl briefly paused at this image, but quickly moved on. Felix didn't notice any other files of note and went to inform the interested party.

"Have anything new?" Charlene asked Carl as he led her to his room, knowing full well he did.

"I do. A friend of mine, or I should say, of Hermes, at the CIA has graciously allowed me to view the files they have on Sol. There's quite a bit of information to filter through, but I've already picked out some of the more promising documents for you to look at. Here."

He handed her a seemingly custom made tablet with the sharpest and clearest definition she had ever seen. The thin but sturdy device displayed a slideshow of various images. On entering his room, she began to swipe through the pictures and documents, hoping to get to the still Felix described. In due course, she came across the sought after image and confiscated a moment to closely examine her adversary's face, being it was the first time she had actually laid eyes on her. It was difficult to make out definite features in the hazy image, but she thought it was enough to point her out in a small crowd. She was a head shorter than Sol, thin, very dark skinned, and had a stern face, signifying she was the cruel woman Felix said she was.

"That's her," said Charlene, handing Carl the tablet as he sifted through the archives on his desk computer.

He gave a shrewd stare at the screen and then tapped it to reveal a pinned document, which he read noiselessly to himself.

"I see," said Carl when he was done. "According to their records, Sol was meeting with some arms dealers. It didn't turn out too well for them. There weren't even any bodies to identify. Just piles of ash. In regards to the woman, the CIA assumed she was a translator for Sol and likely killed with everyone else. It's good to know how she looks like, but I'm afraid a single eight year old pic is not enough to go on. Please, see if you can pick out anything more of interest. I'll restart my own climb of the mountain and send anything I think you should look at."

She sat down on the chair from before and did as she was requested. There was plenty of old information on Sol, but Anashe was stereotypically absent for the next few hours. She expected Carl to chat away while they worked, but he precipitously assimilated the form of his father as he silently and diligently worked at his desk behind her. Two hours passed hastily by, and, at the beginning of the third hour, Gretchen came in with two mid-sized bowls of ice cream sundaes.

"A great weakness of mine, Miss Fade," said Carl. "Care for one? I'll be forced to eat both if you don't."

"A quick bite. Thank you, Ms. Travis."

Both Charlene and Carl continued searching for information between their mouthfuls. She had her back to him and Gretchen left the room, so she felt comfortable letting her scarf down to eat.

"You wouldn't know by looking at him, but I get my sweet tooth from my father," said Carl. "His favorite food in the world is chocolate ice cream topped with Skittles, Oreos, and chocolate syrup."

"It's a little hard imagining that."

"It's true. I once caught him having cake and ice cream for his meals the entire day. When I called him out on it, he told me, 'I'm a fucking billionaire! I can do what I damn well please!'"

Charlene giggled half politely and half because it was amusing.

"Gretchen is good at making these," continued Carl, "but if you tasted the ones my father makes, you'd look like Mammoth in a month."

"You've met her?"

"Yes, and she's just as jolly as she is on television, if not more so, but what else would you expect from a Canadian?"

"Why doesn't she join the Stewards and be with her sister?"

"She's an honorary member, on account of her contributions to various relief efforts, but she wouldn't harm anything if it wasn't already fried. It's understood official Stewards need to be prepared to kill whenever necessary, and Mammoth simply does not have the demeanor, despite the obvious strength she could contribute to the organization."

Felix broke in, saying, "Mention her sister, Medusa, again. Hermes did her."

"It's difficult to believe Medusa is her twin," complied Charlene. "They couldn't be further apart in looks and personality."

"If Mammoth shed four hundred pounds or so then the physical similarities might shine through better, but yes, her personality is pretty different."

"Can Medusa really turn people to stone just by looking at them?"

"Not exactly. She likes to have people think she can, but she does need to touch someone in order to petrify them, and the effect is not instantaneous, although, it can happen fairly rapidly if she wants it to."

Just as she was about to swipe to another file, Felix shouted, "Stop!"

She nearly responded out loud, but stopped herself in time.

"Lesedi Afolayan," dictated Felix. "That's the name she uses when she has to sign something official. I only saw it a couple times, but I know that's it."

She rescanned the document, which was a sort of itinerary written by Sol. She saw the name Felix was referring to in the middle of the page, hastily written sideways and in a sentence that said: *'Meet with a Lesedi Afolayan at the large courtyard at noon.'*

Felix continued with, "I'm sure Lesedi is not her real name, but I'm also pretty sure Anashe isn't either. In any case, Lesedi Afolayan must exist on paper or in the digital world somewhere, which means it can be tracked."

"Miss Fade?" Carl inquired to the pause Charlene had created.

"Oh, Carl, I think I have something." She put her scarf back up, almost forgetting to do so if it wasn't for Felix, and went over to show him the name.

"Hmm, I can't conceive the CIA ignored a name," said Carl. "Hold on and let me check what they have on it." He proceeded to tap the file and rifle through the attachments. "Here we go. They did make a file for her." He started to hum Beethoven's fifth as he read what the CIA had stored. "There's not much," he said after a minute of scanning. All they found were some stocks and minor property holdings. Nothing to indicate she was any kind of threat and worth keeping permanent tabs on. In fact, they concluded Sol was seducing her for money and ended the relationship some weeks later."

"That's wrong."

"It wouldn't be the first time the CIA was wrong about something, or the last."

"That makes me feel secure."

"Says a girl who can't get hurt."

"There's more than one way to hurt someone, Mr. Myers."

"Indeed."

"When did this investigation happen?"

"The itinerary's date is unknown. It was discovered a decade ago in a raid of Sol's apartment while he was staying in Paris for a time. The case on Ms. Afolayan was closed in the same year."

"I'm assuming you can do a better job in digging up something on her that happened in the last ten years?"

"With her resources and possible criminal enterprise-"

"*Actual* criminal enterprise," corrected Charlene.

"Yes, like I was saying, if she's trying to keep herself incognito, then it's likely she has a program that informs her every time someone looks up any of her names. If someone publicly searches her name on a system connected to the internet, which is most systems, then the program detects it and traces the origin.

Kind of like a fancy version of Google Alert."

"You have one, I presume?"

"Yes, and if anyone looks up both Carl Myers and Hermes at the same time, I send diamond robots to attack whoever looked it up."

"How do you get around it?"

"A secure connection from a place not connected to me. In my position, I can usually request a secure line for clandestine business deals. It shouldn't take long for me to have everything on her ever entered on a computer by noon. Good enough?"

"Make it by ten and I'll be eternally happier."

"Flirt alert!" exclaimed Felix. "Code blue!"

She was glad Carl couldn't see her contorting face as she held back laughter.

"Ten it is then!" said Carl. "Now, do you wish to continue our mining operation or do you wish for some repose?"

"Oh, I can go all night."

"Code red!" bellowed Felix. "Full on flirting! Abandon ship!"

Rolling her eyes, she grabbed the tablet off the desk and restarted her search for more information. The two physical beings began talking again within the next few minutes.

"If we can officially get the Stewards involved, then what is the protocol in dealing with a telepath?" Charlene wondered aloud.

"Telepaths are difficult to pin down, but once you can track them, they aren't too challenging to lethally pacify from a distance. There is a limited range a telepath can influence someone's mind, so a sniper at a distance of two hundred yards should easily be far away enough to safely fire at the target. I think the farthest a telepath has been known to control someone's mind was around four hundred feet, but it could be greater depending on the variables. If you want to capture a dangerous telepath alive, then it's getting close to safely subdue them that's the trick. The best option is using a tranquiller rifle, but they have a fairly limited range compared to their lethal counterparts. It usually means entering their zone of influence. It's also beneficial to hide in a crowd. Telepaths have a much harder time focusing in on someone the more people there are."

"I heard there have been tests by the military to see if they could come up with a way to prevent telepaths from reading minds and taking control in the first place."

"There have been numerous efforts to find defensive and offensive countermeasures the day telepaths were first exposed. Unfortunately, I know of no experiment that has shown to actually protect someone from the influence of the mind benders, excluding their own kind, but there has been greater success in reducing their power once they have been apprehended. Certain drugs can be periodically injected to virtually make it impossible for them to concentrate enough to implement their power. I also heard, for a more crude method, electrocuting them breaks their focus quite well, but that only works while they're being stunned. Or else, the key is to hope you remain at a safe distance."

"Another reason I'd be invaluable to help you take her down."

"And why is that?"

"Fading isn't my only power. Have you wondered how I found your father so quickly even when he was in the panic room?"

"That has crossed my mind."

"Well, I can sense an individual's presence from about five hundred feet away. I can even tell if they're either a Regular or an Ex. Right now I can sense that Ms. Travis has been standing outside your door for the last minute."

He laughed and hollered out, "Is that true, Ms. Travis!? Are you out there!?"

"No, Mr. Myers!" shouted back the muffled woman's voice, making him laugh again.

"Well, Miss Fade, any other powers you care to mention?"

"Other than the natural powers given to a woman from birth? No, no others."

.C Clemens

Chapter Twenty

The rest of the night provided no other major clues regarding Anashe. About an hour before the first rays of morning light would enter the window, Carl received a text.

"It seems my line has been secured. I'll have to go for a few hours, but I should have something when I return. I assume you'll wait here?" His visitor nodded. "I'll let Gretchen know you'll be staying then. She won't trust you if I allow you to wander the house, so I'll have to ask you to remain in this room. Just let her know if you need anything." He pointed to the intercom panel by the door as he prepared to exit the room. "Other than that, the room is yours, even the bed, if you require some rest."

"I bet he would like to see you on that bed," teased Felix.

Charlene barely suppressed a giggle.

"Did you say something, Miss Fade?"

"Nothing, only, thanks again."

He gave her a suspicious glance, but he left without saying anything more.

"Don't do that," she told Felix when she felt Carl walking away. "It would help our cause if I didn't burst out laughing from stupid innuendo."

"You're the one laughing at stupid innuendo, Miss Fade."

Wanting to rest her eyes for a while, Charlene and Felix separated so she could lie on the red leather sofa by the window.

As usual, anytime she found herself lying down comfortably, tired or not, she fell asleep. She was awakened a couple hours later by the feel of Felix's ghostly hand striking her feet. He informed her that Gretchen was heading their way. Charlene only had time to sit up, put on her sunglasses, and adjust her scarf before the housekeeper entered the room holding out a breakfast tray.

"Ah, you're up," perceived the old woman. She set the tray down on the small round table between the two chairs. "Please, Miss Fade, feel free to eat up. I know a late night sundae couldn't have filled you up."

"Thank you, Ms. Travis. I am a little hungry."

She went to sit by her meal. She removed her sunglasses and was waiting for Gretchen to move for the door to take down her scarf, but the maid sat herself opposite of her. Gretchen picked up on the hesitation.

"Oh my God! Are you really worried me seeing your face will ruin you?"

"There are some pretty good sketch artists out there."

"How about the little old lady takes off her spectacles?"

"That's not necessary."

She knew Felix didn't like it, but he offered no verbal protest, figuring he knew enough of Gretchen to know she was simply annoyed at what she considered a loathsome disguise instead of trying to trick her into showing her face. She lowered her scarf.

"See? Not so bad, is it?" rhetorically asked Gretchen. "I see you do indeed have a lovely face. Now, I hope you're not one of those girls who starve themselves. Go ahead and eat."

Felix added, "Remember when I said she might have been easier to convince than Victor? Never mind."

After Charlene scarfed down several bites of the best scrambled eggs she had ever eaten, Gretchen grabbed the remote from the arm rest and turned on the television. She changed the channel to a financial program.

"I may play no part in the success of their stock, but I can't help keeping myself apprised," said Gretchen.

"Ask about the Myers family," recommended Felix. "It's the only thing that makes the old bag happy."

"How long have you been connected with the Myers family?" Charlene asked.

"When I was only a little older than you," replied Gretchen. "I was a friend of Carl's grandfather in college, but before I could graduate, a family emergency forced me away. My family fell on hard times and things looked pretty bleak for my future, but dear Cameron Myers heard of my plight and presented me a job to be the head housekeeper at his father's newly bought mansion." She patted the chair. "I haven't looked back since. I know that sounds very passé of me."

"Not at all. People should do whatever makes them happy... as long as it doesn't hurt someone else's happiness, of course."

"Precisely. Most people think I get my kicks from dusting

old paintings or scrubbing the floor, but when I first saw a little wide-eyed Victor become excited to see me, I knew this is what I wanted to do. Now I've seen his son grow up. I only hope Carl gets some sense and settles down before I'm fully spent. God knows I only have a good decade left... How do you like your meal?"

"Oh, it's great. I'd start my own diner or something if my eggs were this good."

"You cook?"

"I've only been forced to cook breakfast for my younger siblings. I'm kinda a mess at any other time."

"You're the eldest then?"

"Yes."

"Does your family know of your talents?"

"My mother."

"And your father is...?"

"Out of the picture."

"I see. It was the opposite for me. In fact, of just about everyone in my family, the only one I really cared about was my sweet old father, God rest his soul. My mother always preferred my older brother to me, even when he became the hopeless delinquent after father died. He broke into this very house once, using one of my set of keys to get in. He didn't get very far after I called the police on him. That was the last time I ever spoke with him."

"I'm sorry," said Charlene, not knowing what else to say.

"Don't be. If there is a hell I'm sure he's in it. The coward didn't even come to our mother's funeral just to avoid me. Don't forget your family in all this Ex-human business. Carl was lucky to be born in a family that wouldn't shun him."

"When did he find out about his power?"

"Actually, it was with me. He had just turned twelve. Already very mature at that age. We were in the library when he suddenly lowered the gravity in the room and everything started floating to the ceiling, including me! Quite the experience. I broke a rib when he managed to turn up the gravity again and I fell roughly on the floor. Poor dear was crying and thought I would be mad at him. When did you first learn of your ability?"

"Close to a year ago."

"Late bloomer, eh? Ah! Look at that. It's up two points!" Once Charlene was done eating a handful of minutes later and Gretchen was in the process of taking away the tray, the venerable maid said, "Carl told me he would be back before ten, which means I wouldn't expect him before noon. Don't be shy about using his bed. I clean it often."

Gretchen turned out to be fairly close in estimating Carl's return, who arrived five till noon.

"I apologize for not making it by my promised time," said Carl when he crossed into the room, "but I had to make a detour regarding another case I'm on."

"It's fine, Mr. Myers," said Charlene, meeting him in the middle of the room. "What were you able to dig up?"

"That Ms. Lesedi Afolayan still exists and looks as

inconspicuous as she did when the CIA last checked her. Officially, she's a business woman with minor ties to the diamond and gold trade, and some of that income goes to retaining part of a private nature preserve, along with a few other properties, usually a type of residence. Intrigued, I looked into the other owners of the preserve and discovered a pattern. The three others also have connections to either the diamond or gold industry and none are involved in public affairs. I found nothing that indicates these people exist anywhere except on a few pieces of paper. On top of that, their records are all remarkably devoid of the slightest hint of possible misconduct."

"So they're *too* clean."

"Exactly. These names are likely the ones she uses to funnel in the money from her endeavors and to keep snooping creditors off her back."

"This doesn't sound enough to get the Stewards involved."

"I'm afraid it will take a little more than clean financial records of people that *might* exist to force the Stewards into action."

"Are you sure Anashe won't find out you were looking her up?"

"Even with my secure line, she might have, but she would also find out countless other names were being searched at random by a messy cyber-attack. I doubt she'll disappear into the jungle because of some faulty internet security."

"Oh, okay."

"Another thing. Her private plane was listed under the Lesedi name and I noted it landed in New Delhi, India yesterday, after a brief stop in Johannesburg."

"Then she must have left my friend there before moving on to whatever she's doing."

"According to the flight logs, the plane was in Washington D.C., before the capital it was in San Francisco, and before it was in America it was in Frankfurt, Germany. I wonder what she's trying to accomplish? She wasn't in any of those cities for more than a couple days." He remained in silent contemplation for several moments.

"Mr. Myers? Shouldn't we use this opening to do something?"

He snapped out of his trance and said, "We have no idea how long this opening will last. She could be back before I hastily put something together."

"Or she could continue her globetrotting tour and we could end up wasting a good opportunity to obtain the evidence we need. If you want to keep waiting that's fine, but send me to Johannesburg and I'll check her listed property holdings. Let me at least find out where she's keeping my friend. I won't intervene, I'll only be scouting."

"You couldn't even enter my home without setting off the alarm. I can't in good conscious send you to a situation that can go very wrong very quickly."

"I didn't care about setting off an alarm in a place I knew

there wouldn't be severe consequences for me. Besides, I'm here to ask for your help, not your permission, Mr. Myers."

"Strong words for someone who, I suspect, can't afford to fly to Africa, stay there at your leisure, and return. You also do not hold all the information you need."

"Look, I know you've seen nothing so far to fully convince you about the danger Anashe poses, but I know I can get something for you and the Stewards if I go to her home."

He sighed and said, "Your earnestness and conduct have convinced me this is a serious affair, Miss Fade, which is why I want to proceed cautiously."

"But this is the best time to go. Who knows if she'll ever leave Johannesburg again when she returns? Someone has to go there at some point, don't they? Nothing here will convict her. Trust me, Mr. Myers, I have a very strong conscious warning me what it will mean if I screw up, and I know I can't save my friend without Anashe completely out of the way. Plus, with my abilities, I can be five hundred feet away and still confirm if my friend is at a certain location or if there are other Exes to worry about. Who else can do that?"

He studied her with a look of both amusement and serious deliberation for several seconds before finally saying, "You make a strong case for yourself. Let me check something…" He began to lift his hand.

Seeing what was coming, Felix yelled out, "Fade!"

Just as she obeyed, she felt her body become heavier, but

the feeling faded as she did, though there was still a lingering feeling something was off balance, as if the room was tilting.

"I told you, no power can affect me," she said when she realized he was using his ability to affect gravity, walking up to him to display her point.

"I had to test you to be sure. Very well, Miss Fade, we shall go to Johannesburg."

"Really?"

"Under several conditions."

"Of course."

"First, if Anashe returns before we settle ourselves, we leave. Second, you must do everything I tell you to when we get there. You must rely on my judgment and experience. And thirdly, you can no longer hide your identity from me. If something happens to you, I would like to know whose family I wronged."

"I see your point."

She created a brief pause to indicate to Felix she wanted his feedback.

Taking her cue, Felix said, "I knew there was no way to keep your identity from him forever anyway."

"My name is Charlotte Fields, though I prefer Charlene. I lived in Seattle most of my life and I'm currently attending Washington State University."

She separated her sunglasses from her face and pulled down her scarf as she spoke. It was too subtle for Charlene to catch, but Felix saw a pleased expression flash on Carl's face before it fashioned back to his default aspect.

Charlene's paranormal partner said, "Now he knows you're hot. Good luck not being seduced. Oh, and don't bother telling him you have a boyfriend, that will only change his approach. I doubt if you told him a ghost was following you that he would be deterred any."

"When do we go?" Charlene asked Carl.

"A private jet can take off anytime. When are you ready?"

She didn't want to leave Devin without seeing him in person first, so she answered, "Give me an hour."

"Perfect. I'll see you then."

Chapter Twenty-One

Half an hour later, sitting in his jeep, Charlene finished telling Devin about the expedition she was about to undergo. He gave his blessing and, after some discussion, it was decided he would return to Pullman, since there was no way to know when she would return and guessed Carl would pay for her flight back home. On her arrival back to the estate, by still going through the woods and keeping her disguise on to avoid getting her face on any cameras, she found Gretchen waiting for her. She was conducted to an airy upstairs room, which was essentially converted into a great closet filled with a sundry of clothing, shoes, and accessories for both genders and all sizes. It was much like a miniature clothing store.

"Mr. Myers expects your ensemble is getting tiresome for you and will no longer do for your journey," said Gretchen. "Feel free to pick out what you like."

As Felix left her to change in private, he advised half seriously, "Nothing too skimpy, young lady!"

She ended up abiding to his appeal through her own solidarity and came out in her new outfit, consisting of practical sneakers, blue jeans, a black shirt proclaiming "I Believe in Unicorns," and a dark blue windbreaker. She had also secured her flourishing hair in a ponytail and sported a Yankees baseball cap, though she kept on her original shades. Gretchen grabbed her old clothes and showed her back downstairs, where Carl was waiting.

Glaring disapprovingly at her headgear, Carl said, "Ms. Travis, make sure there are no other Yankee mementos in this house." Turning back to Charlene, he said, "My driver will be here shortly."

"Should I worry about paparazzi meeting us?"

"No. I'm going to use an Anashe trick and take off using a plane registered under a pseudonym."

"Fake names are piling up fast. I guess I'm not the only one who doesn't like their given name."

The driver and his car arrived less than five minutes later. She could not help wondering what the driver must have thought seeing Carl with a much younger woman. From what Felix told her, Carl preferred women his own age, but was positive his range stretched from legal and beyond. Regardless, she found it didn't particularly provoke or amuse her.

In what seemed a very short drive, the car parked itself next to the waiting jet and she was whisked up to the ladder a moment later. At first, she was excited being in her first luxury jet, but finding out the flight would take at least eighteen hours tempered her outlook somewhat. After the plane lifted off the ground with only the two pilots, the owner of the jet, and herself as the occupants, Carl went into the diminutive bedroom at the back of the plane to dress in a more casual style, coming out in sneakers, jeans, a blue shirt, and a stonewashed brown jacket. Being the only passengers allowed them to talk freely in the extravagant aircraft cabin. She sat on the dark linen couch adjacent a table on the right side of the cabin while he generally kept to a rotating chair on the opposite side.

By using his gift of gab, Carl helped to move the early part of the flight along at a decent pace. Charlene perceived that his tone carried a mixture of both seriousness and aloofness she didn't think was possible. It gave even the most mundane of topics an air of prominence. Simply by using his facial expressions and changing the pitch of his voice the charismatic Ex could grab anyone's attention. She had little doubt that even without his billions he would likely still have his reputation with women. She told him so.

"Thank you. I sometimes wonder how well I'd do without the Myers name attached."

"Or Hermes."

"There's less opportunity on that front."

"But still some."

He presented her with the incredulous smile she most enjoyed luring out of him before he said, "Some, yes. I'm becoming very wary of you, Miss Fade. It sounds you know more about me than I first conjectured."

Completely ignoring his comment, she continued by saying, "Gretchen tells me she wants you to settle down. She wants another little Myers to help rear."

"She often tells me so. Sadly, I do not yet feel the inclination to bring a smaller version of myself into a world where Hermes still exists."

"And how long will he exist?"

"A question I ask myself daily. I am well aware there is not a particular accomplishment that would suddenly make Hermes an unnecessary figure in the world."

"In the world or *your* world?"

"You'd make a fine psychoanalyst, Miss Fade. For now, I feel Hermes benefits the world. When I feel he doesn't, I'll stop. If I'm not careful, I could end up suffering the fate of Icarus."

"Is your drive that strong, Mr. Myers?"

"For a particular person."

There was only one person he could have meant.

"Your mother?" she said demurely, not sure whether to touch on the sensitive subject.

He sullenly nodded and his expression acquired the aspect of a warrior's resolve. "There would be no Hermes without her. Her death, her murder, showed me how much resentment there was towards our family's support of Exes."

"It seems incredible whoever was responsible could hide for so long."

"For over a decade I've searched for those responsible for the car bombing, but to no avail. The trail went cold by the time I started looking into it myself two years later. Whoever did it must have had some wit, some means, and perhaps a bit of luck."

"If you'll allow it, as a sort of thank you for helping me, you can call on me anytime you need help with anything."

He chuckled. "You're a generous young woman. If time shows we can be trusted friends, and gives you the required experience, I will gladly accept your offer."

Carl advised they each attempt to grab as much sleep as possible before they arrived, insisting Charlene take the bed while he used the couch, so much of the middle of the flight was spent with each of them sleeping. It was in the latter stages of the voyage did they begin to discuss their objectives more intently. There were upwards of two dozen properties Anashe appeared to own in South Africa, including those with the possible faux names. Carl charted a route that would efficiently take them to all eleven properties in and around Johannesburg. Charlene wanted to also visit the nature reserve owned by the group of presumed aliases located a hundred miles northwest of the city, but Carl had objections. He argued that, while the reserve was relatively small, it was still too large an area to scout easily, and if Anashe did have something hidden there, it was undoubtedly well-guarded. He was also recommending they would unlikely enter any of the structures owned by Anashe for fear of cameras and hidden microphones.

It was here that Charlene began to think telling Carl about her secret weapon would be beneficial. She didn't want to limit their scouting trip to only what they could see if there was a way to safely gather information by otherworldly means. Knowing it was easier to ask forgiveness than permission, Charlene skipped the discussion with Felix and asked, with no real lead up to the ostensibly unbefitting question, "Do you believe in ghosts, Mr. Myers?"

Felix groaned loudly.

The query made the wealthy Ex raise an eyebrow. He studied her momentarily before answering, "I like to believe I have an open mind considering all I've seen, but I can't say I've ever personally experienced a supernatural encounter."

"Well, I'm forced to believe in them."

"Alright, I'll bite. Why do you believe in them?"

"Because one told me Carl Myers was Hermes."

It was impossible to read in his inflexible countenance what Carl was thinking when she revealed this to him. There was a pause in his eyes as he tried piercing what her attitude was. He saw that she remained composed and stoic.

Meanwhile, Felix could clearly see Charlene's angle, and could even understand why this was necessary, but still remained irritably silent as he saw how this would unfold.

Carl eventually asked, "This is your answer to how you

learned of me?"

"Yes. He learned of your dual identities about ten years back while he, uh, roamed Boston, and he stayed with you for a couple months. When he found me nearly a year ago, he told me some secrets he learned, including yours, and when she came into our lives, about Anashe. We eventually discovered he could give me the ability to fade and sense auras by being close to me."

Carl was quiet some moments, but didn't appear alarmed or repulsed, he was simply studying her. "This is a first," he finally said. With a slim grin, he continued with, "I've never met anyone who could give me as many surprises as you could, Miss Fade. The ghost is here now, then?" She nodded. "Very well, to prove you don't require treatment of some sort, I'm going to the bedroom and I'm going to both write a number and hold up some fingers. When I return, will he be able to tell you what they were?" When she confirmed he would, he went through with his design. On returning, she told him the two different numbers. "Really, I have rarely been so flabbergasted. Either you're telling the truth or you have far more abilities than any Ex known. For the sake of your disposition, I'll go ahead and assume you're telling me the truth. Tell me more about this phantom of yours."

She told him what she thought appropriate: his name, when and how he died, and how they met. He listened with his customary thoughtfulness until she concluded her tale.

"A tragic story. I'm sorry your friend suffered in solitude for so long."

"He appreciates your sympathy."

"No I don't," said Felix truthfully.

"I can see why you decided to tell me about your spectral ally. He will be of great use in our endeavor. An undetectable spirit spying for you… I've never quite been so dumbfounded in my life, if I may repeat myself. The possibilities this brings up boggles the mind. He says there aren't any other spirits or mediums like yourself?"

"He told me there are a few other ghosts he's run into, but they're broken souls who don't speak intelligibly. I don't think I've encountered a spirit before Felix, and I can't say I could even interact with them. Felix could be the only one I could connect with for all I know."

Carl appeared to wholly collect his outward emotion and calmly stated, "Fascinating. I wonder what makes a medium? It would be unusual if you were the only one."

"Your guess is as good as mine."

"I know this could be a touchy topic, but I can't help but ask. How has this affected you religiously?"

She was briefly flustered by the question. It was here she realized that the revelation of Felix never really affected her views on faith. She considered herself a Christian, but was admittedly not an active churchgoer. There was then a sense of disappointment at Carl. He was viewing Felix more as a symbol rather than a person. With a hint of touchiness in her tone she didn't think would come out, she answered, "Felix hasn't really changed my beliefs. The way I see it, he doesn't prove or disprove anything."

Carl picked up on the mildly resentful tone and said, "Forgive me, Miss Fade. I've gotten ahead of myself. I did not mean to offend. I should focus on the matter at hand. Yes, with Felix we could do more scouting than I first surmised. It will clearly be invaluable for him to tell us what he sees in the properties, even in the reserve."

Chapter Twenty-Two

They arrived in Johannesburg at 2:00 p.m. local time, losing six hours of time hurtling towards the sun. A rental SUV was already waiting for them to use. They made their way to their first destination with Carl behind the wheel. The day was clear and crisp. The skyline of the city to the west glimmered as magnificently as thousands of gold rings reflecting the light from the great flame churning in the black of space. There was not a small part of her enjoying the fact she had flown on a luxury jet, was in a new city on another continent, and the current partner of one of the most notable men in both the Regular and Ex-human world.

Felix could see and sense her contentment at the new path her life was taking. He ventured to think he should resign himself more to the idea of her living the life of an Ex if it truly made her happy. He could only hope he could shield her from the suffering he saw many other Exes go through and help her avoid becoming a cold and disillusioned hater of the world, like it had done to so many others. *I will not only protect your body, but I will do my utmost to guard your heart and soul,* he vowed to himself. He would have mentioned her mind if he didn't believe it already exceptionally fortified. Truthfully, it was she who was keeping his mind from faltering.

The first property they visited was already interesting to their ethereal radar. It was a modest one-story home under Lesedi's name and in a neighborhood at the outskirts of the city.

"There's an Ex aura in there along with two Regulars," Charlene informed Carl as he slowly came up to the home. "Though Felix doesn't recognize them."

"I do recognize the positions," said Felix. "I'd say they're enjoying themselves."

"Just go and get their descriptions and check the house," Charlene ordered Felix.

Felix conformed to the plan and exited the vehicle, which continued driving slowly around the block. He found nothing too interesting inside the house itself, so he went into the master bedroom to observe the three lovers and imprint their auras for future reference. The Ex turned out to be a white woman in her early thirties, and while she had a good body, her face left something to be desired. The other two were black men, who appeared to be male escorts. Felix had seen enough sex to know the difference between the free kind and the kind you paid for. In the few minutes he was in the room, he didn't see what the possible power of the Ex was and went back to the SUV when he thought he could give a good report to Charlene.

The next few hours held this pattern of information gathering. A few properties were empty, but the majority typically had an Ex. It didn't matter if the property was owned by Lesedi or any of the other bogus names. Near night's approach, the reconnaissance group learned of seven different Exes, three of whom Felix recognized. The most intriguing of the assortment was a middle-aged Chinese woman, known as Sleet by Americans, who had evaded capture after attempting to assassinate Japan's prime minister, nearly killing him when a lance made of ice punctured his lung. Carl was handed more evidence of Charlene's imperceptible partner when his own eyes were able to confirm Sleet was inside the upper-class home. Carl believed knowing Sleet's location would unquestionably attract the Stewards attention. As they meandered in the western section of the city, the sun starting its dip into the horizon, Charlene and Felix felt Paul's aura high above in a forty-story high-rise apartment building.

"He's not alone," Charlene told Carl after notifying him of the news. "Sol is with him."

"I must apologize, Miss Fade," began Carl. "To discover Sleet, Sol, and Paul, plus a slew of other Exes, in a single day, this has been a very productive little trip. I'm sorry for doubting you."

"It's understandable, Mr. Myers. You're forgiven. I know it took a leap of faith to trust only my words. You still are, really. I had expected to force the issue more to get you on my side."

"I admittedly give women the benefit of the doubt more often than I should, but I can't help it," he answered, a boyish grin on his face. "In any case, now that we have found your friend, I propose we check in the hotel room I reserved, have a bite to eat, and restart our inspection of the other properties after the repose."

"Are we going to the reserve today?"

"Yes. It will be dark by then, but I do prefer going when light is scarce. The reserve is not open to the public and going near it will likely draw unwanted attention. It will be easier to hide from meddling eyes in the dark. In any event, isn't that when ghosts do their haunting?"

"Okay, let's go then."

A little to Charlene's and Felix's chagrin, Carl chaperoned them to an upper-class hotel. One of the highest suites was reserved for them. They would have preferred more subtlety out of their dwelling, but Charlene did enjoy the dinner of fried fish brought by room service, her shower in the spacious bathroom, and would later learn why Carl preferred upscale hotels with balconies that looked out to sprawling views of the city landscape.

As Carl was taking his shower and she was lying prone on her bed, absentmindedly flipping through a fashion magazine, Felix joked, "Do you want me to tell you how big he is or do you want to find out the old-fashioned way?"

"Tell me, truthfully," said Charlene whimsically. "What would you say if I actually ended up sleeping with him?"

Her tone was an attempt at a serious one, but Felix could catch the levity buried in it and replied with, "Ha, ha, ha. If I actually thought you would cheat on Devin, I wouldn't be joking about this. However, to answer you, I would let you do whatever you want."

"You wouldn't stop me from cheating on Devin?"

"This is getting uncomfortable."

"No, this is your punishment for cracking all those dumb jokes. Come on, tell me."

"No, I wouldn't stop you. I have no vested interest in who you sleep with, as long as he's not a complete douche, anyway. It's your life and I'm not going to interfere unless you asked me to. I'm your friend, not your conscious."

Something bothered her about his answer, but she couldn't be sure what the origin for it was. "You wouldn't think any less of me if you knew I was a cheater?"

He wanted to say she could never be thought less by him if her hobby was kicking kittens into live volcanos, but he wasn't sure how she would take it, so he actually said, "I would be surprised, sure, but it's none of my business."

There was another slight pang of aggravation at his words, but she only had a second to dwell on it before Carl came out the bathroom.

"Were you just talking to him?" he asked, putting on a gray sports jacket.

"Yeah, I often do."

"What were you talking about?"

"Girl stuff. Nothing you'd like."

"Does he like it?"

"No, but he doesn't have a choice."

Around the time most began thinking about sleep, the trio restarted their mission. It wasn't long before they unveiled yet another Ex residing in a home.

"That's nine total possible antagonist Exes so far," Carl pondered aloud. "The Stewards will have their hands full apprehending them if they really are all devotees of Anashe. She must be planning something significant if she's gathering followers. Apart from the Stewards, I've never known an amassing of Exes to mean anything good. Most prefer to remain anonymous, even among their own kind."

"Do you think you might have trouble getting the Stewards to act?"

"I have enough clout to get someone to pay attention and investigate. What you won't like is how long they will take in confirming my word. Understandably, they don't just want to send a dozen Stewards and UN soldiers into some corporate people's homes without cause. They would also like to know what they're up against. Finding out what abilities the unknown Exes have will likely save lives if they resist."

"Will you be part of the team that helps to capture them?"

"Depends when and if they do. The Stewards often favor keeping treacherous groups under surveillance for as long as possible until they either think they learned of all conceivable connections or know lives are in imminent peril."

"I don't want to be on the sidelines when they move in. I don't mean actually taking down Anashe or do anything hands on, but I really need to make sure Paul comes out okay in all this."

"I know. Let's see where this goes."

Chapter Twenty-Three

They initiated the drive to the reserve late that night. The road they trailed when they neared the remote reserve was ill-used and secluded. Only a few small towns were within twenty miles of their goal and, according to the map, no constructed roadways led directly to the sanctuary, meaning they would have to drop off Felix several miles from the perimeter.

Charlene asked Felix, "Are you sure you won't get lost in the dark? Everything kinda looks the same."

"I never needed a good sense of direction after I died, but I think I can manage. South shouldn't be hard to find when the sun comes back up."

"Okay, just try and meet us back here in the morning."

"I won't make you wor- I mean, wait all day for me."

They unglued and Felix ran towards the beginning of the animal reservation, determined to finish the task as quickly as possible. He didn't think Charlene could worry about a dead man, but he still felt like he shouldn't keep her in suspense.

As Carl drove to the hotel a hundred miles back, he asked, "So you're unable to use your power when he's not near you?"

"That's right."

"Then you must not like leaving him for long."

She thought a moment on his comment, recognizing she had generally taken Felix for granted. He was always there when she told him to be and believed he kept away when she requested him to be. What would happen if she needed him right then and there? She was suddenly very aware she was in a foreign land with wild animals and dangerous Exes conceivably nearby. Even knowing Carl was alongside her did not diminish her abrupt recognition of her vulnerability and powerlessness. She did not like Carl being the transmitter of this fact, even if she knew he was only being inoffensively curious about their relationship.

Finally, she answered, "No one likes to separate from their friends for long, Mr. Myers."

In the meantime, Felix was busy running through the plains of Africa hoping to not get too lost and end up in Egypt. There were no true reference points to keep himself from wandering out the premises. According to the maps they had studied, there was a small river a few miles to the east that made the easternmost border of the reserve. They hoped this would be good enough to give him a good starting point and something to head back to once he believed he scouted for as much as he thought able. All he sensed were wild animals for the first couple of hours. The overcast night made it difficult to make out anything unless it was just a few yards away. In the time he followed Anashe, he never saw her enter the reserve, or even knew she had one, but something told him there was something out there. He didn't think she would buy uninhabited land for the sake of some wild beasts.

Just as the clouds were clearing to reveal partial moonshine from the waxing crescent moon, he felt some confirmation to his suspicions. As he wandered to the west, three fast moving Exes he had never felt before were heading north fifty yards ahead of him. He ran as fast as he could to catch up to the Exes and soon saw an obscure dirt path, apparently used fairly often, given the deep and numerous impressions of the tire markings. Making his way speedily up the path, he was able to keep the Exes within his outer awareness. After following them for several minutes, he felt them stop when they met with the aura of Sol. When Felix had fully caught up to them, he could clearly see two of the unfamiliar Exes were standing by a battered, military-styled jeep and facing Sol, but he could not see the third, though he knew by the aura that the Ex had moved to stand behind Sol about three yards away. *An invisibility type?* speculated Felix.

The ghost next saw one of the observable Exes was a mature, regal looking bald man with a clean white beard. He looked out of place in his pressed, black suit. Despite the heavy bearing this elder carried, he was surpassed by the tall and beautiful young blonde woman standing next to him. Her aura was undoubtedly one of the strongest Felix had ever felt, and she carried a poise that he thought would equal the greatest warrior-kings of old. She did not look happy and it was perceived in her German accent when she spoke with Sol.

The first words he overheard when he was within their vocal range were her asking him in German, a language he could understand if not quite speak fluently, "So she isn't here?"

"No," answered Sol in English, a minor quiver in his voice. *Was Sol afraid of her?*

Sol continued. "She believed we had the results we needed and went ahead with the next phase."

"It wasn't her decision."

"She told me she thought you would approve, but if I thought there was any chance you wouldn't, I would have told her so."

The blonde Ex sighed and eased her frustration slightly, but not enough to stop sounding displeased. "I know you would have, Sol, and perhaps I should have made myself clearer about my intentions when we reached this junction, but I'm still surprised you took this step without my consent."

"Everything was going so well, we didn't see a reason to hold back. Also, not to make excuses, but we did try contacting you for a week before we went ahead, but you were on the move again and we didn't know when you would settle down."

"You're right, that isn't an excuse. I didn't partner you with Anashe to follow her every whim. I recommend you don't destroy the lab. If something unexpected happens with the contagion, then

I would like to know we can correct it on our own. I don't want to have to rely on anyone else anymore."

"Yes, ma'am."

"Is the timetable the same?"

"Anticipate the most graphic symptoms to appear in a week or so."

"Very well." Turning to the old man, she said in flawless English, "Let's get out of this God forsaken land."

She stepped into the driver's side of the jeep and the two other auras stepped in with her. The invisible individual never revealed themselves as they drove away.

Felix felt he should follow this new group of Exes, but as her last statement implied she was going out of the country, he didn't think it was practical. Instead, he stayed with Sol to see what he would do. Before the jeep was out of sight, Sol strode several feet beyond the end of the dirt path, where a motorcycle was leaning on its stand under a tree. Felix was sure he was about to leave, but as an alternative, Sol grabbed his keys, pushed a button on a small control pad linked with the keychain, and snatched a duffle bag off the bike. A motorized noise could then be heard originating a few yards passed the tree. When Felix went towards the sound, he saw a part of the ground was opening to expose a ladder leading straight down for some eight feet. On reaching the bottom, Sol flipped a switch and a dull light lit the surprisingly large underground room. The space appeared to be the lab the blonde Ex had referred to earlier. After going by a decontamination room, where there were some biohazard suits hanging, Felix could see the lab looked to be top-notch, accommodating some distinctive electron microscopes, vials of various drugs and chemicals, computers of all types, and abundant biohazard dispensers.

Sol rambled about the room and started to dismantle some brick sized objects and place them in a duffle bag he had brought with him. On closer inspection, Felix recognized the bricks were C4 plastic explosives. Sol collected enough of them to fill up the bag. When the explosives were all accounted for, the Ex left the lab, closed the secret door, and mounted his bike. With no reason to hop on with him, Felix let him to ride off on his own. The rest of the night was spent tracing the dirt path as carefully as he could to make sure he could convey to Charlene where the lab was situated. At dawn, he was able to chart the path onto the road he was pretty sure was the one he used to get there, though he imagined most would look identical. He marched along its easterly direction in hopes to meet his ride or, at least, the actual road he was supposed to be on. A few hours of doubt later, he saw the acquainted black SUV coasting towards him. He allowed himself to get in front of the vehicle, phase through the hood and driver's seat, and settle in the backseat. At any other time he would have eavesdropped on the pair for a few minutes to wait for a good time to interrupt their conversation, but he felt the situation was too grave for any of his timewasting games.

"Did I miss anything good?" Felix asked.

"Loads of kinky stuff," Charlene answered with a bigger sense of relief she would have thought strange before her comprehension of her growing reliance on him.

"What was that?" asked Carl.

She laughed. "Sorry, I was talking to Felix. He's here. Did you find out anything?"

"Nothing much. Only a secret laboratory apparently used to create some sort of virus."

"I hope you're kidding."

"Sorry, I'm not."

He went on to explain what he saw and heard, which was promptly relayed to Carl.

Once Carl had a moment to process what he heard, he said, "This strongly implies Anashe is actually an underling. No matter where she lies in the pecking order of her organization though, it seems they are evidently working on a pathogen of some kind."

"Oh God, do you think that's why Anashe is going around the world?" asked Charlene. "To spread this virus?"

"The Stewards might have to involve themselves sooner than I expected," reflected Carl. "You said there were symptoms that will begin showing up in a week?"

"That's what Felix overheard."

"With any luck, Anashe might still be at the testing stages, but if they were prepared to destroy their lab, then I fear we might be too late to completely stop them." He bore a more melancholy tone as he spoke through the sentence. He pulled out a phone

Charlene noticed was not the one he normally used. He chose a contact and called it. After several rings, someone finally answered. "Noe? It's me... Yes, I'm fine, but I've stumbled across something that requires immediate attention... I'm in South Africa... Everyone is always busy, Noe. I wouldn't have called you if this wasn't serious. Listen, I believe there's an anti-Regular terrorist group working out of here that might already be in the process of spreading a contagion in some parts of the world... No shit, Noe. There's too much info to go through just now, but I'll start emailing and texting you everything I have so far... Yeah, Sol has something to do with it, but he's just the tip of the shit pile. We're going to need many of the Stewards on this if we're going to effectively apprehend everyone involved... Thanks Noe. When you're not being a smartass you can get some shit done. Bye."

"Who's Noe?" asked Charlene when he hung up.

"He's a young Ex who works for the CIA. He's been my contact there since Madam X retired."

"Oh..."

Knowing what she was contemplating, Felix said, "Not now, of all times."

Taking his hint to move on, she asked, "Couldn't you have contacted the Stewards directly?"

"For unofficial business, but with us, in all probability, needing many of their assembly to aid in the cause, then I have to go through more official channels. The CIA will quickly realize this operation will necessitate the support of the Stewards and will involve them."

"What do you think they'll do with news of a possible contagion loose?"

"Once Noe tells me he's contacted the U.N. I'll be able to check personally what their plans are and we can act accordingly." The car began to slow down until it came to a complete stop in the largely empty road. "Do you mind driving the rest of the way? I would like to start sending Noe the information." He opened his door, meaning there was only a single answer available.

"Uh, sure." Once they sat back down to their new stations, she asked, "What are we going to do in the meantime?"

"If you have nothing terribly important to go back to, I would like for us to remain here until I know how everything is going to turn out, which could be a few more days."

"Good. I want to see this through."

Her response went unheeded as Carl was already at work sending what he could to his connection.

"You're going to tell them about Paul?" she asked, after a few minutes silence.

"I have to," he replied without looking up from his phone. "It's possible he could be influenced by Anashe and become a threat, but you shouldn't worry too much. The Stewards should be able to subdue a young, inexperienced Ex without injuring him. Even if he has become brainwashed and attacks them, their first resort won't be of the lethal kind."

There was a growing concern for Hannah and her family if

Anashe was really dispersing a virus around the world. The telepath had been in San Francisco after all. She ended up texting her friend, who was still with her family, and warned her about going outside or meeting with too many people for fear of an impending pathogen Anashe could have been distributing while there...

Carl received a text while they were secured in their hotel room later that evening.

"Noe says an agent will be sent from Cape Town to meet us early tomorrow morning to confirm what he can of the information we have."

"How is he going to do that? Much of what we have based on what a ghost saw, heard, and felt."

"The key is Sol. If he can get a picture or video verifying he is where we say he is, then that will go a long way to trusting the rest of our words, though I imagine getting Sleet and some of the other Exes will be needed as well."

"Where is he meeting us?"

"In the bar of another hotel."

"Are you going to wear your Hermes disguise?" she asked jestingly.

"Impractical in most cases. No, I find a simple wig and sunglasses are all that's required to remain ambiguous."

An hour before they had to meet their contact, Charlene awakened and was informed by Carl that Anashe's plane had landed in Beijing.

"She's now hit two of the most populous countries in the world," noted Carl. "Based on her trajectory, I would say this is her final stop before she returns."

"That gives us at least another day, if not two."

"That's hopefully enough time to get all the evidence we need before having to worry about a mind reader in our way, assuming none of the other Exes are telepaths, but if we treated every Ex like a potential telepath, we would never get anywhere."

Shortly after the update, they began preparing themselves to go out. In the afternoon before, the two had went to a nearby shopping center to acquire more clothing. Charlene once again went for the hooded look, along with her baseball cap and shades, while Carl wore a blue blazer and jeans. What brought a laugh from Charlene was when he put on his untidy, dark haired wig. She told him it made him look like a rocker from the eighties. However, the persona was shattered by the thick glasses he put on next, instigating another fit of laughter. As they walked out the building and into the parking garage, she was sure no one who saw the pair could predict what their relationship was, who they really were, and what important mission they were undertaking. It created another swell of exhilaration and anticipation. She had to remind herself of her vital mission a few times.

It didn't take long to enter the hotel bar even more luxurious than the one they had left behind. It was still early and mostly empty. They sat themselves a couple tables away from the bar and he ordered a Jack Daniel's on the Rocks while she had an iced tea.

"Really? This early?" she said after they gave their order.

"When in Rome…"

"Become an alcoholic?"

"I assure you, I can handle my drink. In fact, I don't think I've even become drunk in the last year or so."

"That's too bad, but I do seem to recall a video in TMZ that came out a few months back when you were in a club and-"

"Ah, yes, the fiasco with the Ferrari and the, ahem, professional dancers. I was quite in control, actually. If anyone really paid close attention to me that night, they would have found it difficult to believe the amount I drank would have been enough to set off those events. I'm not the type to drink for pleasure, Miss Fade. I tend to partake in the evil when I'm alone and my more melancholy thoughts threaten to overcome me."

"Then let's toast to keeping back those melancholy thoughts."

Clink.

Chapter Twenty-Four

It was twenty minutes later when they saw an ebony skinned man about Carl's age donning a light gray suit and carrying a black suitcase enter the bar and proceed to their table after spotting the pair.

"Mr. Harris?" he asked Carl with his heavy South African accent.

"Yes," Carl replied. "You have a car?"

"Yes."

"Good, we'll talk in there."

They all exited the hotel and followed the agent to the car he parked by the road a block away. The agent advanced the conversation as they walked.

"My name is Agent Beasley. Am I correct in saying you two are the ones responsible for the information we received?"

"Yes."

"And who is the woman? You didn't mention her."

"My invaluable assistant in all this. Exactly who she is does not concern your agency."

"I see." They soon reached a shockingly old black mini-van with deeply tinted windows. "I know what you're thinking, but her insides are much more updated, and the outside will hide us in plain sight." Once they entered the automobile, with Carl in the passenger's side and Charlene in the backseat, he said, "You're the famous Hermes, then?"

"That's right."

"I know you have this reputation of helping us, but we can't just go by your word alone."

"Yes, I understand, my friend. We're prepared to show you as much proof as we can. I'm sure you received the update on Anashe?"

"Yes, she's in China now, at least, her plane is, but Sol is the more interesting one to us at the moment."

"Take us to the last residence he was in and we'll tell you whether he's there or not."

The two men talked more in depth about the other information they gathered while Charlene preserved her silence, though she noticed the agent often managed to take glimpses at her in the rearview mirror as he drove. It was quickly evident that the agent knew Johannesburg well and transported them without much instruction to the destination.

When the apartment was within her range, Carl looked back at her and asked, "Is he there?"

"No, but Paul is there with another Ex. The very first Ex we learned of, in fact. They're near the top."

"How do you know that?" asked Beasley.

"The lady knows and let's leave it at that," responded Carl.

"You Exes expect trust from us and never want to give us the reason to provide it," remarked Beasley. "She's not reading my mind is she?"

Before Carl could answer for her, Charlene tackled the subject herself. With some ire, she said, "No, sir, I cannot, and maybe Exes have not shown much trust in Regulars, but that's probably because the other side has not proven they have earned it."

Carl chuckled. "As you can see, Agent Beasley, I call her my assistant, but she is really quite independent of me. In reality, I would say we are the ones assisting *her*. Now, we could argue the particulars of the Ex and Regular relationship all week, but what is it you wish to do next, Mr. Beasley?"

Agent Beasley thought some moments and said, "We can check back here later. Sleet is another who we would like to confirm. We'll head for her supposed hideout next and check her situation."

They were at Sleet's upscale suburb after another short drive. Charlene felt Sleet was home alone, which she transmitted to the living men. Agent Beasley parked the mini-van at the edge of the block and had a good view of Sleet's two-story modern home settled three houses away on the left side of the block.

"Okay, now what?" asked the inexperienced and more impatient Charlene.

"We wait," said the agent, reaching for his briefcase in the backseat and opened it to take out a small high resolution camera with a long lens.

"Won't someone call the police about an old, strange van in a ritzy neighborhood?" she asked.

"They'll check the plates and discover its administrative origin," assured the agent. "The worst they'll do is ask us to move to make it look like they did something."

About half an hour of waiting later, Charlene could feel Sleet's aura was moving in three dimensions in what had to be her backyard. "She's outside," she said. "I think she's swimming."

Agent Beasley wordlessly started his car and began to drive to the other side of the block. The houses were on large properties and filled up the entire width of the block, meaning they could see the backyards of the homes when they reached the other side. The sought after view was blocked by a red brick wall heavily concealed by shrubbery.

"Damn, no luck here," said their governmental partner.

Felix had an idea. "You know, no one is home next door."

Charlene understood what he meant. The home neighboring Sleet's was devoid of auras and she observed that one of the second story rooms overlooked her backyard. "Agent Beasley, hand me the camera and I can get your pictures."

"What?" he asked. "How?"

"Her neighbors are out and I can sneak in and take pictures of Sleet from that window."

"So, from what I can gather, your power involves detecting people somehow?"

"That's right. I know no one is home and so I won't get caught, plus, with another power, I won't even have to worry about opening a door to get in."

Agent Beasley gazed at Hermes for his assessment.

Answering the stare, Hermes said, "I have no qualms about it."

The agent gave a moment to think about it and responded by mutely handing the camera to the girl. Without troubling to open the door, she phased out the vehicle and sprinted to the target home, hoping a random South African household didn't have as an elaborate an alarm system as Carl's. She thought about the possibility the home was watched over by rudimentary cameras, but believed it unlikely, and thanks to her hood, cap, and sunglasses, would still be unable to divulge her identity if she was indeed being recorded. She speedily phased into the fashionable home and went upstairs. The bedroom overlooking the Ex was unmistakably a nursery room for two toddlers, one of each gender going by the variation of toys and colors.

Just as they had suspected, the window permitted for an unhindered view of Sleet's backyard. It was confirmed she was swimming in a long lap pool. Charlene adjusted both herself and the camera as best she could and proceeded to snap as many pictures she believed adequate. Luckily, Sleet came out at one point to sip a pink drink, giving the amateur photographer her best shots. She headed back to the car when she was content with her work. Before handing over the camera, she made sure to wipe off as much of her fingerprints as possible. Agent Beasley looked through the pics for a few minutes and without saying anything in the positive or negative the entire time, started the van and drove off, which was enough for her to feel gratified.

The mini-van traced back its tires to head back to its primary mark. When they reached the high-rise, Charlene sensed Sol was still M.I.A., though Paul and the other Ex were still there. No parking was available on street level, so they entered into a public parking garage located about a hundred yards away—after multiple guarantees to Beasley that the building was within her scope of detection—however, since the garage was on the same side as the high-rise, they couldn't see it directly unless they climbed to the top level. There wasn't much conversing during the stakeout.

After nearly an hour waiting either in the car or roving the garage, Carl and Charlene, to the annoyance of the agent, who had to follow, walked onto the busy streets. The day was fresh and sunny, perfect for taking long strolls. If the unceasing aura of Paul wasn't quite literally hanging above her, she would have almost forgotten she wasn't there to be a tourist. It was gnawing at her that he was so close, and yet, so unreachable. What entirely broke any serenity in her outlook was sensing a fast moving Sol approaching them as they were giving another deliberately slow pass in front of the high-rise.

She grabbed Carl's attention. "He's coming," she said, pointing in the direction he was coming from.

Carl, in turn, told Agent Beasley of the newsflash, who was moseying a few steps behind them. They scrambled to the other side of the street to remove themselves from possibly being in Sol's direct line of sight. When they crossed the street, they saw a helmeted Sol on his motorcycle enter the private parking lot neighboring the complex. A few seconds later and they saw him helmetless. He turned the corner to enter the skyscraper. The agent hastily maneuvered Carl and Charlene to be next to one another while keeping their backs to Sol. He then pretended he was taking an unassuming picture of them, but was actually aiming the camera between the pair's heads and targeting Sol. When Sol went out of sight as he crossed into the building, Agent Beasley began scanning through the images to check if he had gotten what he wanted. To his delight, he captured several good shots of Sol's face.

"Is this enough to bring in reinforcements?" Hermes asked the agent.

"I think so. I need to contact headquarters and tell them we need eyes on the other Exes you found. We can probably get the Stewards to act once we have that."

"Be careful when Anashe comes back," advised Charlene. "If she reads the minds of anyone of your men-"

"Yes, miss," interjected Agent Beasley, though suppressing the rudeness as best he could. "I'm well aware of the precautions we will have to take with a telepath."

As the group returned to the mini-van, Charlene felt Sol, the other Ex, and Paul begin to descend to the ground floor. Shortly thereafter, the Exes must have moved into a vehicle, as they began moving at a steady pace together. She informed the men of this new development, but they agreed it was not worth the risk of tracking them. Agent Beasley eventually dropped Carl and Charlene a few blocks from their hotel and drove off to finish his job. There was little else to do for the rest of that day except to wait for an update, which arrived in the middle of the following day. Carl learned Anashe had left China, but her current route was unknown. It wasn't until Charlene was about to go to sleep did any news from the agency arrive.

"Good news, Miss Fade," decreed Carl when he hung up on Noe. "The CIA has discussed the situation with the Stewards and they will provide assistance in the endeavor."

"What's our next step then?" asked Charlene, sitting up on her bed.

"My next step is to call an acquaintance of mine in the organization and find out what I can from her."

"Right, 'acquaintance.' Got it." Carl laughed at the insinuation. "What is the CIA doing about the potential virus?"

"There's not much they can do at the moment other than keep an eye and an ear on the city hospitals Anashe has visited.

They obviously don't want to panic everyone if the information turns out to be inaccurate."

"And if it is accurate?"

"With a bit of foresight on their side, the CDC and WHO will hopefully have a more effective response by already being vigilant for an outbreak. I would also love to get into that lab your friend found."

Charlene was gently awoken by Carl early in the morning. She was told Anashe had returned to Johannesburg. It was punctually decided to check Sol's apartment and check if Anashe was there. While on the road, Carl also informed her that his message to the Stewards was answered in the night and he had spoken with Medusa. All this Felix had already enlightened her of, but she didn't stop Carl from explaining it directly to her. The Stewards were to send some of their best reconnaissance teams to keep tabs on every property she and Carl had discovered.

"The part that might interest you the most," continued Carl, "was when I told Medusa of my companion's invaluable assistance. She became very interested in meeting you. She thinks you can be rather useful."

"Of course I can be. I've been saying that all along."

"You're not letting this get to your head at all," quipped Felix.

"Would you like to meet her?" asked Carl. "I'm meeting her as soon as she arrives."

"Sure, why not? What's she like?"

"She's strong willed, much like you, but is much less delicate about it. There's a reason she's one of the 'faces' of the Stewards. She's not exactly the humble type and enjoys both the fanfare and facing her detractors openly instead of hiding behind a guise like many of the others."

"Does she know who Hermes is?"

"Yes."

"And you trust her?"

"There are fewer people I trust more. Unlike you, I told her from my own free will a few years ago and she has been instrumental in some of my undertakings since then. She likes to act like there's nothing more terrifying than her, but she has a strong sense of integrity. I think you two will be fast friends."

When they came up to the now familiar apartment edifice, she could once again sense Paul, but he was merely with the first Ex. They figured Sol and Anashe met up somewhere else, supposing it would be odd for them to discuss their work in the presence of their latest member. It was also a strong possibility that neither Anashe nor Sol spent much of their time in this particular apartment and would permanently leave Paul to be watched and tutored by the other Ex, which was both a good and bad prospect. It would be easier to retrieve Paul without having to go through Anashe and Sol, but it also meant Anashe could be more difficult to capture if her whereabouts remained unknown. The number of variables came close to frustrating Charlene, but she kept reminding herself that if it wasn't for her (and Felix), that Paul, along with many others, would be left completely in the hands of more malevolent forces.

Before going to their rendezvous with Medusa when the sun began its dip, they passed the apartment again. She now couldn't sense Paul or any other Ex in the area. His absence concerned her, but there was nothing they could do but to check back at another time. The appointment with Medusa was to take place in Rhodes Park, a well-maintained park at the outskirts of the city center and between the city and the international airport Medusa was arriving from. Fifteen minutes after ambling by the main entrance, Charlene felt an Ex's aura. They headed for it and Carl confirmed it was their expected visitor. When Medusa recognized Carl, who only troubled himself to wear his wig and cap, she gave a girlish shriek and ran up to him. In a half moment, the Exes were embracing and kissing, mostly imposed by her, but not refused by him. Charlene was actually relived to find the passionate greeting did not herald any feelings of jealousy. She was beginning to worry the feelings of enchantment were owed to him and not with the exhilaration of the circumstance she was in.

As Felix was melded with his companion, he could not see her reaction to the affectionate display and so thought it better not to say anything for fear of choosing the wrong comment.

The first impression Charlene had of Medusa was realizing the thirty-two year old was shorter and smaller than she supposed. She was a full head shorter than Carl, meaning she was a couple inches shorter than her own five foot six frame. Charlene did think

Medusa was prettier in person than on TV. She had long, wavy, jet black hair, a naturally rich and golden-brown hue on her supple skin—coming from her Brazilian heritage, (her parents were Canadian citizens due to the more welcoming atmosphere to their Ex children)—and the body, while petite, was clearly toned with sleek muscles.

Carl was the one to break off from the eager lover and bring her attention to the third party.

"This is Miss Fade. Miss Fade, this is Medusa."

Medusa held out her hand and, through her sunglasses, Charlene could see Medusa's brown eyes were perusing her features. Whatever she thought of her, she hid it well behind a friendly smile.

"Charmed, Miss Fade," Medusa said amiably. Spending much of her teenage years and all of her adult life traveling the globe with an assembly of comrades from around the world had fairly eroded her Brazilian accent and given her an understanding of the English language nearly equivalent to the average Canadian.

"Me too," said Charlene, shaking the offered hand. They both gave a hearty handshake.

"Aren't you a young thing," observed Medusa. Then, turning to Carl, she said, "I always thought you preferred the more experienced woman."

"You should be delighted to know that your assumption in the matter is correct," responded Carl. "The young lady and I are only professional acquaintances."

"And yet, she knows who you are," Medusa pointed out with a trifle tone of derision escaping her lush lips.

Charlene hardly picked it up while Felix heard it as a shotgun blast.

"Factors out of my control led to the discovery," Carl replied. "I leave it up to her whether she ever tells you the details of her power and how exactly we met."

Medusa shrugged. "Stories for another time. I was brought here for business, not pleasure."

"I've never known you to shift into your professional mode so soon. I thought I might have to humor you more."

"I've become very mature since you saw me last."

"Very well, Miss Mature. Where do we stand?"

"Many of my colleagues are either already here setting up or are on their way tonight. They're ordered to go through the usual surveillance procedures: place bugs, intercept calls, hack digital devices, all that jazz."

"What's your role?" Charlene asked the female Ex.

"Oh, I'm only here to watch over Hermes. I'm too well known to make for an undercover spy. Once Dad found out Hermes was the one giving us the information, he sent me to keep an eye on him."

"Dad?" queried Charlene.

Carl answered, "The Architect's nickname, the inconspicuous leader of the Stewards." He turned his attention back to Medusa. "Do you have a particular mission in mind for us?"

"Not really. I defer to you since you've been here longer. There are quite a few properties to keep a lookout on and we've been advised not to alert the local authorities of our presence unless absolutely necessary, since that would be like announcing to every Tom, Dick, and Harry we're here, especially if your telepath has someone on the inside working for her. If you can support us with more eyes on our marks, without a chance of revealing ourselves, of course, then I'd be prepared to keep a stakeout with you."

Charlene was the one to reply. "Stakeouts are easy with my ability. I can track people over a good distance without showing myself. No tracking equipment needed."

"Yes, Carl said something to that effect. A useful way to stay out of a telepath's influence. Is that who you want to keep tabs on, Fade?"

"I have a personal interest on another Ex."

"Ahh, right. I read the file on the boy who went missing after attacking his classmate and has now joined forces with pure evil. Fine, where's he at?"

The expanded congregation went in their respective vehicles, Medusa brought a red sedan, and headed for the high-rise apartment. The desired auras were still absent. After a quick debate between Charlene and Carl, they decided to wait at the parking garage and see if Paul would return. Medusa joined them in the SUV, content to lie sprawled out in the backseat and texting to persons unknown while listening to a wide variety of music from all parts of the biosphere when she wasn't talking to Carl. The Steward rarely instigated an interaction with the other woman, but Charlene didn't pick up any malice in it. In fact, both girls were in the stage of sizing each other up, trying to read who the other person was. A pastime that helped to move the ticks of the clock along for each.

Felix had little interest in knowing what Charlene thought about other women, but was vaguely aware of their game. He figured if there had not been time to pass then each would abandon their slow crawl and come out with more stimulating conversation. He couldn't tell how Carl reacted to the unexpected leisurely burn by the normally more straightforward women.

Long after the natural light of the sun was replaced by the artificial ones offered by the city, Charlene sensed Paul's aura enter her scope. He wasn't alone, naturally. Sol was with Anashe's possession and went up with him to their floor. She was relieved to have the ever important targets in her sights, so to speak, and never wanted to have them withdraw again. With the Stewards now involved, in what she considered her operation—whether anyone else did or not—she felt a renewed burden to make sure things with Paul went as smoothly as possible. A part of her wished it was only Hannah, Devin, and herself (with Felix, obviously) as the ones sitting there, however unrealistic that was. Having this many prominent people surrounding her brusquely made her feel as if their auras were overwhelming her. When Carl asked Charlene whether she wanted to leave or stay, she chose to stay, though she wasn't exactly sure how long she was going to do so. It could be days or weeks before the U.N. decided to do anything about the Exes. Only if the warning about the virus became real would they be forced to act, and that was a scenario she was not wishing to come to fruition.

As in their last stakeout with Agent Beasley, they did not only wait in the car, but alternated from walking in the garage, strolling outside, or driving around the block. The night and much of the following morning held this arrangement. Carl made several food runs and the bathrooms in the garage allowed the watch to continue uninterrupted.

Chapter Twenty-Five

By noon, Medusa had notified her companions that every property was being observed and that they had found Lesedi, which the Stewards were officially calling her, in the home of a female Ex Carl and Charlene found in their first day. Later in the afternoon, Charlene felt Sol part with Paul and leave on his motorcycle. As the second evening of their stay was nearing its close, with Medusa in the passenger seat of the SUV while Charlene was lying in the back, the Steward agent received an update.

"This is interesting," said Medusa. "Some of our targets, including Sol, are meeting in some old school in the slums to the north. There are several others on the move, too, undoubtedly going up to meet with them. It looks like they might be having one big bad guy convention. Lesedi and the other Ex she was with are there as well." A little less than thirty minutes later, she said, "That's all of them. Everyone we have an eye on is at the school."

"Give me the address," instructed Carl.

"What? We're going?" asked Charlene.

"*I'm* going," corrected Carl. "Stay here and keep a lookout on your friend. I'll go as a precautionary measure, in case they're up to something. It's probable this is only a routine assembly for them, but if it's not, well, I would like to be there and help prevent carnage. Medusa, I'm taking your car." The Steward gave him the keys and the address. "Keep an eye on our new ally," he requested of Medusa as he exited the SUV. He would have flown if he wasn't worried someone would spot him and spread the fact Hermes was in Johannesburg, thus spooking the lawless Exes.

Charlene wanted to go with him and was close to debating the point, but she knew how the discussion would turn out. She had promised to listen to him and, in the end, Paul was her primary goal and responsibility. The rest of the objectives she would have to leave to the specialists.

"Is anyone still keeping watch over Paul?" Charlene asked Medusa once Carl had left.

"Someone was assigned the boy, but they know I'm here so he went to reinforce those surveying the meeting."

"Don't you mean surveilling?"

Medusa mouthed the words to herself, before saying, "Same difference."

Some twenty minutes after Carl left, Charlene felt Paul go down to the lobby and seemingly meander there for a few minutes.

"What the fuck is going on?" asked Medusa sharply,

looking at her phone.

"What? What happened?"

"The goddamn police showed up. They've surrounded the area Sol and the others are meeting in."

It was here when Charlene heard what she thought was a clap of thunder ripping across the darkening, cloudless sky, made louder by the fact the windows of the SUV were halfway down, but she knew thunder alone couldn't make several auras high above Paul instantly vanish.

"A bomb?" guessed the experience of Medusa.

"I felt some auras disappear in Paul's building, but he's still safe in the lobby."

"So they're dead then? If an aura disappears, that's what that means?"

"Y-yes." This was the first time since Madam X's death had she felt lives being lost. The immediate, cruel vaporization of these lives struck her all at once, making her body shiver. What stopped her from concentrating on that fact more, and possibly shedding a tear or two, was focusing on Paul. She next noticed Medusa was starting the car while also trying to reach someone on her phone.

As the SUV was backing up, Charlene heard Medusa say, "I think I just heard an explosion in my position. Stand by for verification." The SUV rolled onto the street and as soon as they gained the appropriate angle, they saw the smoke rising from a cavernous hole from where Lesedi's floor was located. "Explosion confirmed in Afolayan's level, but the Ex known as Paul is alive on the ground floor."

The sounds of ambulance and police sirens were heard soon after, forcing Medusa to head farther down the block and away from the wounded building. Expectedly, a mass of auras was exiting the high-rise structure, including that of Paul's, who proceeded to walk in the opposite direction of them.

"Go around," directed Charlene. "He's going the other way."

Medusa had to move farther up and turn to another street to avoid the increasing obstructive traffic and throngs of people.

Six, thought Charlene to herself. She was sure it was six people she felt lose their lives. Her train of thought was derailed when she felt an unexpected aura enter her range.

"Um, Medusa?"

"Yeah?"

"I feel Sol. He's heading for Paul."

"You sure? They haven't told me the situation in the slums is any different. He should still be there."

"Well, he's not. He's on the other side of the block and going in our direction."

"Shit." On her phone, the Ex said, "I need to know if you have a current visual on Sol." Then, back to Charlene, "Carl gave you his number, right? Call him. I'm still on the line with my people."

Charlene did as she was bid. Soon after Charlene revealed

her identity to him, Carl had thought it prudent they could contact one another in an emergency and gave her one of his numbers. This appeared to her to fit the criteria for an emergency. Technically, she didn't have Carl's number, but of his millionaire's smokescreen.

As her phone rang, she overheard Medusa's line state, "Sol spotted approximately three minutes ago."

After a few more rings, Charlene heard Carl's voice on speakerphone.

"If this is about the explosion, I already heard about it," said Carl.

"No, it's about Sol," clarified Charlene. "He's here."

"What? That's not possible. There's a whole army of the Johannesburg police force surrounding the area and our spotters say they still sometimes see Sol and the others."

"I don't know what else to say except I see Paul getting on a motorcycle with him right now. His face is under his helmet, but, Carl, it's him. Auras don't lie."

"So if we're somehow not seeing the real Sol, then…"

"They're setting you up," Charlene finished. "The meeting, the cops unexpectedly showing up, the explosion-"

"Someone tipped them off!" cried Medusa, completing everyone's thought process. "Fuck!"

"Carl, what do we do?" Charlene asked.

"I'll tell you what we do," interjected Medusa. "All bets are off now. We follow Sol and subdue him when we find an opening."

"Medusa," said Carl firmly, "don't do anything rash. He's incredibly powerful. You won't be able to handle him alone."

"But I'm not alone."

"Dammit, just follow him and wait for me to back you up."

"Will do," she complied lackadaisically.

"But how is this possible?" asked Charlene. "How did they trick the Stewards?"

"I don't know," answered Medusa. "Maybe Sol has a twin brother, maybe he has a clone or two, or maybe he made a lifelike cardboard cutout of himself. All I know is that he's making us look like his fucking bitches right now and he's in my sights. God dammit, you better be right about this, Fade."

"I'm right," she said defiantly, adjusting her sunglasses and taking out her scarf to wrap it around her mouth.

The women continued tailing the motorcycle for several blocks until it parked its passengers in front of a skyscraper, not caring the area did not allow vacant vehicles. The commuters then went into the office tower. Medusa and Charlene mirrored the same scheme. Going through the revolving doors revealed an expansive lobby, nearly empty except for a receptionist and handful of people drifting about. On the other side of the space were three elevators, the middle of which held their goals. They were already heading up. Each pursuer approached one of the other elevators to check which one would open first. Charlene's reacted first.

As they started their vertical journey, Medusa informed her line of which building they were in and to send reinforcements over.

"What the hell is he doing here?" Medusa asked herself and quite possibly Carl, who was still on Charlene's phone.

Felix figured out the answer when he felt a Regular's aura hovering high above them. "I think there's a helicopter landing over us," said the ghost.

Charlene repeated his insight.

Medusa's response was to put away her phone and pull out her firearm from her shoulder holster beneath her jacket. Felix recognized it as her trusty Glock.

Aiming her lips to Charlene's phone, Medusa said, "You better be here in the next couple minutes, Hermes. Shit is about to hit the wall."

"Fan," amended Charlene. "Shit hits the fan."

"Oh, that makes more sense. I've been saying 'wall' all this time."

A second elevator needed to be used to reach the top floor. There was a trace of good luck when their quarry needed to wait a moment for the elevator to come to them, but they still kept their lead. Before they came to their last stop, Medusa quickly went over a few scenarios of what was likely to occur and told Charlene what to do if any of those transpired. There was no time to go over them a second time. The doors slid open and they rushed to find the door to the roof's helipad. Following the easily read signs promptly led them to find the sought out access and burst through it just as straightforwardly. Directly in front of them, Charlene could see Sol and Paul only steps away from entering the waiting helicopter.

In the loudest and most commanding tone Medusa could muster, she yelled out, "Both of you get on your knees and put your hands behind your head or I will fucking shoot!"

Her demand was confirmed to be heard when the fleeing Exes stopped in their tracks, but it wasn't followed beyond that. For Charlene, time was going slow enough for her to count the times the helicopter's rotor blades spun on their mast. She could also see Sol begin to spin around as fast as the propeller blades and discern a bright light originating from his hands. Medusa was accurate in thinking Sol would respond with violence. Fulfilling Medusa's role for her in this event, she began to run towards Sol.

The felonious Ex finished his 180 degree turn and saw the two women, one of whom he saw dashing towards him, and the other pointing the gun. His honed instincts told him to outstretch both his arms and fire his power at each of his adversaries. A blast of white hot light emanated from his palms as he fired a line of intense plasma from each one. The crack of a gunshot reverberated at the same time.

When the line of bright plasma harmlessly passed through Charlene, Felix felt the impossible action of his heart skipping a beat. He was thankful to confirm that even the hottest of flames couldn't touch his source of sanity. Meanwhile, they could touch solid Exes.

Charlene heard Medusa shriek in pain and glanced to see that she was still on her feet, but had an ugly black mark on her upper left arm. Concentrating on Sol again saw him giving his staggered attention at her. He appeared to have been shot in the right kneecap and had collapsed on it. Paul wore the same expression as a newly caught fish while these events unfolded. She continued advancing, trying to keep Sol's foreboding thoughts and eyes focused on her. The commotion, meanwhile, was too much for the pilot to handle and he started to lift the helicopter off the pad.

"Wanna try your luck again, asshole!" shouted Medusa, who, despite the black burn on her upper left arm, was steadily holding onto her pistol with her right hand.

It turned out he did, but as soon as he was charging another blast of plasma, a bullet struck his right shoulder. He fell on his back writhing in pain, but he started to laugh wildly.

"Paul, please get on your knees and put your hands behind your head!" Charlene yelled at the dumbfounded boy when she was within a few feet of the fugitives. She wished she could say more to him, but she didn't want to show any preference to him in front of his captor.

Hearing his name snapped Paul back in control of some of his senses. He looked at Sol on the ground holding his shoulder and shakily did as he was told.

When Medusa came up next to Sol, gun primed to yield

another volley, she said to him, "If I even see your watch reflect any light, the next one is going right between the eyes."

After a stinging chuckle, Sol replied, "You don't have to worry about me, Medusa. My bloody ride's gone and there are quite a few Stewards here, as I understand it. I know when I'm beat."

"Where are Lesedi and the others? Are they also not in the slums?"

"I don't know what you could mean," he uttered with a grin.

"Fucker." Medusa noticed Charlene glancing at her burn. "Don't worry 'bout me. I don't even feel it anymore. I actually dogged it. If I didn't, I wouldn't have the arm right now."

Charlene looked around and saw the door they came from had a burning hole in the middle of it, caused by the plasma shot that had phased through her. Sol's voice brought her attention back to him.

"You're a new one, aren't you?" She only gave him silence. "Welcome to the club."

"Shut up," demanded Medusa vehemently.

Charlene wondered if Medusa would use some of her ability to petrify Sol's hands, but Medusa never made a move to do so. Charlene could only guess the reason her companion didn't perform the act was due to inability to use her dangling left arm, meaning she would have to let go of her gun to touch Sol and activate her power. It was also conceivable that making contact with someone who could emit extreme heat was not a good idea.

After a few uncomfortable minutes of watching over the runaways—despite the two bleeding bullet holes, Sol was awake and lively—Charlene felt Hermes' aura soaring towards them. Turning to see him land on the roof, she identified he was wearing his mask, a sturdy white acrylic materiel that Charlene thought made him look like the Phantom of the Opera.

Hermes scanned the scene and said, "A couple choppers are not far behind." He then saw the burn. "Medusa, are-"

"I'm fine," replied Medusa to the unfinished query, not taking her eyes off Sol. "What's the situation back in the slums?"

"The Stewards have informed the authorities of our presence and they're ready to storm the meeting, but I advised them to give me some time to bring over someone who can be very useful."

As he was finishing his sentence, two police helicopters were approaching. The first one landed and Charlene felt a male Ex come out to meet them, followed by a U.N. soldier. The Ex wore no facial disguise and looked to be a decade older than Carl, donning a military style trim on his graying hair and, other than being very pale and bulky, had no distinguishing physical traits she found noteworthy. He was outfitted in the black SWAT-like uniform frequently worn by the Stewards when working on the field.

Yelling over the whirling of the propellers, Hermes said, "Miss Fade, this is Gaia. I've told him of your aura ability and how it was you who helped capture the real Sol. He would like you to join him and feel out the situation in the slums. I'm going to keep watch over Sol and Paul. Even wounded he's too dangerous for me to feel comfortable leaving until he's fully sedated."

In the duration of his explanation, Sol and Paul were being carried and led into the helicopter. Medusa went in after them. The flying conveyance quickly pushed off the roof to let its partner pick up the others. Charlene nodded to Hermes and he lowered the gravity around him to follow the captured party. She saw Gaia's eyes track the vigilante with what she thought was a look of loathing. When the second helicopter landed, Gaia told both Charlene and the soldier who stayed behind to board it.

Settled in the cramped police chopper, with Charlene sitting in the back and facing Gaia and the pilots, Gaia went on his radio and briefly summed up the situation he just observed. He next gave the newcomer the formulaic up and down glance and asked her, in a coarse voice that gave Charlene the impression he coughed a great deal, "You're a vigilante? Like Hermes?"

"Technically, but I'm not his protégé or anything, if that's what you're thinking."

"What I'm thinking, Miss Fade, is that once this business is done, you'll do none of the paperwork."

"Are you in charge of the operation?"

"Second in command. My boss in scouting missions is Peregrine. His farseeing eyes make him the natural choice in surveillance operations."

"And your power?"

"I can control soil, the earth."

"You must hate flying then."

"Despise it."

They said little else to each other until they neared their destination.

"Hermes tells me you can 'feel' people from a good distance."

"From about five hundred feet."

Gaia turned to the pilots and said, "Hover three hundred feet over the school."

They continued moving forward, but began dropping in altitude. She was soon able to feel a flood of auras at ground level, the great majority belonging to Regulars, but an Ex or two was sprinkled in. The airborne vehicle presently came to a complete standstill.

"We're over the school, Miss Fade. What can you sense?"

It was too dark by then to make out anything distinctive down below with her eyes, exempting the circle of blinking police lights several hundred feet from the school, but her gift provided the appropriate vision for a more precise conclusion. "There's an Ex down there. I felt her before when Hermes and I were scouting properties."

"*An* Ex? As in just one? Nobody else?"

"Tell him I sense at least two squirrels," said Felix, feeling Charlene wouldn't be as nervy with Paul in hand.

"No, no one else, sir."

"Peregrine," said Gaia into his radio, "The girl says she only senses a single enemy, a woman, apparently. If Sol was fake then the rest are too. They have to be illusions of some kind created by that lone Ex."

The radio replied, in a smooth Italian voice that was quite the opposite of the former hoarse speaker, "Agreed. We've wasted enough time fidgeting. All squads prepare to storm the school! Gaia, stay in the air and tell us where the Ex is."

"Copy that," said Gaia grumpily.

A couple minutes of garbled radio chatter later, Peregrine asked, "Fade, was it? Can you sense the Ex led squads below you?"

Gaia had to hand her the radio for her to answer. She said, "I feel three groups, made up of three people each. They're separating from the main, uh, gathering."

"Good. Squad three, begin moving to the main entrance… Fade? Do you feel them moving? Good. Squad two, circle to the back. Squad one, begin flanking the left side. Fade, who's closer to the target?"

"Squad three." She hoped not to get too confused, but she was comforted knowing that there was another mind also concentrating on the activities below.

"Alright, give them one last warning to come out peacefully," instructed Peregrine to whoever had the megaphones. "Tell them we know it's all a trick."

Those in the chopper were too high up to hear the message being given out, but Charlene could feel the response. "Peregrine," she said, "the target is on the move. She's closer to squad one now."

"All squads storm the building! Treat all as hostiles!"

She felt the squads close in on the building, only pausing to bring down their entry points.

Over the party line, she heard someone say in a monotone voice, "Confirmed illusions. They look pretty damn real, but they don't make a sound or move when shot."

"Enough chit-chat!" said a woman's voice, which Charlene assumed belonged to one of the squad leaders. "Just find the real one!"

"Squad one, you're very close to the target," updated Charlene. A second later she said, "You have to be in the same room by now."

"We just see damn illusions!"

"Wait," said Charlene, "The target is on the move again. Oh! I get it! She's under you, squad one! She just crossed under you!"

"Shit, I should be down there! Not babysitting!" exclaimed Gaia. "Dammit! Lower the chopper! Get me closer!"

The helicopter followed his command and began to descend. In a few seconds, the helicopter was suspended twenty feet in the air and the disgruntled Ex opened the door, engulfing the compartment with a gust of wind. He then jumped down.

"Dammit!" screamed the radio. "Get that chopper back in the air!"

Not wanting to stay up, Charlene decided to follow Gaia. She faded, cutting off the radio signal, moved to the open door, and looked down to see she would land near the debilitated playground between the school and the perimeter set up by the police.

"Here goes literally nothing," she muttered under her breath.

She jumped.

Like Felix had mentioned before, falling was bizarre when she couldn't feel the wind rushing past her and gravity not quite affecting her the same way. She landed gently and noiselessly, to her delight. Adjacent her landing spot was a ten foot high earthen tower erected by Gaia to catch his fall. Gaia was at the top of it. The dirt tower began to rejoin the ground and his surprised expression met her on the ground half a moment later.

Regaining his composure, he asked, "So where is she?"

She wordlessly began running to the target aura. In the interlude of her returning to the ground, the illusionist had moved out of the school and was moving speedily under the playground and into the surrounding slums.

On the radio, she said, "Gaia decided to join the hunt and I'm here with him. We're heading for the target. She's currently under the perimeter near the playground." As she refaded, she didn't get to hear what the other end thought of the development.

"Gaia! She's under that cop car!"

She saw him stop, outstretch his arms, and immediately pull them back to his chest. At that instant, a muffled rumbling came from the area she had referred to. A massive cloud of dust and dirt shrouded the car and the immediate expanse, forcing back the spectator police officers. The aura stopped in its tracks.

"I think you got her! What did you do?"

"I pushed the earth around the car. That should've destroyed the tunnel on either side of her."

"I think you did. She's moving, but she can't seem to escape the area below the car."

"Yeah, I can feel the vibrations with every step she takes. Now I'm going to tie up the bitch."

He twisted his hands in various contortions. In another moment, she felt the aura below become motionless, but still standing upright. He reported the success over the radio. Before she knew it, two of the squads had encircled the region Gaia had pointed out. The third squad was still sweeping the school. Everyone on these teams wore SWAT-like attire and dark tinted facemasks. A different three crew squadron moved up to them, led by a man in his late twenties and was wearing a simple gray suit, but with a bulletproof vest over it. He wore no mask and so she was able to recognize him as Peregrine. He was arguably the best known Steward, thanks in no small part to his striking looks and animalistic eyes. He was more her type. His facial features were more masculine than Carl's and she preferred the dark wavy locks to Carl's lighter and shorter hair.

He walked up to Gaia and ordered in his bewitching voice, "Bring her up."

Gaia gave him a look very similar to the one he had given Hermes, but proceeded to obey his young commander. A rectangular pillar began to sprout from the ground until it stood seven feet tall.

"Let's see her," commanded Peregrine. "Everyone stay on your toes. We don't know how she creates her illusions and we could see anything if all she needs is an opening."

The top portion of the column crumbled away. The newly visible face was that of a young woman's. She had short blonde hair and her face looked gaunt and innocent, however, her high-pitched words ended any thought of purity. She yelled out several phrases in French, which Felix knew to be vile curses, and tried spitting at Peregrine.

"I recommend you calm down and cooperate, young miss, or we will be forced to sedate you," said Peregrine in pretty good French. "Do you understand?" Another ball of spit struck the dirt, followed by more French profanities. "Reveal a part of her arm so we can sedate her," he instructed Gaia. "She's not going to give us anything now."

Some of the earthen pillar disintegrated and exposed the bare upper arm of the netted Ex. An Ex from one of the squads came up to the column with a syringe and injected it. Charlene felt the aura become languid within a few seconds, reminding her of

Jodie's aura when she met her in the basement.

"Gaia, remove the dirt from her and take squad one through the tunnel. See how far it goes. Squad two, take our French guest to the nearest transport and take her to the base in Cape Town. I don't want her in Johannesburg. The rest of you guard the crime scene and check to see what it would take to get the local forces to start setting up checkpoints around the city." Turning to Charlene, he said, "You, come with me."

Seeing no reason to object, she followed him as he began to walk past the perimeter and up to a stagnant police chopper. They entered the aircraft and he ordered the pilot to take off and begin circling the perimeter and to continue expanding from there.

"It's a long shot by now," said Peregrine, "but let's see if you can feel the other fugitives. Can you still sense people if the chopper moves too quickly?"

"Everything kind of becomes a blur if I move too fast."

"Just let me know and I'll tell them to slow down."

The deluge of auras forced her to concentrate a great deal in order to differentiate distinct auras. She did have enough of her consciousness to take a glance or two at Peregrine and concluded from his twitching fingers that he was, understandably, apprehensive. For the next half hour, she and Felix worked to find any enemy auras they recognized and had only a vague idea of what Peregrine said on his radio. Gaia and squad one had apparently discovered the end of the tunnel and the helicopter flew to the area and restarted another sweep there. From the descriptions provided by Gaia, the tunnel was impressive. Several extensions led to several rooms stocked with various items and weapons, though most of these rooms were now empty. The end of the passageway reached an abandoned factory three miles from the starting point, and the evidence of several tire marks suggested that the Exes absconded on numerous unknown vehicles. After a distorted amount of time, Charlene heard Peregrine ask her something, but was too absorbed to catch it the first time.

"I asked if you were holding up well."

"Oh, I guess I'm a little hungry," she answered.

In actuality, she was starving. The helicopter was only supplied with a few bottles of water and being melded with Felix for such an extended interval, combined with fading repeatedly, had sapped her energy reserves. She knew the instant she separated from her ghostly partner that she wouldn't last more than five seconds before she fell asleep where she stood.

"Hold out a few more minutes, the helicopter is almost out of fuel, so we can get you a quick break, but I would like to continue the sweep as soon as possible, if you're up for it."

"I would really like to find Lesedi. I know Sol was the priority, but she was the one in charge here."

"It's embarrassing we let as many escape as they did. Unlike you vigilantes, the Stewards are held accountable for these slipups. I should have kept Gaia with me instead of sending him to you. He might have discovered the tunnel earlier."

"It might not be your fault. Did Hermes tell you what

probably happened?"

"About how someone informed them we were here? A disturbing possibility, but, for now, I first have to act on the assumption we fucked up before I or anyone else assumes one of my comrades is a traitor, unless evidence is produced."

"What will happen to Sol, the French woman, and the boy?"

"We'll have to request the Brits to lend us their telepath. With any luck, we can get the potential sanctuaries of the others by reading the minds of our felons, and find out how real the contagion threat is."

"The Stewards don't have a telepath?"

"Nations give a strong incentive to telepaths to be loyal to only their own countries. We haven't had a telepath in our group since its inception. Your power would also be highly sought after. I've never heard of someone able to feel whether a specific person was an Ex or not. Do you know how many people would find that valuable?"

"I have no interest in ousting people of their privacy."

"You'd certainly become quite well-off."

"I could probably rob banks too, but I don't do that."

"I'll have to take your word on that, you've at least earned the benefit of the doubt. We would still be staring at illusions right now without your help. I realized I haven't thanked you for that yet."

"I'll say 'You're welcome' when I get to eat something.

What do you think the Stewards will do about me?"

"Vigilantes are not normally well received and we officially don't encourage it, plus, you complicate official reports and legal proceedings, but your connection to Hermes and the obvious aid you supplied us with shouldn't give us any reason to bring you in for official questioning. Anyway, from what I heard and seen, that would be difficult to accomplish."

"Are there any people at the lab site?"

"Not yet. We've had everyone dedicated on the Exes and any personal attention on the lab might have informed them of our presence, as much good as that did, but we do have the coordinates and have a drone watching the area. As far as we know, the enemy has not tampered with it."

A few minutes later, Peregrine received a message saying Hermes was at the base camp near the school. He ordered the pilot to return to the school grounds. When they disembarked, Hermes met them and the two Exes acknowledged the other with a cool nod. The trio then walked towards an armored van currently in the possession of squad three. They each informed the other of their respective situations. According to Hermes, Sol was in surgery and would be kept under until transferred to a secure facility. Medusa was getting treatment for her burn and would likely head to get the special treatment only the Stewards could provide. Both Hermes and Peregrine assured Charlene the Stewards had a couple Exes who could heal virtually any wound and Medusa would make a full recovery in a few days. For the time being, Paul was currently being held in a jail cell and watched over by U.N. officers.

Charlene was handed some protein bars from the van. While these were terribly inadequate to fill her up, she was too hungry to complain and didn't mind pulling down her scarf to gulp them down. With her insistence, and against the recommendation of Felix, Peregrine steered her into another helicopter to begin another inspection of the area, but she didn't last half an hour before she found herself beginning to tremble from fatigue. The chopper transported her back to Hermes, who found her nearly unable to walk. To her surprise, but not disapproval, he hoisted her up in his arms, carrying her parallel to the ground, and they began floating higher and higher until they were above most buildings. She was too tired to take in much of the sights of the twinkling city below or feel the cooling wind massage her warm face. It was like she was already dreaming. She could only just comprehend Hermes lowering himself on the wide hotel balcony and setting her down on her bed. The fuzzy light in her mind turned off the very second Felix separated from her.

Chapter Twenty-Six

She awoke to some dim sunlight casting soft shadows in the unlighted suite. She saw she was alone. No, she hadn't asked to be alone.

"Felix?"

"Good evening," he answered in a Draculean voice.

"Evening?" she asked groggily. "It's not morning?"

"Nope. You slept all night and day."

"Really? I still feel like I could use another couple hours."

"We've never attempted to meld and fade so much before. At least I can estimate what your limit is now."

"I'm sure I can hold out longer with more practice... Oh, God. It's a good thing you can't smell my breath. Where's Carl?"

"He must really believe you can talk to ghosts. Before he left, he said openly that he was going to see Medusa off. That was about an hour ago."

With her hygiene coming into question, she went into the

bathroom to cleanse herself. Afterwards, she ordered as much as she could from room service as soon as she clad herself into new clothes. While she was eating she watched the story of the Stewards' operation, which dominated the news networks. They had little concrete information and nothing she didn't already know. They did have several pictures of the Exes at large, including Anashe, in order to have the public help in the search. There was no mention of Paul.

Carl came in to witness a ravenous beast eating a hefty cheeseburger and seeing two other dinner plates with the muddled remains of unidentifiable food. "I'm glad to see you're up and doing well," he said. "Did your friend tell you where I went?"

"Medusa," she said with her mouth half full. "Did she go?"

He nodded. "She's fine and she sends her regards to you. I knew she would like you."

"I like her too. What's happened since I was out?"

"Nothing too significant. The Stewards are still scouring the city, but I doubt they'll find anyone at this point. They had a well-organized escape strategy and it will take a mistake by them or luck by us to find them. As you can see, the Stewards were able to get the depictions of most of the Exes and I doubt many of them will be able remain hidden for long if they ever go out in public. I can't believe Lesedi could have another setup like she did here and effectively stash away everyone in her posse. They also discovered the lab, but no one has reported that part thus far. No one has officially said why, but the cities Lesedi has recently visited have had their terror alerts raised. Some have connected it to the operation here, of course, but the U.N. doesn't want to use the word 'contagion' yet."

"Why not? Isn't better to warn people?"

"And almost certainly have an exodus of people evacuate these cities? What if someone already has the virus? Evacuating people will only spread it more rapidly. Not to mention if we're wrong and disrupt tens of millions of lives and billions of dollars for something that might not exist. The lab persuaded the U.N. to give an obscure caution, but it will take more evidence to convince them of the worst. There's also the fact they would have to say the virus was produced by Exes. How do you think the world will react if told Exes have tried wiping out Regulars? How many people do you think would care it was a terrorist organization? War drums would begin beating again and they would beat a thousand times louder than after the Humans First Conference. The U.N. would prefer to avoid that if they can."

"Nothing I can do about that, I suppose. And Paul? Is he still in jail?"

"He's being transferred to Cape Town. He's a quiet boy, but that's to be expected in his current situation. I was briefly able to talk to him when we reached the hospital. I let him know I knew he was no terrorist and that he had a potent friend watching over him and to keep thinking of his family. He didn't seem influenced by the telepath and responded as to be expected, but he will still have to be interrogated. There's no stopping that. He won't be treated like Sol or the Illusionist, of course, but he will ultimately have to face what he did back in the States and become registered."

Charlene hadn't really thought about Paul's future beyond getting him back from Anashe and it was only with Carl's reminder did she comprehend that he still faced a shaky future. There was some relief knowing his sister and herself would support him, but who knew how this would affect his family? How would they treat his father once it was in the open?

"Oh, have they informed his family?" she asked.

"Yes, but Medusa helped convince the U.N. to keep his story sequestered for now. Easy to do when they want to promote Sol's capture as much as possible."

She hauled out her phone to see a couple more messages from her friends and her mother apprising her on her sisters' grades. Her mother, of course, knew nothing regarding her current whereabouts and deeds. She texted Hannah to call her when she could. She sighed. "Is there anything more we can do?"

"The Stewards have everything covered. Peregrine did request your assistance again, but like I said before, I don't believe the effort will attain any results."

"And I believe you need more rest," Felix chimed in.

She didn't want to admit it, but she knew Felix was right. In spite of all the sleep she caught up with and the food in her stomach, she couldn't ignore the feeling that she had overextended herself.

To Felix's pleasure, he saw Charlene had wordlessly

accepted at least one of their arguments and continued eating the rest of her food until she felt she never wanted to eat again. She then slept until she was awakened an hour later by the ringtone of her phone, the song "Crazy Train" signifying Hannah was calling. She activated the speakerphone when she noticed Carl was in the shower.

"Oh, Charlene!" joyously cried her confidant when she answered. "It was you, wasn't it? You and Felix found Paul?"

"We might have had something to do with it," she said, beaming her contentment across as best she could. There was no denying how much her spirits were lifted when she heard her friend's grateful voice. It was mostly the same for Felix.

"When are you coming back? I need to hug you and hear everything that happened."

"I want to see you too, but I might stay here a little longer. I just want to make sure there are no loose ends. How are your parents?"

"They're happy he's safe, but I can still tell they're worried. So am I, but we'll see him soon, and I think I'll tell him he's not the only Ex in the family, that his sister is with him and it won't be so bad after some time passes. I would love if you were there when I tell him."

"I will, just stay safe until then. Remember what I said about the possible virus? That's basically the main loose end I want to tie up before I leave."

"Alright, give Felix my thanks."

"Sweet girl," said Felix when she hung up.

"I think so."

"And how exactly are you going to tie up that loose end you were talking about?"

"I don't know," she said as she lied on her back on the bed. "Ugh, don't mention that right now. I actually feel good about myself."

"You should. You did well. We deserve a nice vacation."

"I agree. I can probably make it for the end of Spring Break if I act now. Have the sun tan me up, get mindlessly drunk at a night concert-"

"Have guys do shots off your bare chest."

She laughed good-humoredly. "I'll let you get away with that one." She next called Devin to notify him of her current plans.

Felix was thankful she didn't place the call on speakerphone this time, as hearing Devin's voice tell her things he wished he could say irritated him considerably.

Ten minutes later, Carl asked, "Are you sure you want to stay longer?"

"If it's not too much trouble for you," she replied. "I just don't want to go tomorrow and then find out I could have helped out if they caught a break."

"It's no problem for me. My father should have things covered for a few more days before he really needs me, but if I can be mildly selfish, I would like a set date."

"How's Wednesday morning sound?"

"Acceptable."

"Could it be extended if the virus does start showing up?"

"Why?"

"Well, couldn't I help then too?"

"No!" exclaimed Felix.

"What? Why not?" she asked louder than normal.

"I'm assuming your friend has fittingly protested?" asked Carl.

"You agree with him, too?"

"I do."

"Seriously?" said Felix. "I have to explain why I wouldn't want you in the middle of an epidemic?"

"But you can tell if someone is sick, right?" she asked Felix, marginally turning away from Carl, who looked a bit tickled at the proceedings.

"I can, but I can't always identify from what and we don't know how the infection spreads. Also, we already know you can't fade forever to avoid it. Please, don't make me further explain why this is a bad idea. It'll basically be a lot of begging intermingled with threats of singing."

She gave in not so much for his argument, but for the tone he was giving it in. It was as close as she's heard him get to the tone she first heard him use when they first met.

"Okay, fine. I guess I am overreaching."

"Thank you. You've made Carl very happy."

She looked back at Carl, who said, "He's convinced you

then?"

"Yeah."

"One of the toughest concepts for a new Ex to handle is learning their limits. The young Hermes once worried about the goals he couldn't accomplish and ignored the ones he did achieve."

"Yeah, yeah, I get it. I'm inexperienced. So what will you do if the contagion is real?"

"It shouldn't be difficult to obtain a sample and have my medical facilities have a look at it. Some of the most knowledgeable experts in the world work for me and will work around the clock to find a cure."

"And then there's a traitor to deal with."

"Medusa thinks so as well, but, unfortunately, there's little they can do to pin down the culprit without more information. A lot of the Stewards were involved in the operation here and back at their headquarters. Anyone of them could have tipped off Lesedi and it might not even have been intentional. Throwing around the word 'traitor' could be too strong a statement."

"How do you not get a headache with all this?"

"Who says I don't?"

On the advice of the two concerned men in her life, Charlene went out to the nearby shopping centers with a credit card provided by the fictitious millionaire persona of Carl. The real billionaire persona could not join her as he kept busy with other ventures on his computer or physically employed himself someplace outside the hotel. She enjoyed the commotion of the animated crowds in the upscale stores at first, buying any piece of clothing that caught her eye the entire morning, having to make a couple trips to the hotel to collect everything, but the memories of the past few days did begin to grind her initial rapture.

Her forever vigilant friend swiftly recognized her downheartedness and did not want her to simmer in it long. He thought he knew what was specifically perturbing her and decided to confront it openly when she came in to the hotel room to drop off her latest packages. Still, he wanted to be delicate as possible.

"I bet you're anxious to see your sisters and mother again," he began as casually as he could, but he knew a minor change in his tone he couldn't control would be picked up by her.

She paused at his comment, trying to figure out what topic he was attempting to get around to, but not being able to guess his angle, followed his lead. "Of course I am. I wish I could tell them everything I've been through. Hopefully, I'll only have to wait until Ann is a little older to tell my sisters what I can do now. As you can see, I've bought quite a few things for them."

"Do you wish to tell them *everything*?"

"Alright, Felix. What are you getting at?"

"Nothing, only, I can tell you're kinda… How do I put this? Low? And you should know by now you can't deny it from me."

"You've had plenty of time to study me. Am I now easy to read?"

"Yes."

"I'm not sure I like that."

"I'm not sure I like you chasing around dangerous Exes. So I guess there are a couple things we don't like about one another."

"What else don't you like about me?"

"How easily you can get me to change subjects."

She moved to the balcony that overlooked a good portion of downtown Johannesburg, sitting on one of the chairs at the patio table. "Can you also read why I'm a little low?"

"It's not hard to guess. Even with my years of lingering the world as a cold specter I still get shivers when I feel auras getting extinguished. It's not something someone can get used to."

"It was just so sudden. It's not like they even had a chance to fight back."

"I can't give you any words that will really make things better. I wish I could, but what I can guarantee to you is that it's a passing thing, like anything else. Damn, I wish I was a better wordsmith."

"You're doing fine. It's not as bad as you think, really. It just hit me all at once. I'll be fine."

"I know."

After a moment in silence, she said, "Felix?"

"Yeah?"

"Thanks."

"Yeah."

A few hours before her requested time was up, Carl enlightened her on the completion of the telepathic interrogation of the caught Exes, including Paul's. He didn't have details, much like the telepath, who gathered what he could in bursts of memory, but it was apparent Sol had some noteworthy information on the pathogen, if not the current whereabouts of the fugitive Exes. The Stewards learned Sol himself had often supervised those who had been working in the lab, though he had little understanding of the processes involved. What was incontestable, however, was confirming that Lesedi was taking her global tour for the express purpose of scattering this contagion. This revelation would force the U.N. in a short while to go ahead and begin triggering full scale measures to prepare for the worst. With this appraisal, it was decided they should leave for home that instant or risk the U.N. shutting down all civilian flights within the next twenty-four hours and stranding her in South Africa for the foreseeable future. Inside the hour, she and all her new belongings were on the private jet and heading for Pullman-Moscow Regional Airport. The flight lasted an entire day, meaning she and Carl had plenty of time to say their farewells, though Carl told her they would keep in touch.

By the time she ran up to Devin waiting for her, she melted into his arms from mental and physical weariness. What came as an agreeable shock was seeing Hannah waiting for her, too. Each girl shed a few tears as they embraced and, even in her exhaustion, she had started telling her closest companions about the details of her exploits all the way to her apartment. Her explanations brought every reaction from them, particularly Hannah, and they both professed their desire to have joined her. There was a necessary dampener on the celebration of her return. The news that an impending pathogen could be days away from appearing across the world would cast a cloud over any festivity. All three stayed up to their limit and slept over at her apartment when it was clear Charlene could no longer sustain contact with the waking realm...

It happened three days after her return. The first signs of an unknown illness began to bud in Frankfurt, Germany, but symptoms of turmoil arose as soon as the U.N. had announced the potential of an artificially manufactured disease created and distributed by an anti-Regular group. Of course, some of the furor was checked by the fact the Stewards were responsible (to the public's knowledge) for the information being exposed in the first place. Naturally, many anti-Ex advocates had no logical ears to take in that detail and had fresh fuel to burn in the fire. Most regions held back from full on violence, but the atmosphere was thickening with storm clouds, ready to rupture with the slightest pinprick.

The nature of the illness did not ease sentiments any as the signs of the illness made themselves clearer over the next several days. It started with symptoms mimicking the common flu, but they rapidly became fouler. Dark, purplish boils would form throughout the body, accompanied with excessively high fevers, intense sweating, and convulsive cramps. More extreme cases had vomiting of blood, deep pain, and seizures. By the end of a week, all the cities Anashe had visited had hundreds of confirmed cases of what laymen uncreatively dubbed "the Ex virus" (it was actually bacterial). In an unprecedented action, nearly all non-essential flights were immediately canceled for much of the world. Nevertheless, scattered pockets of the infected popped up in different areas. One of the few silver linings about the disease was that it did not kill swiftly or often. The end of two weeks had thousands of cases, but only a few dozen deaths.

All the same, businesses and schools closed within dozens of miles of an infected person. The State of Washington had a handful of cases, effectively forcing students from Washington State to find shelter in their dorms or with their families. Charlene and Devin took the former approach in the early days of the spread, but eventually elected to stay with their own worried families. With San Francisco experiencing the most cases in the United States, thus being too risky to head back too, Hannah stayed with her friend. Paul, in the meantime, was still being held by the Stewards. The main concern for handing him over to local authorities so soon after the outbreak was some sort of attempt on his life from anyone who unjustly associated him as a contributor to the terrorist organization. The Stewards were also working to enact the Stewardship Act on him and could hold him for some time.

"My parents think I foretold this after you told me to be careful about going outside and getting into contact with too many people," Hannah explained to Charlene. The two friends were in Charlene's Camaro hurdling for Seattle. With no mission urging her forward, Hannah did not have the motivation to drive herself.

"I just told them I had a bad feeling and forced them to listen by pretending I was too scared about Paul and would have a nervous breakdown if they left. Which was pretty much true, but knowing you were doing everything you could for my brother helped me be strong."

"And knowing I couldn't disappoint you helped me get through both the tough and boring parts."

"Boring? I heard nothing boring about what you told me."

"There was a lot of waiting around, and I'm not just talking about the flights."

"Yeah, but I would never call regularly having a ghost to talk to boring."

"You have a point there, but he doesn't constantly talk."

"That's good too or he'd get annoying."

"I don't know. He can still get pretty irritating."

"Fine," said Felix, "next time Hannah has a brother missing, you can count me out, *Charlotte*."

"Ugh!" exclaimed Charlene. "You made your point. There was no reason to go that far."

"What did he do?" asked Hannah.

"Something he can't get away with a second time," answered Charlene, half sternly and half playfully.

"How were the Stewards like?"

This was the second time Hannah had inquired about the organization. She was now positive she was contemplating revealing her ability to more than just her brother, something Felix had picked up on in her first inquest.

"I don't think they've changed from the last time I answered you."

"I know, it's only, what if that's what's right for me and Paul? I can't hide my power forever, can I?"

"Maybe not."

"Thankfully, it sounds like Paul won't go through anything too bad, and Dad hasn't lost his job or anything, but I know Paul, he'll think he shamed his family. But if I can get into the Stewards and pave the way for him to join... Wouldn't that be the best case scenario?"

"It's a big decision, obviously. All I can say is that it's a very perilous job with both terrifying and brave people all around you. You should think carefully. There are opportunities if you can get in, but not all of them are good."

"I know. What about you? You sound like you could already make a great Steward... Hey, what's so funny?"

"You just made Felix turn in his grave."

"Oh, I'm sorry Felix. I forget Charlene is the only one you can talk too."

This reality compelled Charlene to dial down her laughter and make her want to adjust her seat and mirrors. Being reminded of her significance to Felix always made her feel awkward about the bizarre bond she had with him. It also forced her to start thinking of disconcerting situations, like how her death could actually affect him as much as her family or, even if she lived a long time, what would become of him when she passed away. Could or would she become a ghost as well? Were ghosts around forever? What if he suddenly vanished one day? She didn't like most of the possible answers and she much preferred to think of Felix as he currently was; a good friend. The next Hannah comment restored her mood.

"Do you think I'd find a good husband in the Stewards?"

She giggled. "I didn't have time to pick one out for you, but there's a pretty good chance you'd land one with the features any girl would want."

"Wouldn't that be so amazing? Finding a guy who can lift a bus? Or fly? Or shoot acid?!"

"That would be something," Charlene said, pleased by Hannah's enthusiasm.

"Not that there's anything wrong with Regulars, of course. It would just be easier for a relationship, I think."

"We're young, no need to go crazy about marriage yet."

"The future is all I can think about now. I look at you and Devin and I want that too."

"But with more acid, apparently," added Felix.

"Oh, Hannah, you'll get it, but let's just concentrate on making it through all this mess first."

Her mother's profession meant that the diffusing contagion gained even more import for her oldest daughter. Every time her mother was in range, which included several outings to the hospital she worked at, she would have Felix meld with her to try and detect any trifling change to her aura that might mean she was falling ill. Luckily, the Pacific Northwest was left largely untouched for the next few weeks. Nothing was privately heard from Carl, but his public persona had declared that his company was aiding in the cause to find a remedy to the problem.

The death toll slowly began to pile up and snatched away the health of both the young and old, but she and Felix were under the impression that the disease was not as lethal as they first assumed it should have been. Of course, they could each see this was good news if it preserved this state, but what did it signify? Surely Anashe would have wanted as deadly a pathogen as possible? In any case, by the end of two months, there was a spike in fatalities in India and the death toll was over four thousand, with hundreds of thousands more infected, the vast majority of which were in the dense hubs of India and China.

Chapter Twenty-Seven

One evening, a couple of weeks after the contagion had revealed itself, Charlene noticed the date on the corner of her desk computer matched the commencement of a new era.

"Oh! Happy anniversary!" she declared to Felix, who had been listening to *The Sun Also Rises* on her bed as she browsed the internet from her desk.

Felix was well aware of the date, but still reacted by saying, "What?" as he didn't really expect her to mention it.

"Come on. Don't act like it isn't a big deal. I can

understand why you don't care about your birthday, but this has to be important to you. It's obviously a big deal for me, too."

"Well, you technically learned of me the day after."

"Technically, but whether I knew it or not, it was a life changing day. Anyway, I still first heard and felt you that day."

"Okay. Happy anniversary," said Felix flatly.

"You don't sound happy," she grumbled.

"Hey, this is a big deal for me, but I'm just not the type who's into a calendar dates meaning anything, even when I was alive."

"Whatever, I'll be the only one happy then."

"Don't twist it like that. What I'm really saying is that I don't need a date to tell me I'm already as happy as I'll ever be."

"Hey, what are you…" she began to say as she experienced a pulse of energy she presumed came from the beginning of a meld, but stopped herself from saying anything else when she realized it wasn't a fusion she was feeling. It wasn't too far off from the feeling only Felix could offer, but it was distinctly unique, though still pleasant, in its brief existence. For that split second, she imagined fingers were softly caressing her aura until Felix's voice, originating in his spot at the bed, snapped her back to reality.

"What's wrong?"

"N-nothing. For a second I thought… It was nothing."

A concentrated dose of déjà vu overcame her. It teleported her back to the baseball game a year ago when she first felt Felix touch her aura, giving her that confused reaction. It wasn't merely nothing then, so what was it now? A strong memory? An even more powerful imagination? What disturbed her even more was knowing the clock was far too close to the time when Felix must have first made contact. It made it seem like fate itself was dictating matters. She never liked the idea of higher powers controlling her or anyone else's actions, for good or evil. There was a sudden aversion to the next anniversary.

If I feel this again next year, I'm going to freak out, she thought to herself.

Felix sensed her odd behavior and could tell she was meditating over something. He decided pressing her for answers when she was clearly befuddled by whatever she was musing over would be of no benefit, so he let it go.

Despite the terrible circumstances bringing about her current situation, Charlene found herself experiencing a good deal of enjoyment since she had returned home. Classes were canceled, she was often with her family, seeing friends, and spent as much time with Devin as she could. There was an overflow of vigor when she returned from her exploits in South Africa. Everything there had given life a new luster, generating a little more evocativeness in her, something Devin, to his pleasure, was the direct beneficiary of.

About a month and a half into her forced retreat, one of these nights destined to end in fleshly bliss was going particularly perfectly. The dinner of restaurant lasagna, salad, and bread impeccably eradicated her appetite and everything Devin said was either hilarious or outright turned her on. They were now on his bed hastily abandoning their clothing. He was in rare form. He kissed her on the right places, with the precise amount of pressure, and at the correct times. The same could be said of his hands and other extremities. He even smelled the way she liked him to smell, a light amount of the cologne she had picked out for him mingling with his natural musk. It was going to be the best she had so far, it wasn't even going to be close.

By its glorious end, they were both out of breath and wholly fulfilled. Still panting and staring at the ceiling, she began to compliment her lover. "That was amazing, Fe…" Her breath, body, and heart tightened in that instant, squeezing out every drop of water and oxygen. At first she hoped he wasn't coherent enough to notice, but it was quickly evident that he had.

He sat up and gave her a wild look. "What the fuck did you just say?"

"No, n-no, it was nothing. You were amazing, Devin."

"Were you imagining I was-"

"No! Of course not! It was a mistake! A fucking stupid, stupid mistake."

He turned away and slid off the bed. Hastily grabbing his clothes from the floor, he said, "I fucking knew it."

"Knew what?"

"I don't know. It's all so fucking weird. I knew he would somehow fuck things up."

"It's has nothing to do with him. I've been through a lot recently, but that's why I was so happy to be with you. I love you, Devin. Please, it was just a dumb mistake."

He didn't respond to her and went on putting on his clothes. He was angry and there was nothing more she could say to change that. She had to give him some time. He left his own home without saying anything and she didn't move from the bed for a long while.

How could I slipup so badly? she repeated to herself over and over. She eventually had to conclude it was solely the consequence of spending so much time with Felix. Her mind started drifting off into profounder territory, but she dismissed it as quickly as possible. She began to dress when she noticed Devin's parents were due to come home in another few minutes. There was no way she could head home straightaway. Felix was there and she was in no humor to talk to him in her flustered state. He would know there was a fight—not that she didn't think he wouldn't respect her wishes to drop the subject or ask him to leave her alone for a while, which she thought she would have to ask of him anyway—but she didn't want to even give him a hint about what had happened. She wanted time to collect herself enough to say and think the right things. She went in her car and rode to a friend's home, staying there for a couple of hours.

"Have a good night?" Felix innocently asked when she had returned to her room late that night.

She sighed. Even the two hours of organizing her thoughts didn't take away the guilt she felt at having to ask him to leave.

"Felix, could you… I feel like being alone today. Come back tomorrow night." She knew it wasn't his fault and she held no resentment towards him, but she felt it necessary to have some space from him for at least the day.

"You okay?"

She had briefly debated a few times during the drive whether to tell him what had happened, but thought he might take the incident as meaning there was an issue she didn't believe existed, and might make things very awkward in the near future.

"It's nothing you need to worry about. Please, just give me a day."

"Alright. If you need it, I'll give it."

He figured it had to be something to do with Devin, but he couldn't guess what exactly. She didn't look too distraught at whatever happened, so he conformed to her request.

Charlene texted Devin throughout the morning, but he never responded. She informed him how he had a right to be upset, how she only wanted to hear from him, but he continued to ignore her. At the lunch hour, she met with Hannah in the basement, which her friend was still using as a guest room, and told her what happened. There was a need to tell somebody, which was why she had almost told Felix.

"I don't know what else I can tell Devin. How I can convince him it didn't mean anything?"

"So Felix isn't here right now?"

"No. I told him I needed some space, but I didn't say why."

"You trust him that much?"

"I have to. If I was always paranoid about him, I'm pretty sure I'd go crazy."

"But you *actually* believe he's not here?"

"Don't you trust him?"

"Sure I do, but I'm saying if you have confidence enough to know that he isn't here, then maybe you saying his name *did* mean something."

"I know where you're going with this, and no, it means nothing except we've spent too much time together."

"You know what usually happens when two people spend a lot-"

"Stop!" In more of a whisper, she continued with, "Hannah, he's dead. I can't see him, we can't... That's not it."

"Do you think, you know, he loves you?"

This was why she needed to tell to someone. When she pondered over the unique relationship she had always dismissed some notions before they could fully materialize. Now someone else could do what she couldn't do; say things she didn't want to begin considering, but knew she would someday have to. The possibility that Felix loved her made more sense and was a better starting point instead of trying to reflect on exactly what her own feelings for him were.

"Thanks Hannah, like I didn't have enough on my mind," was her guised response to the small relief she felt on allaying the burden of having to develop the idea on her own.

Devin finally responded later that afternoon by asking her to meet him back at his home. She was glad to hear from him, but his message gave her some mild annoyance when it specifically said to meet him alone. Regardless, she met him with a determined goal of not upsetting him further. She was encouraged by seeing he had regained his usual casual demeanor as she sat next to him in his living room couch. The TV was on a cooking show, but it was muted. His first words heartened her further.

"Do you think we might be the first couple to have fought about a ghost?"

"I can't imagine there have been many," she said, the early stages of a smile on her lips.

He exhaled deeply, a sign he was going into a more serious zone of conversation. "I really want to believe it was just a dumb mistake. And the more I think about, the more I know it had to be. Still, I can't help be a little jealous of him."

"Jealous?"

"I can't help it. He might be dead, but bottom line, it's a guy hanging around my girl. That's not an easy thing to wrap my head around."

"I know it can't be. I'm impressed you never seemed bothered by it until now, until I screwed it up. Maybe we should have talked about it earlier."

"You know, I expected it would be him who would screw it up. I know you say you can feel when he's around, but in the back of my mind I think he could be tricking you and seeing anything he wants and that you would find out somehow and become scared of him or something."

"Don't do that."

"What?"

"Don't make me mistrust Felix. I wish you could hear him, and then you would know why I trust him. I really think you would be friends if you could actually have a normal conversation."

"Would we? What does he think about me?"

"I know he likes you. He says he wouldn't have a problem telling me if he thought my boyfriend was an asshole. He doesn't insult you. He knows that would upset me if he did it without any reason, and you've never given him a reason."

"How long do you let him hang around you?"

"It depends. When I know I'm going to be with you he stays out of the way most of the day. I'm not even sure where he is now. I asked for some time alone after our fight."

"You didn't tell him we fought?"

"No. He probably suspects we did, but he didn't prod." Devin became silent for several moments as he had another question or two churning in his mind. "What is it? Ask me anything. We need to clear the air."

"The thing is, I'm not sure I want to know, but here it goes. How exactly does he give you your power?"

Of all the questions he could have asked, this was the one that made her blush. "Oh, um, can I just say he has to make contact and leave it at that? That part is not a big deal, really."

He shrugged. "If you say so. You know, to be honest, I couldn't help sometimes thinking I was a little crazy for believing my girlfriend was actually talking to ghosts."

"Ghost. There's only one so far," she said with a fuller smile.

"Do you think that will matter to the therapist?" he asked, his smile almost matching her own. His hand found her hair and began coiling some of it with a finger.

"Everyone knows it takes at least two ghosts to be considered crazy. That's just science."

"I like your longer hair," he said as he scooted closer to her.

Some of her smile went away when a flashback reminded her it was one of Felix's comments that first gave her the idea to grow it out, but she recovered in time to say, "And I like that my boyfriend likes girls who are a little crazy."

They were kissing with wild abandon on his couch a half moment later. However, in what should have been uninhibited lovemaking, was dulled by a nagging splinter in the back of her mind. She was now restrained by making sure she never alluded to *him* at this juncture and restart a fiercer argument. There was also the added worry Devin would use the previous incident as a weapon in any quarrel they would later have. They were reconciled, but she knew things had changed. Devin was wary of her relationship with Felix and would inevitably affect momentous life decisions. They were no longer a carefree couple. There were serious conditions to consider if they decided to move in together, marry, or have children. All these concepts ran through her head the entire time. It was over before she knew it.

She was home early that evening. Felix was still absent when she learned that the Myers Corporation had announced a promising treatment for the Ex-virus and that a few more tests would soon make it available for mass production. The declaration lifted her spirits to nearly their level before the name incident. A few more hours passed and was surprised to notice her mother came home from her after-midnight shift before Felix returned, or so she thought. A few seconds after hearing her mother being met by Ann downstairs, she heard Felix declaring his presence by loudly singing "Raindrops Keep Falling on My Head" outside her door. Her aura waved for him to come in.

"Where were you?" she asked "I was expecting you a little earlier."

"Can't you guess? I was watching over your mother. No change by the way."

She couldn't explain it. Telling her he was looking out for her interests had her on the verge of tears. No. She could explain it if she allowed herself to consider it for even a single complete thought, which she finally did, several, in fact. She had been in denial. She had become dependent on his company, and not just because he gave her power or found him a loyal friend, but because she found him linked to her very happiness. She felt desolate when she asked him to be away and hated to do it. She still believed she loved Devin, but she could no longer reject a prodigious affection for Felix. The change in her bearing was bound to be perceived.

"Charlene? Is something wrong?"

She didn't want to tell him something she was only starting to grasp herself. Her quick mind found a replacement motive. She answered, "Did you hear about the possible cure Myers might have? It will be nice to have a conclusion over this mess. I can stop worrying about Mom and everyone else so much."

"Yeah, I heard at the hospital." He believed her reason. He thought he felt her keeping back some emotion since coming back from Johannesburg and he was relieved she wasn't holding it back anymore. "People were very happy there too."

She needed to keep talking. "I thought you were bothered by hospitals." She immediately regretted pointing that out, knowing what his answer would be. Fortunately, he chose modest words.

"They used to. There's no reason for them to affect me anymore."

It was enough to compose her. "I have to get ready for bed."

"You sure everything is cheesy? With Devin, I mean."

"As cheesy as it will ever be."

She changed into her pajamas and went to bed, but her giddy nerves wouldn't approve of sleep for a few more hours. Her erratic mind settled on nothing definite, but constantly on Felix, finding he brought the most peace back into her cognizance. The trouble began when she thought realistically. What was there to do next? Time was her answer. She would give it time.

Felix was downstairs feeling Charlene's aura rarely at rest for long. She was tossing and turning more than usual, making him think he misread her emotional state or something more serious happened with Devin. However, when he saw her the next day, she was as cheerful as he ever saw her. This extra cheeriness wasn't so obvious to anyone else, she veiled it well, but he could pick it up. There was little purpose for him to interfere on the cause of her sudden change. If she didn't tell him herself, then it wasn't his business. He could only conclude that the combination of her evident resolution with Devin and the news of the incoming cure provided enough explanations to brighten her day.

Chapter Twenty-Eight

Two days after these proceedings, Charlene received a call from her tremendously well-off friend through his millionaire persona's line.

"I've been given an update you and your friend will find intriguing," began Carl. "Medusa has informed me that the Stewards have received information on a certain telepath's current location."

"Where is she?"

"Medusa won't tell me, not until I agree to only offer my services under their supervision. You see, the only ones who know of this are Peregrine and Medusa and they agree they should not inform the rest of the Stewards or risk Anashe getting tipped off again, but they would like my help. I told Medusa I promised a certain friend I would inform her if our telepath was found. So, my certain friend, would you like to join us?"

"When do we go?"

"I had a feeling you'd agree. Medusa and I are on my jet right now. We'll be there in five hours. I'll pick you up just outside the airport and Medusa will tell us where to go next."

"I'll be ready."

Telling Hannah and Devin about the newest opportunity presented no problems of secrecy, it was giving an excuse to her family that proved slightly problematic. It was Hannah who came up with the pretext. She had wanted to get back to her family for some time, and with the news that a cure was not far away, thought it no better time to head back. Charlene's ruse was to tell her mother she would go with her friend and possibly stay with her for a little while. Ms. Fields was understandably concerned about her daughter heading for one of the cities initially contaminated by the contagion, but San Francisco, along with the other U.S. cities, had the outbreak relatively under control and had barred it from scattering wildly. The disease spread easily from person to person with a simple sneeze or cough, but a simple skin test was found able to accurately expose the early stages of the illnesses. While it was unconfirmed if Exes were entirely immune, it helped knowing Hannah and Charlene (in Ms. Field's mind) were Exes and likely resistant to the Ex created pathogen. Her offspring left by promising to call often.

A few short hours after and she was dressed her usual disguise, had been picked up by Carl outside the airport, and was embracing Medusa.

"How are you?" Charlene asked Medusa. "Are you

completely healed?"

"Daddy fixed me right up in a few days."

"That's his power? To heal?"

Carl interposed, saying, "That's why he's known as the Architect. He can rebuild anything in the body. An unconfirmed story says he restored a heart minutes after it was struck by a bullet, and this seriously wounded person was successfully brought back with no ill effects."

Somewhat cynically, Medusa said, "He's amazing, but he can't bring back a burned arm without resting every few hours. I doubt even in his youth he could have healed a major organ without killing himself in the process."

Carl shrugged while smiling at Medusa. "Most Stewards do tend to embellish their stories a bit."

"Hey, all of mine are true! Sure a couple of them may have an extra detail or two, but nothing crazy like restoring entire hearts."

"We'll be here for this story, in any case. Where do I tell my pilots to take us?"

"Oh, right. Frankfurt, Germany. Our telepath is nearby in a small town I can't pronounce. Peregrine will be waiting for us there."

"How did you find her?" Charlene asked.

"Luck. Well, luck and a massive database scanning every type of communication we've been able to dig up on her and her fake identities. The data search alerted Peregrine of a call taken by

Lesedi originating from a German house just after we arrived in Johannesburg. It was the last form of communication her known connections received, which means it was likely the call that tipped her off of our coming. Once Peregrine discovered this link, he went to the address the call came from and lo and behold!" Medusa pulled out a high-contrast photograph of Anashe from her inner jacket pocket.

The picture showed Anashe standing outside a door of a large cottage-style home wearing a light windbreaker over some casual clothing. She didn't look like one of the most dangerous Exes in the world.

"What's she doing there?" Charlene wondered. "Wouldn't she know you would trace the call there?"

"Our thoughts exactly. We think she's possibly waiting for a safer, uh, safe house to open up. She might also think she's secure so long as her inside man can tell her if she's been found."

"That's why you want to try and take her now," said Carl. "Time is of the essence. Either she moves again or the possible conspirator finds out we found her before we can move in."

"That's the situation," confirmed Medusa.

After the plane refueled for the eleven hour journey and leveled out at thirty thousand feet, Charlene asked Carl about the forthcoming cure.

"The tests have been promising," he answered. "I'm not a medical major, but my people are very encouraged by what they've found. Apparently, the contagion is molded after the bubonic plague, but with extensive alterations. Much of the technicalities go over my head, but I'm told by modifying a medication already approved by the CDC we should have an operational remedy to inoculate everyone, effectively ending its potency and curing the early stages within a few months."

"Doesn't that sound strange though?" asked Charlene.

"You're thinking this is getting off easy, don't you? I'm of a similar sentiment. It could be that they didn't have the technical proficiency to create a disease to both keep Exes safe from it and kill off only Regulars, but, as I mentioned, this contagion was heavily altered, meaning there were people with knowledge working on this for a considerable amount of time. Perhaps there's another phase to the plan that only Lesedi herself knows about."

"All the more reason to capture that bitch," added Medusa.

"What is our plan?" asked Charlene.

"Peregrine is the plan guy," replied the Steward. "I'm sure he'll have a few when we get there. He does know the area around the cottage is secluded, meaning it will be easy for her to sense anyone within her range. This pic came from one of those little hummingbird-sized drones we have. Even with his eyes he won't risk getting close with a regular camera."

"Does he know I'm coming?"

"I think he assumes you are. If she really can't sense you in your faded state, then that will make things easier for us."

"We can't forget that other Exes could be with her," Carl reminded the girls.

"I'll find that out too," said Charlene.

"I like your spunk!" declared Medusa. "Stop hanging around with loco vigilantes and join up with us already. Peregrine and I will make sure it happens."

"A talk for another time," she said, more for Felix than herself.

"We do have eleven hours to kill," Medusa pointed out.

"Then I'm going to sleep. I haven't had the chance for a full night's rest yet."

"Ah, it's a good thing we didn't ruin the bed for you," Medusa said, giving an impish smile to Carl. Looking back at Charlene, she said, "FYI, I wouldn't sit on the couch I'm sitting on."

"Noted," said Charlene as she closed the door separating the bedroom from the cabin.

Felix overheard a conversation between the other two passengers several minutes after Charlene fell asleep.

"Do you like her?" Medusa quietly asked Carl.

"She's a fine girl."

"That's not what I asked, dickhead."

"And yet you say you don't get jealous."

"I'm not. That's why I can freely ask such a question."

"Why don't you believe me when I say I really do love you? That if our situations were only a little different that I would have married you by now?"

"Bullshit. If you really loved me, then we would already be

married and you'd stop fucking anything that bashes their eyelashes."

"And if you were really serious about us, then you would have agreed to my plan."

"That would take too long. It's unrealistic."

"And so we remain at an impasse."

"So that girl is not better for you?"

"She has more baggage than you might think. If you two become closer and she tells you her secret, you'll know what I mean."

"She has a secret?" This instantly perked up Medusa's enthusiasm and overshadowed her previous frustration. "Tell me! You know what your reward will be!"

He laughed. "Tempting, but this is something far too serious. Moreover, I have a feeling I won't get away with it, no matter how discreet you'd be."

"No fun! Parade pooper!"

He laughed again. "It's party pooper."

"Whatever, asshole... Do you want to do it again?"

"So much for holding back your reward, but with-"

"I was just kidding. Jeez, you take everything sooo seriously."

Charlene awoke a few hours later.

"Felix?" she whispered.

"I'm here, Miss Fade."

"Don't call me that."

"You came up with it."

"For other people, not you. Have they said anything interesting?" After surmising the few dialogues of note, she asked, "Do you think they really love each other?"

"I think they love each other more than they love anyone else, but I'm not sure how deeply promiscuous personalities can love. From what I can tell, those two will never quite settle down with anyone."

"Is that something you can tell if people have? True love? Have you seen it before?"

I feel it. "That's tough to say. I've studied people, but at the same time, I've never really cared to analyze relationships too deeply. It doesn't make a solitary ghost feel much better to see happy people all the time." *Why was she being so serious? Did it have something to do with Devin? Did he propose and she was wondering if she should accept? Or did she accept already? Was that why she was acting a little odd lately?* "Is this about Devin?" he asked after a moment of silence had passed.

She sighed sullenly. "It'll have to be, at some point."

"You're not going to tell me what's going on in that head of yours, are you?"

"I'll have to, at some point, but can you be a little more patient? Discussing this in a whisper while going to arrest a dangerous telepath is not my idea of an ideal situation."

"That's funny, because that's exactly my idea of an ideal situation."

He saw her smile a tad, but she said nothing more as she tried falling back into her slumber. He was as confused as ever. What on earth did she want to discuss? She had given signs of both bliss and anxiety, and he felt tenser than when he had first decided to speak with her that very first time in her class. The only thing he could conclude was that whatever was on her mind had nothing bad in store for him. He didn't think she would tease him with bad news, so it had to be something serious concerning her boyfriend or family. Still, his intuition harassed him and told him something different was to be expected.

Chapter Twenty-Nine

The plane landed at Frankfurt airport with the only incident they experienced was momentarily flying into heavy turbulence that awoke Medusa from her nap on the couch and made her spew curses in multiple languages. As one of the centers of the outbreak, it was mandatory for any and every traveler to have their skin tested on arrival and before departure. A U.N. medical officer with a white mask over his mouth, but otherwise wearing only his long-sleeved white coat and khakis, boarded the aircraft and swapped each of their skins, including the two pilot's. He then put the swabs in a vial filled with a purple solution meant to detect any signs of the infection. Once a few minutes passed with no reaction from the solution, he let them proceed to their waiting van.

"Here, put this town in the GPS," said Medusa, handing Carl, who was in his prearranged civilian disguise and sitting in the passenger seat, a piece of paper. "Peregrine says he'll see us coming into the town and meet us there. It's less than an hour from here."

Charlene observed that in that hour the setting sun would be well below the horizon.

"Too bad we probably won't be able to visit some beer halls while we're here," continued Medusa. "Ugh, I've visited practically every major city in this world and haven't experienced ten percent of them."

Almost as soon as they had left the city behind their rearview mirrors, the van entered a scenic forest. A strong inclination to drop breadcrumbs passed over Charlene as she watched the woods from the center row of seats. As Medusa had indicated, Peregrine's car met them as they came upon the small postcard village. Peregrine bade them to follow him and he led them passed the town and into a thicker patch of forest. The two vehicles stopped by an obscure dirt road a few miles beyond the settlement. It would have been entirely missed in the dark they were incased in if Peregrine didn't already know where it was. Before they exited their respective vehicles and congregated between them, Carl put on his Hermes mask. It was dark and virtually noiseless, but it was a calm, nearly soothing bleakness.

"Thank you for coming," Peregrine expressed to the vigilantes.

"It would be nice to end this tonight," said Charlene.

"That should be considerably easier to do with you here," admitted Peregrine. "Are you positive that fading ability of yours prevents her power from working on you?"

"I guarantee it."

"Well then, let me tell you the lay of the land. The cottage she's staying in is fairly isolated, as you can see. I've tripled checked for any possible cameras or alarm systems, but haven't found anything by the road here. This dirt path goes about 180 yards straight through dense forest and clears a bit after that, with the road turning into a quaint stone trail. You can see the house itself thirty yards farther down at that point. This would currently put her out of your range, correct?"

"Over a hundred feet out, yes."

"This is as close as I've been, but I didn't see a problem inching up this close if you didn't feel her or anyone else. It should mean we're well out of her range as well."

"Now what?" asked Medusa.

Peregrine's answer was to open the trunk of his car and pulled out three bullet proof vests identical to the one he was donning. They put them on. At the shoulder clasp was a radio, which Peregrine asked to be turned on.

Once they confirmed the radios worked, Peregrine said, "I would like for you, Fade, to head for the cottage until you can get a good feel for the area and see if you can feel anyone else before we continue. Can you do that now?"

"Sure."

"Don't go too far in yet. I haven't been able to see if there are any security systems beyond this road."

After a nod, Charlene faded and headed into the forest, noiselessly using the dirt path to guide her. It didn't take too many steps to begin to feel Anashe's aura and a few more steps to confirm that she was alone and stirring about. She went back to give them her impressions.

"That's what I thought," ruminated Peregrine. "I haven't seen anyone entering or leaving the premises since I arrived. She's unguarded except for a potential security system nearer the house."

"What's our next play?" asked Medusa.

"The night has only started. I would prefer to wait for her to fall asleep before I shut down the power to the house by cutting the utility lines. That should take care of any alarm system. I can't imagine with the setup she has that there are any backups reinforcing her power supply."

"You found where the lines are buried?" asked Hermes.

"Yes. It wasn't a problem getting the town layout from their little record building. The cottage is still connected to the grid of the village, despite the distance. A little poking around and I found a good shallow spot not a hundred yards away. Medusa, I'll show you where the lines are so you can cut them when the opportunity arises. I'll go set myself up on a good perch." As he spoke, he seized a long black case from the trunk and opened it to reveal parts of a sniper rifle. "There's a good high up spot about three hundred yards from the cottage I can use to oversee the area. One wrong move and I'll be forced to go for the kill."

"What's plan A?" asked Charlene.

"That involves you vigilantes. I have a long range tranquilizer rifle, but *long* is a generous term. Even my skills won't allow for an accurate shot unless I was within her range. Incidentally, I know someone who can get much closer to use the close range version."

In a hushed tone, Felix said, "I think he's talking to you."

Peregrine hauled out a smaller case and handed her the tranquilizer gun inside it.

"Do you think you can handle it?" Peregrine queried Charlene.

"Just show me how to use it," she answered as confidently as she could.

As he displayed the best way to handle the non-lethal weapon, he proceeded to explain, "To be precise, this particular gun in not holding a tranquillizer, it's loaded with the formula meant to disable her telepathy."

"Why can't we just sedate her first?"

"Because we want her alive. The concoction needed to take away her ability will probably kill her if we inject it with the sedative already in the bloodstream. In fact, we need to wait at least five minutes before we attempt to sedate her. That should give it enough time to dilute itself. On another note, the nullifier takes away her ability by critically disorienting the mind. She won't be able to walk and don't be surprised if she begins to vomit."

"Okay. So who sedates her?"

"Hermes will. After you radio that you've injected the nullifier, then Hermes can quickly fly in to your position and safely sedate and subdue Lesedi after the allotted time."

"Great," said Medusa approvingly. "What's our cue for all this?"

"My perch can see into her bedroom, and even if the drapes prevent a clear line of sight, the thermal camera will be able to tell me her position."

Charlene added, "I can probably sense if she's sleeping. Check with me when you think she's in bed and I'll give you my take."

"Very well. That will be our cue. If I believe she's in bed then I'll leave it in your discretion whether you believe she's asleep and go ahead with the plan. Once Fade lets us know she's on the move, Medusa will cut the lines and Hermes will wait until Fade gives us the second go ahead to do his part. I'll keep myself back. If something goes wrong and Lesedi exits the home alone, and there's no radio chatter from Fade or Hermes, I'll be forced to go for the kill. Anyone need clarification?"

"Ask how many snack and bathroom breaks you'll get," said Felix.

When no one he could hear responded to him, Peregrine said, "I'll go show Medusa where I already dug up the lines I want her to cut. If you two don't mind, I want you to take the vehicles and hide them in the forest. No one really takes this road, especially at this time, but I don't want anyone calling in and tow them away. We'll get into position once that's done. We'll wait this out until we either accomplish the mission or new developments force us to change our strategy."

The makeshift squad was within fifteen minutes of settling themselves in their respective positions. Except for Peregrine, Charlene could feel everyone inside her range. She was near the dirt path facing the cottage with Medusa about 350 feet to her left while Hermes was a hundred feet behind her, choosing to be as far as possible from Anashe's scope of detection. Her fading ability allowed her to be less wary, but still kept a respectful three hundred feet from the house. Felix, without being asked to, prevented the otherwise static night from testing Charlene's nerves by occasionally humming any song that came to mind. He would have sung them, but he only attempted the feat during less serious situations when it would not matter if his terrible singing elicited either aggravation or laughter from his host. The clear night progressed in this way for the next few hours. Anashe was more or less active during most of that time. Peregrine provided them with intermittent updates when he had her in his sights. A particular notification picked up Charlene's expectation for her to go to bed soon when it was guessed that Anashe was taking a shower. The suspense proved productive. The target went to bed several minutes after the rinse, but the convict closed the curtains as well, cutting off Peregrine's direct line of sight.

Thirty minutes later, Charlene walked back to where Hermes stood and asked Felix to see if Anashe was wholly asleep. Felix did as entreated and rushed to the cottage. It was a fair-sized, single story home, looking as picturesque on the inside as it did on the outside. He guessed Anashe loathed the style. There were modern conveniences, like a large fridge, an impressive plasma screen in the small living room receiving satellite channels, and seemingly every gaming device known to man scattered throughout the home, usually connected to other plasma screens. Felix found Anashe in the largest bedroom at the back of the home, though it was still small by American standards. A minute of close observation convinced him that she was in a deep slumber. He dashed back to inform the necessary individual.

Once Felix melded with her, she told her superior she was ready. When Peregrine informed that the power had been cut, she began sprinting through the forest. It was a bit disconcerting to run into the open expanse between the forest and house due to the light of the full moon easily divulging her presence, but it was wiped out as she stepped into the dark building. She thought it fitting that the shadows now brought her more comfort than the light. Heading for the spiritual beacon led her straight into Anashe's bedroom. The curtains opposite Charlene blocked much of the light, but her well-adjusted eyes could make out nearly every detail. The queen-sized bed occupied up much of the room and alongside it was a digital clock resting on an ornamental nightstand with no numbers on its screen. Like Felix had described, Anashe was sleeping on her right side, facing Charlene, and was draped with a thin blanket that did not look to pose a significant problem for the dart to penetrate. Stepping a bit closer, she could personally make out, for the first time since she was informed of her existence, the visage of the Ex who had helped cause so much panic. Sleep had turned this potent Ex into an inconspicuous, middle-aged woman who didn't appear capable of summoning the malice to menace a flock of sparrows.

Charlene raised the tranquilizer gun and prepared to switch off her fade, when the shrill ringtone of a cellphone coming from the nightstand made her jump.

Her mind would have stayed blank for an unspecified amount of time if Felix didn't yell out, "Shoot!"

In the interval between the ringing and Felix's order, Charlene heard Anashe groan from the interruption and shift to lie on her back before beginning to sit up. As the Ex turned her head towards the intruder she did not yet know was there, the ejected dart struck her right arm. The spectral girl had refaded by the time the telepath's eyes recognized a human figure standing in her room. For a long moment, the trespasser and the target stared at one another as the distant ringing of the cell continued unabated in the background. Anashe could not see into Charlene's eyes, nevertheless, she felt like the Ex was reading everything about her while her own judgments drew a blank. This second of inadequacy was swiftly removed by intrigue as she saw the concoction begin taking its effect. Anashe's eyes rolled back and her head swiveled as it lost its bearings. The criminal Ex ensued to hastily toss back her covers while attempting to keep her head balanced with her hand. Words in her native tongue spewed forth, and while neither Felix nor Charlene could understand her, it was safe to assume it was not suitable for children. Her effort to get off the bed was met with clumsy success. She banged her knees on the wooden floor as she stumbled out of bed, and began breathing deeply and rapidly. Charlene kept motionless and mute during this inept display until the phone's sudden silence reminded her of her next step.

After taking a couple steps back, she switched on the radio and said, "She's nullified."

"On my way," was the response.

Anashe endeavored with great effort to stand up, but landed roughly on her knees again. She could only raise her head up and look at the reason for her current condition. She snickered smugly at Charlene. In a highly stressed tone, Anashe asked, "Are you... a fucking... traitor?"

"I haven't betrayed anyone, though I'd be grateful if you're willing to tell me what or who tipped you off back in Johannesburg."

She chuckled, but it sounded more like a gurgle. "I would like... to know... how you found me. Tell me that... and I'll tell you... who created... the contagion."

Charlene heard the front door burst open.

"We know it was your people. We found your lab in the reserve."

She began to madly cackle. It was a horrible laugh Charlene hoped wouldn't stick in her mind for too long. Hermes entered the door Charlene had opened once she heard him coming down the hall.

"What's she laughing about?" asked Hermes, turning on a flashlight to help reveal the syringe he was holding.

"I mentioned finding her lab and she began laughing," Charlene explained.

"I'm laughing because you think... that lab was enough... to create the contagion."

"Save your breath," said Hermes. "We'll soon know everything you know."

The fugitive restarted her laughing fit. When she gathered herself, she said, "You'll know because... I'll *let* you know. You see-" A coughing attack interrupted her for a few seconds. She was close to vomiting, but held it back. "The contagion that's out there... is not *my* contagion. My contagion should have killed every... last... Regular. It had to have been changed by those... who really did make it."

"And who did make it?" asked Hermes.

"I'm getting to that you fucking..." More coughing. "Maybe the contagion being a sham... will turn out... not to be so worthless. At least now... the Myers Corporation will be no more."

"The Myers Corporation?" Charlene wondered openly. "What do you mean?"

"They're the ones who did most of the work... We had someone on the inside for a long time... and even after she was murdered... we were able to keep our ties."

"After who was murdered?" Carl asked, a sharp edge to his voice.

Charlene could see the answer coming. Anashe could only mean one person with the hints *she*, *murdered*, and *Myers*. She could see Carl was expecting it as well. His normally relaxed body looked ready to pounce on some helpless animal.

"Selma Myers, of course!" responded Anashe with more repugnant glee than Charlene saw anyone ever convey. She couldn't imagine how much more pleasure she would derive if she knew the son of the deceased woman was standing before her. "Isn't it wonderful? Now you... you have to investigate them! And you'll find out that they created it! We used them... and they must have believed they could... make fools of us! But I'll get the last laugh! Find the bastard who betrayed us! Maybe it's even that dumbass she had to marry! Or... or her son! Wouldn't that be great?" Anashe was cut off when she had to dry heave, but she was able to conquer the disturbance.

Carl remained stoic throughout her rant, simply waiting for her to finish. Charlene could only guess what was going through his mind. Did he believe her? Was he scouring through memories? Even if he had his mask off, she thought it unlikely that it would clarify matters any. Charlene herself had the uncomfortable impression Anashe was telling the truth. Felix had an even stronger conviction, but did not express it.

Wanting to change the subject, Charlene attempted to distract Anashe by asking, "Back in Africa, there was a young blonde woman ordering Exes around. Who is she?"

Anashe's eyes cleared up from their fuzziness to reveal a

wild stare beneath them, as though it was an affront to mention that particular person.

The image of the mysterious blonde woman zoomed through Felix's non-existent brain, triggering something akin to a mini-epiphany. With the vague recollection of Selma's appearance still in his mind, he said aloud, "You know, this might just be a coincidence, but now that I think about it, that blonde woman looked a lot like Selma."

Taking his cue to push forward, Charlene pressured with, "Does she have a connection with Selma?"

This statement really set Anashe's already hard features into a fury, but the attempt to lunge forward was promptly met by an increase in gravity. Hermes had pinned her face first to the floor and calmly walked up to her, preparing to inject the sedative.

With unreal willpower, Anashe fought against the concoction flowing through her body and Hermes' control to say, "Too late, motherfucker!"

Anashe's eyes then completely rolled backwards into their sockets, made a freakish wailing noise, and her tongue sagged out of her mouth.

"Shit," said Carl. He stabilized the gravity and felt her pulse for a moment. "She's dead. I think she might have..." He went on the radio to finish his assertion. "Lesedi was given the concoction, but I think she was still able to wipe her own mind."

"What?!" exclaimed Medusa in disbelief. "Shit. I'm already heading for you."

"Me too," said Peregrine. "Try not to touch anything. The Stewards will look over everything."

Hermes kept himself crouching by the body, clearly in deep thought.

"Hermes?" Charlene asked after several seconds of viewing the scene.

He stood up and guided her out of the room. "You did well, Miss Fade, but this is no sight for someone as young as yourself."

"What do we do?"

"Leave it to me."

Peregrine was the first to arrive. "What happened?" the leader of the mission asked the vigilantes as he headed for the room Anashe was in.

Hermes answered, "I entered to see Fade had successfully inoculated Lesedi, but before I could give the sedative, she went into the state you see her in now. I believe she used her own telepathy against herself, wiping her mind of all cognitive function." Medusa reached them at that moment and was given the same explanation as Peregrine skimmed the body. "There's something else," he continued. "She began explaining how the contagion was not primarily produced by them, but by the Myers Corporation. She indicated how she had someone on the inside, and that they're the ones who double-crossed her and sent out a lesser version of the contagion originally meant to be spread."

"The Myers Corporation?" Medusa said doubtfully. "Are you sure that's what she said?"

"I don't believe she was attempting to deceive us. It would actually answer why the contagion doesn't have the potency first projected. Perhaps someone couldn't prevent the spread of the disease, but were able to weaken it."

"Or they wanted it to spread," supposed Peregrine. "Didn't the Corporation recently announce they already had a possible cure? I did think it strange they found a treatment so quickly."

"Wait," said Medusa, "let me get this straight. You're saying Lesedi's inside guy decided to go against her and make a lesser version so he could sell the cure? I mean, this is all just to throw us off, right? The words of a clearly desperate criminal."

"But you'll have to investigate, won't you?" shyly questioned Charlene.

"Yes, we'll have to," said Peregrine. "She might have been desperate, but if her allegation is true... Well, I've learned not to trust too many felons and I know the Myers family have treated us Exes well. Why would an Ex use them of all options? What will you do about it, Hermes?"

"I'll investigate what I can and share anything I find, but you don't have to worry about me doing anything rash. I'll leave the Stewards to do the heavy lifting."

"Fair enough. I've already called the cavalry. If you don't mind, Medusa and I will handle it from here." Peregrine offered Carl his hand, which he took. "Thanks for the help, and yours as well, Fade."

"Anytime," said Charlene in the most professional tone she

had.

The first opportunity Charlene had a chance to ask Carl a personal question occurred when they were back in the van heading back to the airport.

"Are you going to tell me what you're thinking?"

He removed his mask and answered, "If what Lesedi said is true, even partially, the Stewards will have to involve themselves eventually, so I thought it no harm to tell them what we heard."

"But not everything."

"No, not everything."

She knew he didn't want to talk about it, but she felt she needed to make sure he wouldn't do anything impulsive, though she had no idea what that would be.

"What are you going to do?"

He gave her a soft smile, one that seemed more real than any he had given her before, and said, "Give me at least until we're in the air."

She reluctantly agreed and sat silent for the drive. Felix knew the restlessness in his hostess' mind and began to talk.

"Uh, this won't exactly make you feel better, but I think Anashe was telling the truth, at least, partly, and her look when you mentioned that blonde woman tells me she definitely has a connection to Carl's mother. A relative, I guess. This also implies Selma was an Ex, except, if Anashe's telling the truth and Selma was their inside woman, then how does she not know her son was an Ex? An Ex who could control gravity. Selma must have not told them, or Anashe would have surely guessed who Hermes was. And there's also the fact Selma died. So who is the connection Anashe and her group kept to make the contagion? Ahh! My head hurts! I have an idea. Just fade into the countryside and you'll live off the land. You'll become a new German fairy tale. You'll be known as Der Geist Dame, I think that means the Ghost Lady, and we'll make money by solving crimes for forest creatures."

"Felix," said Charlene in a mildly chastising tone, who was at the precipice of laughing at the image of her in a trench coat and holding a magnifying glass over an acorn with a squirrel on her shoulder.

"Sorry. I hope she was simply trying to throw us off the real trail, or make us suspect the cure the company is preparing is tainted or something, but I guess we'll find out sooner or later. Darn, if only I died a few years earlier. Then I would know more."

After their plane leveled in the air, she made herself more comfortable by unwrapping her scarf, taking off her sunglasses, and pulling down her hood. She stood up to stretch. As she did so, Carl began to head into his room to change and came out a little later in clean, more casual clothing.

"Now will you talk?" she inquired, still upright.

"This could finally be it," he began, as if talking to himself. He started pacing the cabin. "All this time I assumed my mother was killed because she supported the rights of Exes, but perhaps she was killed because someone discovered *she* was an Ex. Whoever kept the tie with Lesedi after her murder must be the one responsible."

"So you think it's true, then?"

"It makes the most sense. For nearly two decades I searched the outside world, when all this time it was an internal hit. There's only one person who could pull all these strings from inside the Corporation. Dr. Joseph Fitzgerald."

"Who's that?"

"My father's best, oldest friend. The only person who's been with my family business longer than Ms. Travis and who knows who I am. He's now in charge of research and development at our company, in fact, he specializes in the medical field."

"Well, shit," said Felix.

"You're going to confront him?" she asked.

"I would normally be less blunt, but if he is the culprit and has already created a medication he's still holding back, simply for the sake of following a procedure he likely followed months or years before, then I need to expose it and give it to those who need it."

"I want to go with you."

"You've done enough-"

"No, I haven't," she insisted. "I won't have done enough until all this is over. Let me help you."

"I believe I can handle this personal matter myself."

"What will happen if you meet him? Won't he only deny it? And won't you be inclined to believe him? Won't you hurt him if he turns out to be innocent? Let me confront him."

"Why wouldn't he deny it from you?"

"Because I can pretend to be somebody else. He doesn't know about me, right? What if I act like I'm blackmailing him? I'll say I know what he did and I want money to keep it quiet from you and your father." Carl sat down on the rotating chair with a milder expression on his face. She was glad to see it. She could understand why he would be agitated, but she felt his mind was contemplating things that weren't usual to his regular demeanor. Not wanting to lose a possibly brief advantage, she continued speaking. "If he's innocent, then it won't matter if I offend him. On the other hand, if he is the culprit and thinks someone is on to him, then there's a better chance he'll panic and do or say something to reveal his true intentions. There's less harm if I try. It's not like you won't be able to intervene at any time."

Carl closed his eyes a moment.

"He's going to agree," Felix predicted.

Carl sighed in defeat. "It's not a bad proposal, Miss Fade."

"So we'll do it my way?"

"I have yet to witness something going against your wishes. In any case, all this began with you, you do have the right to see it through."

"Thank you, Mr. Myers." She sat down after her victory and began to wonder exactly what she would say to the doctor. "What's this Dr. Fitzgerald like?"

"He's a bit of the opposite of my father. Eccentric and incredibly intelligent. Dad might have more book smarts, but Dr.

Fitzgerald is more versed in the real world. He never struck me as someone who would do something purely for money. If he's someway involved... then I don't understand his motives, but I'm certain he's the one who it has to be. No one else could have the access and control he does... It just doesn't add up. I don't have a single bad memory of her. She was never stern with me and she looked so proud when she found out I was an Ex. Surely she would have told me at that instant if she was one as well. Nevertheless, there's no denying Lesedi's expression when you mentioned her and that blonde woman your friend saw, a woman your friend says Sol and Lesedi were obeying."

"We'll know everything soon, Mr. Myers."

Chapter Thirty

The trio brainstormed the exact approach they would use to confront Dr. Fitzgerald during the rest of the eight hour flight back to Boston. The first agreed upon action was to get him into a location where he would have little chance of escaping if he tried to flee. The answer turned out to be the Myers yacht. The scheme they came up with was for Carl to text Dr. Fitzgerald that he needed to see him on some pretext, but it would be Charlene who would meet him on the vessel. Carl would be hiding in the boat while she spoke with him, recording the conversation on the security system. The private plane landed in Boston at 2:00 a.m. It was decided they would eat and rest at Carl's home and go ahead with their plan in the early sunrise…

"What did you text him?" Charlene asked as they headed for the docks in what he called his 'nondescript' car, a black Jaguar, a few hours later. "I suppose I should say, what did *I* text him?"

"That I have alarming news about my father and I need to speak privately with him."

"Carl? What will happen if he did create the contagion?"

"He'll go to prison."

"You know what I really mean."

"Our stock will crash, and even if my father and I had nothing to do with it, the public will condemn us. I doubt I'll be a billionaire much longer after that."

The comparatively light attitude at which he explained the demise of his company struck her as peculiar. "You aren't worried?"

He turned to her and said, "I assure you, Miss Fade, I won't become a vagrant. I said I would no longer be a billionaire, but my father and I still have a good bit of credit stashed away and we will be able to keep the remnants of our company. We'll start over and rebuild trust with the public. Maybe someday they will forgive us, maybe not, but work is work, whether I'm earning a million dollars an hour or minimum wage."

"Your father thinks the same way?"

"He's the one who taught me to think this way. If all this is true, he'll be more concerned about my mother and his best friend than any numbers on a screen."

"Have you talked to him yet?"

"I told him to make sure not to contact Dr. Fitzgerald this morning as I had pressing business with him. He knows nothing else for now."

They parked a couple blocks from the inner harbor and walked to the pier. The early morning was warm, clear, and only a slight breeze accompanied them. There were many different class of boats docked in the harbor and a handful of people strewn about the area. The Myers ship, christened *The Little Nautilus*, was pretty much exactly what she expected, if perhaps a bit smaller than she had imagined. It was a sleek, glistening white powerboat about forty-five feet long and had darkly tinted windows running along the middle. It had been years since Charlene had boarded any kind of ship. Her father had owned a little sailboat her unbroken family had sailed in when she was very young, but recalled her mother had made him sell it so they could help pay for their new home. They went aboard the broad stern, a wooden table and three chairs set in the middle, and Carl stepped up to a portside door and unlocked it, which Charlene could see led into a large cabin. Carl also opened the starboard entry. The latter entrance had a little ladder that headed downstairs.

"He should be here in the next ten minutes," informed Carl as they entered the large cabin, locking the door behind him. "I texted that I would meet him in my room below deck. Once he enters, you'll follow him and close the door behind you. I'll make sure it stays closed by making the door far too heavy for him to open, so don't worry about him trying to run out if he sees you. I'll then turn on the security system to record your conversation."

"Sounds good," she said while putting on her standard masquerade.

He handed her his phone and said, "So you can show him you were the one giving him the texts. You ready?"

"Yeah. I think I know what to say."

"Whatever happens, I believe it might be prudent of me to hire you full time."

"You'll have to pay the both of us."

"That's an idea. Perhaps I can begin a business for the undead. Well, let's see how this goes."

Felix soon felt the nebulously familiar aura heading for them. They next heard the older gentleman embarking the ship and open the contrary door, saying Carl's name as he did so. After hearing him close the door behind him, Charlene hurried towards him, feeling him move farther down the hall. She phased through the door and inaudibly walked down the short flight of stairs. She saw the back of the elderly man's head, the top of which was bald and the sides were laden with thin, gray hairs. He wore a tan overcoat.

"Carl? You in here?" he called out in a mousey voice.

"Show time," said Felix.

In the most formidable tone she could pull together, she said, "I'm afraid, Dr. Fitzgerald, that Carl isn't here."

Felix thought she pulled it off and found he quite enjoyed her chilling tone.

The doctor turned around, looking shocked at the source of the voice in his half spectacles. "W-what? Who a-are you? W-where is Carl?"

"Carl is fine, doctor," she answered, holding up his phone. "He's only missing this at the moment."

He began backing away, going closer to what was Carl's room at the bow end of the yacht. He pulled out his own phone. "Stay b-back. Get out now or I'll c-call the police."

"I wouldn't do that, doctor, unless you want your best friend and his son to find out about you and Selma." He stopped cold in his tracks. A good sign for some bad news. She used his hesitation to continue her speech, walking slowly up to him at the same time. "I wonder who the police would be more interested in? Someone who broke into a boat? Or the murderer of a beloved and prominent woman? Or how about the person responsible for the Ex-virus going around?"

"You're talking nonsense," he said, recovering some of his poise, but not enough to convince her he was really refuting everything.

"Let's not drag this out with denials, Dr. Fitzgerald. Our connections in South Africa might have dispersed, but they left behind enough information for me to use against you. Did you know the reward money for any lead that leads to the arrest of Selma's killer is three million dollars? I would be content with that amount and not have bothered you, but when I found out about the contagion, well, I thought I deserved a little more. Don't you think so?"

"You have nothing, only a fanciful story," he said defiantly. "There's no evidence you could possibly have."

"I think Hermes and Victor might see differently. What I have might not be enough for the police to force themselves into your files, but for a child and husband desperate to take any leads they can, don't you think they will take the easy step to go through your offices? It at least won't take them long to discover you already have the cure to the contagion stored away and ready to sell for huge profits. Once they find out you're nothing but a greedy old man, it will take no great leap to see you had the means and access to kill Selma."

He panicked at those last words. He spun around and rushed for the door to the bedroom and slammed it in her face. This presented no obstacle to her, of course. She phased through the impediment and came in to see a stunned old man fumbling with his phone, proceeding to drop it. His much younger challenger was able to swiftly pick up the fallen object and was able to fade before her elder lunged at her. He unexpectedly passed through her arms and fell to the floor. The sight made her feel wretched at what she was doing to such a feeble old man, but she had to see this through. She next saw him on his feet, reopen the door, and run down the hall. She leisurely followed his desperate form to the end of the hall where he tried vainly to open the exit. Soon beaten, he gave up, walked back down the narrow stairs, placed his back to the wall, and slumped to the floor.

"I just want some money, doctor. Ten million dollars and I'll go away. You'll remain free, the cure will eventually get out, and no one will know you betrayed both the Corporation and the terrorists."

"*I* betrayed!" he said with rekindled fire in his eyes. "You don't know as much as you think you do."

"And what don't I know?" she asked, knowing they were at the precipice.

"That *I* saved the company from *her*! *She* was the one making the contagion that would have wiped out half of humanity!"

She felt Carl's aura move and head for them. She dropped her commanding tone. "So you really did do it."

He noticed the abruptly softer tone and looked up at her with a tangled mix of confusion and bitterness. His open mouth was about to disgorge some words, but he was interrupted by the opening door. The gaping mouth stayed open when he saw who it was and it exclaimed, "Carl! Thank God you're here! This wom-"

"Enough, doctor," coldly stated Carl. "I heard everything."

Dr. Fitzgerald steadily stood back up and said, "Carl, I was-"

"I said that was enough," Carl said quieter, but more firmly. "What do you mean you saved the company from my mother?"

The old man looked at Charlene and back at Carl, either trying to find an escape or some aid. Finally, seeing no path open, he started slumping back down to the floor. Before he could reach the ground, Carl caught his arm and gently lifted him back up.

"Let's go to my room, doctor." Carl guided him forward

until they reached his room. He released him alongside the bed. "Have a seat." The timeworn man did as he was bid. "Now, doctor, I need to know everything."

The doctor stared at the floor for a good while. Charlene was sure they were frozen long enough for her to see the light from the windows becoming brighter from the rising daylight.

Ultimately, the doctor looked mournfully up at Carl and said, "I could never tell you or your father. I know you can never understand my actions." He inhaled deeply. "And, at the time, I didn't know the extent of her hold over you and him."

"Hold?"

He nodded. "Your mother was an Ex with the power to force people to follow her whims by using powerful pheromones emitted into the air. When I learned of this ability, I knew she had used it to attract Victor and make him marry her."

"How did you find out?"

"It was little things at first. In fact, I can honestly say it was the very first time I saw her with Victor that I initially became suspicious. I had seen Victor in love before and what I saw in him when he was around her was outright absurdity. Over the years, however, his passion fluctuated a great deal. One day would have him acting like he couldn't live without her and the next had him barely remembering she existed. Then, about five years after you were born, she began intermittently asking me for some unusual favors, such as wanting for me to check on various diseases and viruses. You see where I'm going with this? And it wasn't just me, she did this with several of my associates as well. So I began investigating her background. Eventually I found interesting or muddled gaps of information, such as how her orphanage conveniently burned down her history, but there was nothing concrete I could pin her down with.

"My eyes were always on her present self, not just her past. I began to diligently converse with anyone she spoke with, and while I found nothing as extreme as your father's case, I did find similar symptoms. I did blood tests on those she spoke with and gathered air samples as often as I could. I subsequently found the smoking gun. They didn't last long either in the air or within the blood, but they were there. Pheromones, pheromones that can make anyone she wished liable to act out her commands. It doesn't last forever, which is why your father experienced those highs and lows. The pheromones dilute in time and need to be reinforced every so often. Around the same time, you would have been about ten or eleven, I was looking through old Ex documents and I discovered the picture. *Her* picture. It shocked me, but it provided the opening I was looking for."

"What was the picture of?" asked Carl.

"A World War II photo of a woman who looked remarkably like Selma. She was standing in chains among Nazi soldiers. It required a lot more digging and expense to reveal the circumstances of that photo, but I eventually learned that the woman in the photo was a captured Ex, an Ex rumored to have the power of immortality. The Germans captured her and experimented on her until the Russians discovered the lab at the end of the war. According to a few Russian forms hidden from the public, this Ex escaped during the transfer, but it also told of a child they were able to secure. *Her* child."

"Holy crap," said Felix. "That blonde Ex I saw in Africa must have been Selma's mother."

The doctor continued. "I don't know what happened after that, but it was clear Selma grew up with a hatred for Regulars and somehow fled from her captures, or maybe her mother went back for her, I can't say."

"If she had such influence, how did you escape it?" asked Carl.

"My sinuses have been horrible my whole life. You should know that well enough by now. Ironically, my nasal infirmity help prevent the power of the so called 'superior race.'"

Charlene's ears fully opened and her mind grasped the doctor's situation. She said, "But it didn't completely inhibit the effects, did it, doctor?" He gazed at her in what appeared to be trepidation filled eyes. "Or, at least, you were worried you weren't totally immune. You were in love with her, weren't you?"

The doctor bent his head and buried it in both hands. After a moan, and without lifting his head, he said, "I tested my own blood and found nothing to indicate she was regularly pouring her pheromones, and yet…"

She felt sorry for his miserable figure. A glance at Carl showed he didn't seem to carry any type of emotion.

Carl broke his former friend's silence. "What happened next?"

"I never thought about killing her, even after I found out she was an Ex and manipulating your father. I thought I could attempt to find a way to permanently eradicate the pheromones effects and gain the advantage over her. I thought I could expose her. I was alone in my struggle. Victor would reprimand me if I ever spoke ill of her and I could not trust anyone who knew her. I tried keeping Victor away from her, but she was wary and going any further would surely have put my life in jeopardy. But I soon had an opportunity to possibly gather hard evidence. She came to me one day and began asking me to undertake very illicit actions concerning lab activities. I played along so as not to provoke any doubts on her part. I wanted to get closer and see if I could find out what she was doing and who else was connected with her. My forbearance paid off. I was able to infer she had ties to South Africa and concluded that the group wanted to create a special contagion tailor made to exterminate Regulars. Even recognizing that Exes were capable of these genocidal thoughts didn't send me over the edge."

"Then what was it!?" Carl asked with swelling impatience. "Why did you kill her? Why did you feel you had the right to murder her?"

"It was when I learned you were an Ex." Dr. Fitzgerald paused, seemingly reliving the moment everything changed for so many lives. "My outlook changed when Victor told me the news. I saw her take a new interest in you. I saw a mother treating her child with cold calculation, only using you for what would be her benefit and for that of her kind. I saw a never ending cycle of Exes trying to take over our world with whatever means necessary, unless someone stopped them."

Carl didn't say anything. He was as speechless as Charlene had ever seen him in the short time they knew each other. She decided to advance the conversation herself.

"How, doctor? How would you stop them?"

"I formed a different design that would use their contagion against them. I would create a disease that I would be able to cure with a simple inoculation. The disease would have to be prevalent and frightening enough to force as many Regulars and Exes to take the treatment, yet still be tweaked not to be especially fatal. To accomplish this meant having to get rid of Selma. Her direct oversight endangered my plan and, all things considered, I couldn't be sure I could always resist her. I first made sure I could keep in contact with her group so they would not be forced to move on. I still wanted them at hand so I could use them and later reveal them to the authorities. After that… well, I had to make certain you were not with her when it happened. I found a day when you would be in school and she was to go to a charity auction. You… you know the rest."

Nothing came from Carl. No emotion or new line on his face suggested anything but a blank mind. There was more to learn. Charlene pressed on.

"You said you wanted your new disease to be able to frighten everyone into getting the inoculation. Is the inoculation the final phase of your plan?"

He stared out the circular port window looking out to the water and answered, "The samples I sent Selma's group fooled them into thinking they were exactly the Regular killing contagion they were after, but it would be the cure that would end the growth of their kind. The inoculation is my magnum opus."

"What does it do?"

"It sterilizes anyone with an Ex gene."

"What? But that would affect people who have Ex genes, but aren't Exes."

"An essential sacrifice. While Exes are more likely to conceive Ex children they are not the majority carriers of the Ex genes. Up to five percent of the total population carries the genes and the number will only propagate if left unchecked. In twenty years it will double and then triple in half the time after that. In just a few generations, having a child born an Ex won't be as rare as it is today. My treatment won't get rid of it completely, but it will significantly reduce their numbers. It will give humanity time to prepare and keep the advantage from your kind."

"You can't possibly think no one will notice what your 'cure' does."

"They will, but when it's far too late. The CDC is pressured by the frightened public to give them something to prevent them from getting sick. They won't hold back my treatment to test the long term effects on Exes, of all things. Once it shows to effectively cure the contagion with only minor side effects on the healthy, it will be in every hospital in the world within weeks and millions will be inoculated in days. A billion by the end of the month. Don't you see? It's the solution with the least bloodshed. There will be war if we don't do this! Everyone knows it's coming! If it wasn't for me the Exes would already have landed a devastating first blow!"

"Can the cure still be changed from its sterilization capability?"

He ignored her and looked pleadingly at Carl, saying, "Carl, the plan will work. The company will be in ruins if you turn me in. The Stewards will get someone to read my mind and they'll find out about Hermes and do who knows what. This is our chance to avoid a war that will cost the lives of countless innocents."

Carl's features softened and there was finally a vibrancy in his eyes. However, his voice was still icy when he said, "There's nothing I can say to you that will bring either of us comfort. Speculating on what could happen won't excuse what you facilitated bringing about. Your disease has killed over four thousand people in the last two months and you murdered my mother over seventeen years ago. You will be the one to bring down a company you have worked so hard to help build. You killed, we caught you, and you'll be miserable for the rest of your short life. Those are the facts." He turned to Charlene. "Keep an eye on him for a moment while I make a call." He stepped out of the room, closing the door behind him.

Yeah, go ahead, Carl, this isn't awkward at all, Felix thought to himself.

The doctor removed his spectacles and hid his eyes with a hand. "I know I sound cracked," he began, to Charlene's surprise, "but I do understand not all Exes are evil and out to get us. I hold no ill towards you if you are a friend of Carl's." He put his glasses back on. "There is a pure version of the cure I planned to give to Exes whom I deemed worthy of it, one of which was Carl, of course."

"So Exes can get sick from the 'Ex-virus?'"

"It's difficult to say, but I think it possible. More than that, they can at least carry it and spread it to others. A small vile of the purified cure is in a safe at my main office."

"Why tell me this and not Carl?"

"I will, but this is in case I die in the next minute. I'm surprised I've lived as long as I have with the strain on my sickly heart, but I suppose my mission kept me going. Now I feel nothing preventing my heart from giving out at any second. Something else I have yet to mention. Maybe my mind is cracked... I think I've seen her."

"Who?"

"Selma's mother. I never found a name she goes by. Once the news gets out that I was the one to trick them, she'll have me killed."

"You'll be watched constantly. I don't think she'll risk it."

"I wouldn't underestimate her. I always felt someone in the background of everything I looked into during my investigations. When I saw her, or thought I saw her, then I knew it was her. She's out there and has amassed supporters, but at least you now know how she looks like."

"You're an intelligent man, Dr. Fitzgerald, but you seemed to have flown too close to the sun."

"It won't mean anything anymore coming from me, but, please, tell Carl I'm sorry for everything. I just need to know he'll hear it."

"I'll tell him."

No you won't, Felix foretold.

Carl came in a minute later. "You can go," he told Charlene while giving her his keys and a credit card. "Go to any hotel you like. I'll contact you later."

"Are you sure?"

"This is the end of your role. Thank you, Miss Fade."

She left for his car, feeling anti-climactic about the whole thing. Felix allowed her time to process the event and they kept quiet up until Charlene entered her Motel 6 room she rented. They separated from the meld and she collapsed on the bed, but had no intention to sleep. She texted Carl to inform him of the purified cure the doctor told her about, just in case.

"I feel… blah," she said once the message was sent.

"Is that the official diagnosis on yourself?"

"Do you have a different one?"

"No. That's pretty much the natural reaction to seeing a frantic Ex wipe her own mind and a sad old man losing his will. I'd be worried if 'blah' wasn't your reaction. I only prescribe some time with your family and boyfriend to get over it."

"Why not with your family? Don't you think it's time we talk to them? I think my summer just cleared up." She heard no response for several rotations of the oscillating ceiling fan above her. "What's wrong?"

"I'm just imagining how it will go."

"And?"

"Either very well or very bad."

"Don't you trust me to convince them?"

"I don't trust the pope to convince them."

"I've convinced other people that you exist. Wouldn't it be easier to sway your family?"

"But they saw my dead body, they found closure years ago, and… so did I. Let me think about it."

She was surprised at his reluctance, but it was something she could never understand, or never hoped to, at any rate.

Felix sensed her disappointment and knew she merely wanted to keep her mind off the depressing events they witnessed. To appease her desire, he said, "You should speak with my sister first before anyone else. Persuade her and she'll be able to convert everyone else. She's the most levelheaded of the bunch. My mother will throw holy water at you and Dad will be nice, but he'll just think you're an amusing homeless lady."

"And your brother?" she asked, effectively diverted into a better mood.

"Oh, he'll just call the police as soon as someone enters his yard, well, unless you're wearing a cheerleader outfit or something, but that goes for any guy."

"Maybe I'll finally get to see how you look like," said Charlene.

"Just remember the pictures you'll see were before I obtained my incredible muscles and underwent major facial surgery."

For the next hour he continued with stories of his family he had previously withheld. He had always thought it presumptuous to talk about his family to her, not wanting it to make it seem as though he were pressuring her to take him to them.

It wasn't until a little passed midnight when Carl contacted her and asked for her location. He was in the room shortly after, looking fairly worn, but not at all distraught.

"How are you?" she asked him.

"No worries about me, Miss Fade," Carl replied in a tired voice. "The Stewards have the doctor in custody. He's confessed and has shown us all he had on his previous investigations."

"So you found the purified cure?"

"Yes. It will be solely handled by the CDC and they'll synthesize more of it."

"When will the news get out?"

He smiled softly and looked at the blank television.

"You've avoided any connection to the world, then? The news that a crazed doctor and board member of the Myers Corporation is responsible for the contagion has already broken about ten minutes ago. As you can imagine, I'm needed for interviews and other such articles of business. I come to give you this airline ticket and say my goodbye that will likely last a good while." He handed her said ticket. "You're welcome to use the Jaguar to get to the airport."

She held the ticket, not knowing if she should ask what she wanted to ask. She didn't feel like possibly leaving him on a sour note. Instead of asking, she said, "I'm sorry about your mother."

He nodded slightly. "The woman who died that day is the only woman I remember and the only one I can mourn, no matter what someone else says. True or not. What I do know is that Lesedi did not know who I was, which can only mean Selma never told anyone in her group about me. Does that mean she wanted to someday use me against them? Or does it mean she wanted to protect me from them? I'll never know. I would like to say it was the latter, but in the end, it doesn't matter so much. Get home to your family. I'm sure we'll see each other again if you wish it. Farewell, to your friend and to you, Miss Fade."

He warmly shook her hand and left.

Chapter Thirty-One

She continued to ignore the news as much as she could. It would only be filled with the loudest people who cared little for anything other than having their opinion heard on a matter they could not entirely understand. How could they if she had experienced it and could not? Inescapably, she did here the talk of the effects of some of her actions over the next couple days. The Myers Corporation stock sharply declined, many supporters deserted them, and congressional hearings would be held for the foreseeable future. Victor and Carl shared in the responsibility, though many on the board did fight to keep them as heads of the company, seeing as there was no evidence saying they did anything wrong, moreover, Dr. Fitzgerald stated he was alone in his actions. The doctor's public account did not mention Carl was an Ex like his mother, but many became suspicious and wanted him to take a blood test. Carl agreed, saying even if it proved he had the genes, it did not mean he carried any latent abilities. The positive test still didn't force him from his inheritance, since it was technically legal for Exes to inherit businesses if the owners had it in their wills. Little was disclosed of the security recording she was a part of, likely meaning Medusa was able to induce the Stewards from disclosing it to the public, seeing as the two parties involved were instrumental in the case and in previous others.

Four days after she spoke with the doctor, he turned up dead in his cell under "mysterious circumstances," as the initial reports characterized it. The official cause of death converted to a heart attack, but an anonymous guard in an interview stated that he was first on the scene and described the puncture wound of a syringe on his arm, fueling speculation he was indeed murdered by someone able to sneak into the penitentiary.

It didn't take long for the CDC to confirm that the purified cure was an almost side effect free cure to the contagion and would not need much time to begin distributing it. There was no true public consensus on the closing of these events. Extreme Exes were attempting to wipe out humanity and vice versa. No punch was able to land wholly on their intended target as both extremes were kept from their full impacts. In a sense, prevailing attitudes settled back to their pre-contagion situations. It was the loudest ends of the spectrum who became brasher and barked for changes in business and government policy. Charlene saw an example of this after she and her sisters stopped playing on their PlayStation in their basement one evening. The channel had a news anchor speaking with a government official about the latest petition sent to the White House by those wanting all public officials to have to reveal if they had Ex genes in their genetic code.

She turned off the TV and stretched herself on the couch as her sisters went back upstairs to eat. She was on her back and staring up at the ceiling, though really looking well beyond it. She was in this state for some moments before she told Felix, "I can see why you didn't want me getting involved with Exes. Things are only gonna get more complicated, aren't they?"

"Things have always been complicated. It's only my presence that forced those complications on you. Sorry about that."

"You really think you've made my life worse?"

"Not worse per se, just more complex. Higher highs, lower lows."

"What do you think you'd be doing now if you were alive?"

"I'd be right here. A thirty-five year old man staring creepily at a twenty year old."

She laughed. "And what type of girl do you think you would…" That wasn't the question she really wanted to ask. She had, in fact, been thinking all day about asking him the question she found becoming more prevalent in her mind. She could not hold it back any longer. After some time deliberating on how to exactly approach the topic, she decided being blunt would be her best option. She interrupted herself. "Felix?"

"Uh, yeah?" he answered, confused at her unexpected

change in tone.

"Do you love me?"

There was a pause. He was surprised, but not shocked she asked him something she must have suspected for some time. He chose to answer plainly. "Of course I do." There was an even lengthier pause as they each let their words echo in their minds. "Is that a problem?" Felix finally asked, more timidly than he would have liked.

"You're right. You have made my life more complicated. A year ago I could picture my future perfectly. I would go to college, get my degree, and study to become a doctor, probably a pediatrician. Devin would be with me and become a big shot football coach. I imagined we'd have two girls and two boys, no real order, and we'd visit my sister's families in big get-togethers. You changed none of that Felix. You loving me changed none of that. It's when I realized I was in love with you that changed everything."

Not since he first saw her react to him in the baseball game did he receive such a jolt of unbridled emotion. He had never expected to hear someone tell him they loved him for the rest of his existence. He regarded her closely, but she continued to simply stare at the ceiling and gave no indication she was being anything but serious. He felt horrible. All he wanted to do at that moment was run up to her, take her in his arms, look as deeply as he could into her eyes, and kiss her. But he couldn't. He couldn't show what she meant to him. What was worse was knowing she must have recognized all this and she still told him.

"Damn, Charlene… I don't know whether to laugh or cry."

"You think I know what to do?"

There was a lot he wanted to say. Such as how he couldn't give her all she deserved or how no real prospects existed for her with him, wanting to ask what this meant for Devin, along with a million other questions and comments he could not foresee. However, he knew that's not what she wanted to hear at the moment and he recognized there would be time later.

"Do you want to meld?" was all the words he could gather.

"Sure."

He did what was desired, doing the only thing they could each physically feel from the other. So, for an untold number of minutes, they simply kept the meld, not wishing to worry about what their love meant for their futures.

Fade